THE ACCIDENTAL TIME TRAVELERS COLLECTIVE

VOLUME ONE

MOSTLY WIND BOOKS

To all time travelers past, present, and future

CONTENTS

THE PAST,

or was it?

FIELD AND FLAME

JENNIFER MARCHMAN

~from the world of *The Mender*~

THE SANCTUM, Axis Mundi, the True timeline, 1996

As she and Tophe bowed before the seven elders, Eva trembled despite the familiarity. From the council dais, the elders ruled over the destiny of each Lux Libera member, their decisions echoing through the chamber and beyond. It didn't matter how experienced she was as a mender; being in her superiors' presence always intimidated her.

"You'll get in and get out," Elder Nnaji said. "You shouldn't need to build a rapport. The Christmas party will do that work for you, but you'll be there to ensure Haber's pistol is on his wife's dressing table. If it is, they'll both be dead by 11:39 p.m."

Together, the recipients of these instructions deepened their bows at the waist, hands folded across their bellies. Eva knew it would be an easy job; she and Tophe had been partners since adolescence, both recruited as children to

Axis Mundi, the only True timeline, and they worked in tandem.

"One last thing," Elder Nnaji said. "You will be taking a novice with you. It will be the girl's first mission." With those words, she presented a manila envelope, their orders and operation details.

Tophe stiffened beside her. Neither of them minded training recruits, but they both guessed who would join them. No one else was ready. After a final bow, Eva retrieved the paperwork and followed her partner out the door and down the spiral staircase. When they reached the bottom, Tophe tore open the flap and scanned the instructions, flipping through the pages.

"Lydia."

"I knew it," Eva said.

Groaning, Tophe dropped his arm and threw his head back, slapping the papers against his leg. "*Merde.*"

"She's not that bad. She already speaks German. It makes sense to accelerate her training."

Tophe rolled his eyes. "First stop, the Novitiate House, I guess."

UNLIKE THE HOUSING for consecrated members, the novices' dormitory sat like a swollen toad at the epicenter of the sanctum, a vast dome crouching beneath an ancient Teutonic forest. Tophe held the door open, and Eva passed through. Before they had a chance to ask the on-duty novice mistress to call the girl's room, they heard Lydia, her voice echoing down the entry stairs, laughing...no, guffawing.

She was always a little much. Never unkind but often blunt, shocking even in her word choice. Her thoughts would tumble out like gumballs—you never knew what color you would get—and she might comment so loudly her friends would gasp and look around for their teachers or the target of her thoughtless remark.

The next moment, thunderous footfalls announced her descent, and Eva wondered if Lydia had grown another inch since she had seen her last. Tall for her age, she stooped, clearly self-conscious, with rounded shoulders— her one insecurity, by all appearances. Eva herself had topped out at five feet two the year she had turned twelve, and she resisted the urge to tell the girl to stand up straight, to be thankful for her height, a perfect complement to her long, jet-black hair. Instead, Eva smiled and tucked a strand of her own fine, blonde hair behind her ear.

As the girl rushed past them, Tophe said, "Lydia."

She stumbled at the sound of her name and turned unfocused eyes toward them. Eva watched as recognition dawned, and the novice adjusted her stance to face them, bobbing her head, one hand over her belly. "Brother Christophe. Sister Eva." When Eva explained she would join them on their mission, Lydia's eyes sparked with excitement, and she bounded in place like a tethered rabbit.

Back outside, they crossed the well-manicured lawn and headed toward the outfitting departments. All three would need proper clothing for 1914 Germany, Gold Marks from the sanctum bank, and though they would use Herr Haber's own gun to ensure the timelines merged correctly, additional weapons to arm themselves.

Eva and Tophe knew, should something go amiss, the elders would prefer them to die rather than further compromise a timeline, but after their disaster at the French court of Louis Quatorze years ago, they privately swore to defend each other, regardless of their mission goals. Doing so remained their one secret heresy, and Eva never traveled without knives. Or lock picks.

Lydia walked backward, peppering them with questions. "Why Fritz Haber? Who is he? I haven't eaten lunch yet. We should eat before we go. Unless there will be food at the party. Will there be food at the party?" The next moment, she tripped on her heel and landed with a thud.

Tophe pulled her up, and after she had dusted off, he pressed the manila envelope to her chest. "You should know who Fritz Haber is. You're specializing in European timelines, are you not? Haven't you had Variations in Twentieth-century Germany?"

"Yes," Lydia said, her voice unsure.

"Then, you tell me."

Lydia rubbed her nose and shifted uncertain eyes to Eva.

Eva glanced up at Tophe, who had set his lips in a flat line, then turned her attention back to their charge and said, "It can be difficult to keep so many names straight when you're first starting out. Right, Tophe?" When her partner didn't respond, she elbowed him.

"Sure."

Eva frowned at him, but Lydia seemed to blossom, standing to her full height, overblown confidence restored.

"Let me jog your memory," Eva said. "Fritz Haber created a machine that could turn air into bread. Basically, he invented chemical fertilizer, and billions more people are alive today than would have been otherwise."

"But in some timelines," Tophe said, "like the one where we're headed, he developed the gases used in the trenches of the First World War and the Holocaust, so he also *killed* millions of people."

"At least they were just shadows...all those victims," Eva

said. She couldn't think of a starker example of the double-edged sword of science, or—that is to say—at least how scientific history played out in some timelines, but thankfully not in Axis Mundi, the navel of the multiverse.

Lydia stopped in place. "Do your targets feel real? When you kill them? The reflections? Doesn't it feel like you're killing a person?"

Tophe shrugged. "The first time, it did feel strange, but I knew they weren't alive, couldn't truly feel anything. Just remember, the real Fritz Haber is in our timeline, and he never invented chemical warfare or the pesticide that would exterminate his relatives in Nazi concentration camps."

"I don't understand how they aren't real, too...all these other timelines," Lydia said.

With a huff of impatience, Tophe strode ahead. "Come on, let's keep moving." As they passed the Assembly Hall, he pointed at the stained glass gleaming in the sun. "Didn't Master Singh show you the prism analogy? At orientation? He did for us."

His words reminded Eva of her own long ago first day with the head teacher. Tophe had been recruited earlier than herself. She hadn't met him yet or become his friend, was still ignorant, still giddy with curiosity, still half-believing she might have made a mistake, that her family was real after all, and she should never have left them without a word and come to this strange world, so different from her own birth timeline. But the prism lesson, invisible light fracturing into every color imaginable, had made sense to her.

"Yes, I remember," Lydia said. "Doesn't mean I understood it. So, the world broke apart into infinite timelines at creation. So what?"

Tophe turned, displeasure painted across his face.

The girl raised her hand. "Hold on. Let me get my thought out. What I'm saying is rainbows are beautiful. When Master Singh held the prism up to the window and rainbows spun around the room, I thought to myself, why would anyone want to force all that beauty back into nothingness?"

The question alone made Eva's guts twist, and the blood drained from Tophe's face. In five steps, he returned to them, grabbed Lydia by the upper arm, and put his nose to hers, his fear so palpable it might slither around Eva's fingers if she reached out to touch it. He spoke in a strained whisper. "Don't. Ever. Say that out loud again." His eyes searched the novice's. "Do you understand what I'm telling you? Not only is it blasphemous, but you will be declared apostate just for wondering and thrown into the Abyss."

Lydia reared back, eyes wide. "I know."

But Eva could tell she didn't, not really. She had heard the word "apostate," but never understood the consequences.

"This is the only True timeline," Tophe continued. "All others are false. It is our duty to realign the multiverse into a state of spiritual purity. To end this material world and the chaos we have now. None of it is beautiful."

Nodding, Lydia straightened her shoulders. "I understand. I know. I didn't mean it the way you took it."

Eva placed a hand on Tophe's chest. Every muscle in his body had tightened, and she knew why. Hot tears sprang to her own eyes at the triggered memory. Love. Betrayal. Disbelief. Grief. Scabs on their hearts so new, they could easily crack. "She's not Sakura, Tophe."

"Who's Sakura?" Lydia asked.

"A good friend who was declared apostate early last year before you were recruited." Eva took the girl's hand in her own. "You didn't witness her punishment and execution. We did."

While Eva spoke, Tophe stepped back and ran his fingers through his dark hair. "I'm sorry," he said, then drew a long breath. "These sorts of questions...you shouldn't ask them. The answers never help. They'll lead you down false paths. There is nothing else in existence except Axis Mundi, no other people than the Lux Libera. Everything else is fake. Just...just be careful." Tophe appeared to be trying to smile, but it came out more as a grimace. "You have a tendency to talk too much."

"I do not!"

"You speak without thinking first. Let's say that. That is true."

"I think out loud."

"Well...don't," Tophe said, moving his hands to his hips, voice hardening. "Look, ground rules. You're the novice. No more questions. Do what we say. And go read the orders. If you need it, go to the library and refresh your memory on Germany."

Eva puckered her lips and quirked them sideways, not liking his tone, despite his calm delivery. At least Lydia seemed to take orders from a known and respected superior with good grace.

"We'll get your supplies," Tophe continued. "Just...go study. Please."

Once Lydia was out of earshot, Eva said, "I'm worried, just like you, but we have a responsibility toward her. We need to help her, not berate her."

Tophe grumbled something under his breath, then acquiesced. "If we fail, it's the guilt by association I'm most concerned about."

EVA WAS RELIEVED THAT ELIZABETH, mistress of costuming, hadn't put her in a hobble skirt. "No need for you to be the cutting edge of fashion this go 'round," she had said. Instead, she had dressed her in a lovely sapphire sequined evening gown, and nearby, Tophe exited the changing room and adjusted his cuffs, dapper as always in a tailcoat and top hat. Lydia twirled in her frock, a similar cut to Eva's, though with the higher neckline and longer sleeves befitting a young girl. The jade silk made her green eyes shine.

Having acquired all other supplies and bundled for a German winter night, they had made their way to Yggdrasil, the enormous ash tree every member of Lux Libera traveled through, though more from tradition than necessity. Any tree large enough would do.

Lydia, of course, had practiced traveling many times before being allowed to attend an active mission, and her body outwardly hummed with excitement as she opened a portal. Eva smiled to herself, then laid her hand beside Tophe's and Lydia's on the trunk, expanding the portal further. There was nothing magic about their abilities. As a sixth sense, real humans could move freely through space and time simply by changing reality at the quantum level. A string of pure energy danced at the center of every particle, and by slowing the speed, shifting each tone, one after another, like a symphony, they could teach the tree to play a new song, if only for a moment, while they slipped out of their world and into the next.

The trunk shimmered, hazy and immaterial, and then they were amongst the threads of the multiverse, each a separate timeline, a tapestry woven of light. Previously, scouts had traveled ahead, gathering intelligence and placing a beacon for menders like Eva and Tophe to follow. They located the unique signal and exited the portal, stepping out into a wooded corner of the Haber Villa grounds and a crisp, starlit night. Eva shivered despite her fur coat, breath steaming. Lydia whispered, "Look, I'm a dragon."

Tophe put his finger over his lips and jerked his chin toward the mansion.

Lydia frowned, and then a thought seemed to pop into her head. "Won't it be a shock to Clara Haber's friends that she kills herself and Fritz tonight? I understand why she kills herself in the True line, but she's a different person here. Wouldn't the confusion keep the lines from merging?"

"I asked you before we left if you had any other questions," Tophe said, the words hissing through his teeth.

"I know. But...I'm just wondering."

Tophe pinched the bridge of his nose. "They just do, all right?"

Eva patted her partner on the arm, tapping him out. "Clara's just as unhappy and depressed in this timeline as she is in the True line, and that fact is no secret. Though she won't murder Fritz in this timeline, she'll finally commit suicide when she catches her husband with a mistress and witnesses a successful gas test, but in the True line, Clara is distressed much earlier by his decision to research gas warfare, something he told her earlier this very evening as they were dressing for the party. The news bothers her, but she doesn't act on it. She's a chemist herself, the first female doctorate in Germany, and she has only ever wanted science to contribute to the progress of the world, not its destruction. We're here to make her act on her dismay, just as she does in the True line. The news of their murder-suicide will shock their community, but upon further thought, will surprise no one."

Lydia cocked her head, then nodded, seemingly satisfied.

"They don't really feel those things, anyway. It's just programming," Tophe said. "We just need to line up their actions, and the effects fall into place. It's simple. Don't overcomplicate things."

"Anything else before we head in?" Eva asked.

Tophe leaned toward Lydia. "Actually, tell me the plan so I know you were listening the third time we told you."

With a roll of her eyes, Lydia crossed her arms. "You will find Fritz's military pistol and place it on her dressing table, and Eva and I will introduce ourselves to Clara and mess with her mind."

"'Mess with her mind' implies she has one. We're just reminding her of thoughts she already possesses, fixing her code."

"I don't like it," Lydia said.

"You don't have to like it. You just have to do it." Tophe shifted his weight. "And?"

"And I don't say anything. I'm just observing."

"Right." Tophe tilted his chin and turned on his heel. "On y va."

"Don't you mean, *auf geht's?*" Lydia asked, a little too loudly.

Tophe slit his eyes but didn't stop or respond.

"Yes," Eva said, just to Lydia. "Only German now."

"IS THAT EINSTEIN?" Lydia's mouth dropped open, and Eva chuckled at her sense of wonder, reminded of her own first times running into famous historical figures. The glamour always faded the moment one saw the warts, the pettiness, the anxieties, the small ways all people failed to be perfect, even the accomplished and beautiful ones, and, more disappointingly, the virtuous ones.

"At least you've heard of *him*," Tophe said.

"Who's the man next to him?"

"That's Carl Bosch. Fritz Haber designed the process for pulling nitrogen out of the sky and turning it into food for plants, but Bosch is the man who built the city-sized machine to make it so." Tophe's eyes scanned the heads of the crowded party and the decorative centerpiece, a towering Christmas tree ablaze with tiny candles. "He deserves more credit, I think."

"Do you want to meet him?" Eva asked. "Einstein, I mean?"

Lydia beamed. "Can I?"

Tophe shifted beside Eva, throwing her a questioning look, and she read his mind. "What? We have plenty of time. Besides, Clara is busy at the moment."

Tophe puckered his lips, but then lifted a shoulder. "Fine. I'll steal the pistol off Haber."

As she watched Tophe weave through the glittering guests, Eva worried that her partner's attitude might put them in more danger than Lydia's. He was usually the fun one, coaxing her into side trips before they returned home. Beignets and *café* in New Orleans. Sampling the first edible chocolate in Britain. Introducing himself to this king or that artist. Then again, he only allowed himself that indulgence once their missions were complete and the timelines had merged. They both assumed their small adventures were benign at that point.

Eva dismissed her concerns about her partner. Of

course Tophe was on edge. Lydia irritated her, too, and she posed a real danger to their success; the child didn't yet understand that time spent in Penance Hall was something she would only want to endure once. Eva had been just as naïve when she was younger, but no one survived repeat mission failures.

Regardless, there was no harm in meeting Einstein.

Within moments, they hovered nearby, eavesdropping on the engineer and the physicist, waiting for the men to make eye contact.

"My dear friend, this 'Spirit of 1914'—Germany over all —it is madness. All of Berlin is a lunatic asylum," Einstein said, his dark eyebrows drawing into a bow. "I'd rather move to Mars and view the inmates from a telescope. Nothing good will come from war. Nothing ever does."

"Bah," Bosch responded. "It's still possible the war will be over in a matter of months. Once the Oppau fertilizer factory is converted to produce the ingredients for gunpowder, we'll have an endless supply of ammunition."

Einstein snorted. "Oh, the irony."

To his credit, Bosch grimaced. "Though I'm not a pacifist like you, Albert, I dislike war as much as the next man, and believe me, I see the irony of toiling away to feed people only to turn around and use the same machine to kill them... But it's the only way."

Eva cleared her throat. "Pardon me...Herr Einstein, I presume?" In actuality, no presumption was needed; she had met many copies of him before on other missions, in other timelines.

The two men startled, then bowed before the ladies, clicking their heels.

"I am he," Einstein said, then introduced the man beside him.

Eva inclined her head. "My name is Helga Schmidt, and this is my niece, Anna. We are cousins of Clara Haber. She mentioned to us you are a physicist, and she knows of my niece's amateur interest in the science and suggested we meet you."

A broad grin spread across Einstein's face. "Well, well! Pleased to make your acquaintance, my dear," he said, focusing on Lydia. "What part of physics most intrigues you?"

In Eva's periphery, Tophe inserted himself in the circle of men surrounding Fritz Haber. With her partner away, Eva didn't stop Lydia from answering the scientist, curious to see how she would handle the conversation. As Lux Libera travelers, both knew the ins and outs of general relativity, had studied it in their very first classes after recruitment, but the young physicist had yet to publish the theory. Lydia would need to be engaging without feeding him thoughts he hadn't yet had himself.

Once she was confident the girl was navigating the tricky parameters with ease, Eva kept one ear on the discussion and one eye on Clara Haber. Ten minutes passed before she saw her opening.

"Excuse me, Herr Einstein," Eva said, interrupting him and pulling on Lydia's sleeve. "We haven't greeted Clara yet, and I see she is available."

Einstein clamped his mouth shut, lips thin for a moment, before his smile reached his eyes. "Yes, of course."

With a last bob of their heads, Eva took Lydia's arm and hooked it in the crook of her own. "This way," she said, voice low, anxious to reach the hostess before someone else started talking to her. She spared a glance in Tophe's direction, but no longer saw him next to Fritz.

"My dear Clara! It's wonderful to see you again. It's been too, too long!" Eva plastered joy across her face.

Their hostess's eyes rounded, blank and confused, obviously struggling to recognize the two strangers. Clara took a quick breath and extended her hand. "Yes, it has been too long," she said, matching Eva's enthusiasm, then pressed her lips together as if she would say more but wasn't sure what.

"You remember my niece, Anna?"

At the supplied name, Clara sighed, and a genuine, relieved smile settled on her features. "Yes, of course. My, how you've grown! You're nearly as tall as a man."

Lydia's persona cracked for the span of a heartbeat, and Eva saw the insecure girl underneath before she sealed the breach. Clara might as well have shined a spotlight on the child.

Eva laid a hand on Lydia's arm. "She's turning out to be quite the beauty," she said, smiling up at the girl. "Statuesque."

At those words, Lydia stood a little taller. "Thank you, Aunt Helga."

"But enough about us. We want to hear all the news about you and Fritz. I know you're busy raising young Hermann these days. What of Fritz? I hear he volunteered for the war?" Eva spooled out the lines, deftly creating the illusion of a two-way catching up between old friends. Eventually, Clara seemed to relax, resigned to the notion that she must know these women, for they certainly knew her, and she must have simply forgotten them. How embarrassing.

Finally, Eva said, "Is Fritz working on any new experiments?"

Clara drew back a hairsbreadth, and suspicion flitted behind her eyes, then dispersed. "He was just telling me about a new weapon he's planning to develop, but I shouldn't say much more."

"Do you know what I worry about? Poisonous gas." Eva rounded her mouth and glanced at Lydia for confirmation. "Can you imagine? How terrifying for our brave men!"

Next to them, a footman leaned in with a tray, and Lydia pounced on two canapés.

Clara's face, which had blanched, pinkened again. "It's funny you should say that. I agree; it would be terrifying, but only for our enemies. Such a weapon would end the war sooner. Many more lives would be saved."

For a moment, Eva's mind continued on its original track before realizing what the woman was saying. "But any poisonous gas used by us could also be used by our enemies."

"Not if we surprise them. My husband believes they would be so terrified, we could march to Paris unchallenged."

Eva's thoughts reeled. "It doesn't bother you?" A desperate note came into her voice, and she tried to quash it, to remain calm and reasoned. "You're a chemist yourself. I've always heard you promote science for good. Aren't you appalled to see technology used to kill people?"

"I'm a German first. We must defend ourselves if we want German civilization to continue to thrive."

This was not the Clara she had been told to expect; this timeline's Clara was a patriot. Over Lydia's shoulder, Tophe stepped through a distant doorway and locked eyes with Eva. He shook his head once, then walked toward a refreshment table.

With an inward sigh, Eva excused herself and Lydia to join her partner, and Clara seemed as relieved to move on to other guests as Eva was to leave.

"Well?" Tophe asked, stuffing a pastry into his mouth. Flakes of laminated crust dusted his lapel, and Eva reached up to brush them off.

"This Clara is immune to our Jedi mind tricks," Lydia said.

Tophe cocked his head. "What?"

"Bad intel," Eva said.

"I already knew that. What do you mean, 'Jedi mind tricks'?"

Lydia's jaw dropped. "Didn't you have *Star Wars* in your birth timeline?"

Tophe took another bite, leaning over a bit to catch the crumbs in his free hand. "No," he said out of the side of his mouth.

"How did you already know we had bad intel?" Eva asked.

"The pistol isn't with Fritz. It was supposed to be in a holster on his hip. I've started searching the house. I need your help."

"What about Clara?" Lydia asked.

"One thing at a time." Tophe rubbed his hands together until Eva handed him a napkin.

———

WHILE TOPHE SEARCHED the ground floor, Eva and Lydia snuck up the deserted back stairs. After a hasty reminder to leave everything as she had found it, Eva sent Lydia into the first bedroom, then continued to the second one herself, which appeared to be the Habers' own suite.

She started with the nightstands. Then, the dressing table. Under the bed. Wardrobe. Jacket pockets. Upper shelf. Shoe boxes. Hat boxes. Trunk—thankfully unlocked.

With nothing left to open, Eva stood in the center of the room and let her eyes rove over each piece of furniture, illuminated by a waxing moon, and she peered into the deep shadows, expecting to have overlooked something. When she was sure she had checked everything, she peeked into the dark hallway and listened. Not hearing a sound, she skirted around the door frame and into the next room.

Again, nothing. Her pace quickened as she searched successive rooms down the wing, no longer hopeful. Fritz Haber would have no reason to hide his sidearm in a guest bedroom.

Lydia met her at the top of the main stairway, her search equally fruitless.

Back downstairs, they discovered Tophe waiting for them. "I found a locked drawer in a writing desk. It's in a back room, away from the party. I already tried to pick it. It's not coming loose for me."

"Can I try?" Lydia asked.

"No. Eva's faster."

Eva ignored the look of disappointment from their charge. Now was not the time to practice. "You can watch me."

"No, she needs to be lookout. I can cover you better if I'm with you."

Lydia huffed, and her mouth drew down into a scowl.

"There will be other chances," Eva said. "I promise."

Tophe led the way to a quiet room where an occasional guest passed by, but the hallway cleared long enough for them to slip inside. Eva mouthed the words "Thank you" to Lydia before she closed the door on the girl's pouty face.

Within moments, Eva rounded the desk and knelt where Tophe pointed. Right-hand top drawer. Tumbler lock. She plucked her tools from her bodice, inserted the tension wrench, and then used her rake pick to knock the pins into place. When that didn't work, she switched to her hook; she'd do it one pin at a time.

Through the door, they heard Lydia say, "Excuse me, Herr Haber. Where is the toilet?"

"*Merde*," Tophe said under his breath, then pulled her to her feet. Eva clutched the tools in her fist and threw her arms around him.

As they had feared, the door opened, spilling light and sound across the threshold. Fritz Haber gazed at them, lips parted and eyebrows raised. "What is this? Who are you?"

While Tophe made their excuses, Eva did her best to blush, eyes cast downward, fiddling with her hair; lovers caught.

"A colleague of Bosch's, you say? He's already left, and I didn't see you arrive with him. Besides, he would never presume to invite guests to my party." Haber wagged his head. "I don't know who you are, but I want you to leave. Immediately. Before I call the police."

Without another word, Tophe grabbed Eva's hand, and she hurried after him, doubling her pace to keep up with his long-legged stride.

Lydia wasn't in the hall or the grand rooms they passed. Haber followed close on their heels, escorting them to the door, so they had no choice but to retrieve their coats and leave. At the last moment, Lydia appeared, her brow creased with worry. In her haste to join her mentors, she slipped on the polished floor. Haber's glower turned to fury when he saw her, but he seemed willing to let them go.

Rather than return to the garden, all three strode down the drive and continued along a residential lane. Eventually, the trio reached a street lined with shops shuttered for the night, and they stopped under the awning of a grocer.

For the entire length of the walk from Haber Villa, Tophe had kept up a muttered stream of French curses, but he was silent now.

"We'll just have to wait until the last guest leaves, and then break in," Eva said. "How much time do we have left?"

Tophe's initial response was to cup the back of his head with laced fingers and turn a half circle, deep in thought. His top hat tipped forward, low over his brow. After a moment, he read his pocket watch and said, "It's 10:50. Forty-nine minutes. We should be on our way home by now."

"That lock is going to be a pain in the ass. I can already tell."

"Didn't give me any trouble," Lydia said, holding the gun in her outstretched palm.

A laugh erupted from Tophe. "When did you do that? There wasn't time."

"As soon as you left the room with Haber. I was hiding around the corner. It popped right open for me. Two seconds."

"Thank God," Eva said, hugging her. "Well done!"

"Now who's faster?" Lydia asked, jutting her chin at Tophe.

"You. *Évidemment*." He grinned at her. "I'm sure we loosened it for you."

"Whatever. My father was a locksmith. Bet you're glad I came along."

"I am," Tophe said, tone serious. "I should have done my homework on you."

Lydia scrunched her forehead when she seemed to realize Tophe was no longer teasing her, then she glowed.

"Well," Eva said after confirming the pistol was loaded.

"Nothing to do now but wait, and do this the guaranteed way."

AFTER THE LAST guest turned the corner of the drive, Lydia signaled back to Tophe, who crouched next to the latticed doors that opened onto a side garden. He pushed the edge of a thin plastic card against the latch bolt, forcing the lock to open. After slipping off their shoes and holding them close, all three entered a windowed sitting room. They crept through the house on silent feet. Careful to stay to the side of each stairway tread rather than the noisy center, they ascended, pausing every few seconds to listen when a floorboard creaked.

Each of Lydia's steps landed flat-footed. To Eva's ears, the sound echoed through the chambers, making her cringe with anxiety. Unable to endure another, she turned and pantomimed stealth walking with her hand, rolling it palm to fingers as if it was her foot. Lydia squinted at her, and Eva jabbed toward the girl's stocking toes peeking out from under her skirt.

Lydia formed a silent "ah" with her mouth and stepped forward precisely as she had before. Eva gritted her teeth and told herself it didn't matter. No one else was in the house, just the Habers' young son, Hermann, who had already been put to bed earlier in the evening, and the Habers, whose own voices masked any tiny sounds she and Tophe and Lydia might make. The ongoing dialog between the married couple drifted over the banister to the trio.

At the bedroom doorway, with Haber's gun in his hand, Tophe glanced first at Eva, then at Lydia. Eva would act as backup this time, though she doubted he would need it.

Tophe held up the pocket watch, showing Eva the time. 11:38. After a shared nod, he pushed away from the wall and entered the bedroom.

Clara screamed. So did Fritz, which didn't surprise Eva. Men, startled in the comfort of their own homes, rarely acted with instant bravery.

Tophe pulled the trigger, hitting Herr Haber in the forehead, then turned to Frau Haber and shot her in the chest, exactly where she killed herself in the True line. She had stood from her dressing table but now fell back against it, her disoriented eyes not seeming to know where to land. Tophe. Eva. Lydia. Her husband.

Just as she slid to her knees, knocking a perfume bottle to the floor, they heard a shout from downstairs.

"Who's that?" Eva whispered. The cloying scent of a thousand concentrated rose petals filled the space, a near tangible thing.

"I don't know. Maid?" Tophe replied, shoving the pistol into Clara's hand and threading the dying woman's finger through the trigger guard. From below, someone clattered up the stairs, rattling the banister.

Tophe gestured emphatically toward the double bed, then slipped behind the door. Lydia was already halfway under when Eva, hampered by her fur coat and pulling and tucking her dress as best she could, dove beside her. To her horror, she saw Lydia's shoe on the floor next to the bed, but before she could reach out to retrieve it, a woman rushed through the door.

She didn't scream. Instead, she whispered, "Oh. Oh. Oh...," scurrying from one body to the other and back again, touching neither.

"Mama?" a child's voice called from the hallway.

"Hermann!" the woman said and seemed to snap out of

her loop of indecisiveness. She was beside him in three strides to cover his eyes with her hand. "We need to get help," she said, turning his shoulders to put his back to the scene.

"But Mama..."

"They're hurt, and we need..." The rest of her words became inaudible as she pulled him along with her at a run.

Next to Eva, Lydia sniffed, her lips quivering and tears streaming down her face. Eva brought her mouth to the girl's ear. "It wasn't real, Lydia. It wasn't real. It looked real, but it wasn't real."

"We killed them. Tophe killed them. I killed them."

"No. No, Lydia. Listen. It wasn't real."

"But it's real now. The lines merged, right? It's real now." Lydia's voice fried on her last words.

"Yes, it's real now, but they killed each other, not us. We didn't kill them."

"That boy." Lydia hid her face in the back of her hands. Downstairs, the front door slammed.

Eva's heart squeezed, seeing Hermann's face again in her own memory. "It can't be helped. It's what really happened. We can't change that."

Lydia cried harder, more audibly now.

"When I first started, it helped if I pretended I killed a bad guy. Even though the old timeline wasn't real, you can pretend that we just saved millions of people. Literally millions. Think of all the fathers and brothers who won't be gassed in the trenches, the entire families who won't be gassed in Auschwitz. Little boys, girls, grandparents, mothers." Eva felt herself pleading with Lydia and stopped. The girl was overwhelmed. "I'm sorry," Eva said. "It gets easier. I promise."

Tophe's shiny black dress shoes appeared at the edge of

the bed, then his knees, hands, and face. "Come on." He passed Lydia's dropped shoe to Eva. "Put your shoes back on."

The house remained dark and quiet as they ran down the stairs and through the sitting room, re-locking the door as they left. At the tree, Lydia braced herself against the trunk and vomited on the roots. Tophe wrinkled his nose, hovering his hand over her back, but then seemed to decide his touch might help. Eva gathered the girl's hair out of the way.

"Honestly, I threw up the first time, too," Tophe said.

Eva smirked. "True story."

When Lydia pushed away from the tree, she smiled wanly. "I'm sorry."

"No apologies needed," Tophe said. "You did good. Didn't even talk too much."

"You okay?" Eva asked. "It's not wise to hang out here."

In answer, Lydia placed her hand on the trunk and formed a portal.

———

LYDIA REMAINED silent throughout their report to the elders. Despite the bad intel, they had succeeded in the end, repaired the universe a little more, and survived to make it home. That was all that mattered. Tophe praised Lydia's quick thinking and recommended her for future missions, but the girl didn't smile. They had been allowed to rest the evening before and had come to the council the following day, but Eva assumed she was still processing her experience.

Dismissed and outside once again, she put her arm around the girl's waist. "I'm proud of you."

"Thank you," Lydia said.

"Eh, me, too," Tophe said. "Though I hate to admit it." He shoved her head forward, mussing her hair.

Lydia shied away at first, still subdued, but then fell a step behind and wrapped her long arms around his neck in a rear naked choke. Unfazed, Tophe tossed her over his shoulder in a judo throw and pressed his knee into her belly, laughing. "You'll have to do better than that."

The girl's eyes lit at the challenge, despite the wind being knocked out of her lungs, and Eva was glad to see her solemn face clearing. Tophe grasped her hand to pull her to her feet.

"I'll get you when you least suspect it," Lydia said.

"I'd like to see you try."

As they continued to walk toward the dormitories, no one spoke for a moment, and a heaviness returned to the novice's face.

"I've been thinking...in some timelines that we learned about in class, Fritz Haber didn't invent the fertilizer factories at all. World War I ended in 1915, three years earlier than the True line and the timeline we just merged. Germany was forced to surrender because they didn't have a way to make gunpowder. With the war ending early, the Allies didn't punish Germany so harshly, and Hitler never rose to power. Also, the Germans didn't need to send Lenin back to Russia after being in exile, and the Bolshevik revolution never happened, so no Stalin either."

"That's like my birth timeline," Tophe said.

"And another thing! Is all that fertilizer in the world a good thing? What's it do to the ground? And the water? The animals? Us? Is there some sort of balance it's messing up? And all those billions of more people on the planet? I mean, is that really such a good thing?"

"I don't know," Eva said, and her partner tensed beside her.

"Was your birth timeline better than the True line, Tophe?" The girl stopped moving, and the older two turned to face her.

"It's an irrelevant question, Lydia."

"How is it irrelevant? We're 'repairing the world,' aren't we? Why wouldn't we be making it better?"

"Because it's not real. This is real." Tophe grasped his forearms with his hands and squeezed, then opened his arms wide, taking in the sanctum and all of Axis Mundi. "Only this world. My birth timeline was a fantasy. Is a fantasy. The True timeline isn't perfect, because nothing about this material world, this mistake of creation, is perfect. None of this should exist at all. That's our purpose, Lydia. To put the genie back in the bottle, Pandora back in the box. To return to a state of bliss and unity with God. And we can't do that until all the timelines are recombined with the True line."

Lydia stared off into the middle distance.

"Don't you see? There is no place else." Tophe put a hand on her shoulder. "Do you understand the stakes?"

After a moment, Lydia refocused on his face but didn't speak for a beat. As the novice moved her gaze to Eva, questions brimmed behind the girl's eyes, and a gulf yawned between them. Eva's teachers had explained these inconsistencies long ago when she was still a novice herself, yet a deep uneasiness burrowed into her chest, unearthing loose threads Eva had forgotten.

Finally, Lydia's mouth moved to form words, but then she looked away, jaw set. "Yes, I understand."

Biography

Jennifer Marchman lives in Austin, Texas, with her husband, three nearly-grown children, and the two best dogs in the world. At different times, she has worn various authorial hats, including ghostwriter-memoirist, editor, curriculum writer, educational blogger, grant writer, and addicted social media over-sharer, but now, after many years, she's writing for pleasure.

Besides being a member of the Writers' League of Texas, Jennifer belongs to the Historical Novel Society and #TimeTravelAuthors in the Twitterverse. She also enjoys flamenco dancing, is the proud owner of a white belt in jiu-jitsu, and wishes to compete internationally in mounted archery but lacks a ticket to Kazakhstan. She has toyed with the idea of picking up pottery again, but needs more hours in her day and a husband willing to install (for the fourth time) the necessary electrical outlet for a kiln that may likely go unused.

Jennifer's debut novel, *The Mender*, is a 2022 Finalist in the Writers' League of Texas Manuscript Contest.

TO JOIN Eva on her next mission, visit: https://jennifermarchman.com/. Everything she believes is about to be upended.

THE DARK HORSE

K. L. SMALL

1860

I urged Fireball into a full gallop. The pony responded, and her hooves thundered against the dry ground. Puffs of dust exploded with each footfall. We dodged around clumps of pale gray sagebrush and raced past a herd of buffalo. With every stride, the mail pouches squeaked against the saddle leather, and the wind whistled by my ears.

Barely seventeen, short and skinny, I rode a fast horse, carrying mail across the frontier. Ten days from St. Joe to Sacramento was the goal. Fireball and I were nine miles into this morning's run to Sand Springs Station.

The pony snorted. Her nostrils flared, and her heavy breathing matched the beat of her hooves.

Getting tired.

Her exhaustion pressed into my mind.

"We're almost there. Got to keep going." I tapped my boot heels against Fireball's sides and leaned forward.

We flew over the ground, while the mare's mane whipped against my face. Dust swirled around us, and I coughed. The thrill of the ride coursed through my body. My dead parents would never have imagined their son, little Mike Barnes, riding for the Pony Express.

I spotted the stone walls of the way station in the distance and waved my hat. "Yippee!" Quickly, I lifted the bugle to my lips and blew three short bursts to warn the station master we were approaching. "He'll get my next horse ready."

Fireball tossed her head.

You should go back to the carousel.

"You're right." I lowered the bugle and fumbled for the black cord hanging around my neck. With a tug on the cord, a brass ring emerged from my shirt. I held it in my gloved hand. The sun glinted off its smooth surface.

Once, I had made the mistake of racing into a station, jumping off Fireball, transferring the mail pouches to the saddle on a fresh horse, and riding away on the next leg of the trip. It had taken me a week to reunite with Fireball. I needed her to return to the carousel and my real-time life. I wouldn't make that mistake again.

I closed my fingers around the magic ring and imagined myself back on the carousel in Barnwell Park, Upstate New York. With a blast of cold air and a blaze of colors, I transitioned across time.

When I opened my eyes, I was astride a wooden carousel horse with a bugle carved into the saddle. Smiling, I patted the arched neck before me. "Thanks, Fireball. I enjoyed our ride."

Anytime.

Her warm thoughts settled in my head.

With my wrinkled hands wrapped around the pole in

front of me, I slowly lifted my leg over the horse's back and carefully lowered myself onto the carousel platform. My hips and knees ached from the effort. My body reminded me I was seventy-two, not a youthful Pony Express rider. Heading toward the exit, I shuffled past the brightly painted ponies. Many invited me to join them for a ride. I politely declined. My old body wasn't as agile as it had been years ago.

Before leaving the carousel, I paused next to the dark horse—a plain black jumper on the second row. His eyes were wide in fright, and his mouth open, exposing his teeth and tongue. He hadn't spoken to me yet, so I didn't know his name. "You're the only one I haven't ridden."

Children scampering off the ride avoided me, eyeing me with a nervous expression. I'm sure they thought I was a crazy old man talking to a wooden horse. I suspected my family thought the same thing.

I limped over to the bench by the carousel entrance, where my redheaded grandson, Russell, slumped, his cap pulled low over his face. He always looked depressed. "Russ, my boy, you should ride with me next time. You never know what adventure awaits."

The boy rolled his eyes. "No thanks, Grandpa."

I sighed. Ever since I moved in with my daughter and her family, the relationship with my grandson had gone downhill. Giving up his bedroom for me didn't sit well with either of us, but Carla had insisted.

On the walk home, I told Russell about the challenges of being a Pony Express rider in 1860. The boy gave me a skeptical look. He didn't question me, but the doubt was there in his eyes. Like the kids on the carousel, he thinks I'm a crazy old man, too.

THE NEXT DAY, I sat next to the bedroom window in my
rocking chair, keeping the movement slow and steady. The
wooden slats creaked in a comforting way. Sweet Violet had
loved this rocker, despite my complaints that it was noisy.
Now, I cherished it as a reminder of my late wife, that and
the handmade quilt on the bed. I recalled her working on
the colorful fabric squares, stitching an intricate pattern
across the patchwork top.

The hands on the face of my watch crept toward 3:30.
Russell would be home from school soon. Then we would
walk to the Barnwell Park carousel. Carla insisted the boy
accompany me. I guess she figured the ten-year-old would
ensure I didn't get lost.

At the sound of the front door opening downstairs, I
hobbled over to my chest of drawers and splashed on some
cologne. Violet always loved the woodsy scent. A quick
check of the cord around my neck confirmed the brass ring
was tucked inside my shirt. I slipped on my walking shoes
and headed down to the kitchen.

Russell leaned against the kitchen countertop,
munching a cookie. His shoulders drooped, and his eyes
were downcast.

I frowned. Trying to lighten the mood, I asked, "How
was school today?"

"Okay." He shoved the last bit of cookie in his mouth.

"Ready to go to the carousel?"

The boy shrugged, and I took that as acceptance.

At Barnwell Park, the lively music from the carousel's
band organ greeted me before I could see the shingled roof
of the carousel pavilion. My pace increased in anticipation
of today's ride.

"Russ, my boy. Do you know how many horses are on this carousel?"

He mumbled something I couldn't hear.

"There are sixty horses in four rows, and I've ridden all but one of them."

The boy glanced at me with a raised eyebrow. "How do you know that?"

"I just do." I couldn't tell him that each horse had a distinct personality, name, and history. Or that they talked to me. Not in words that people could hear, but in my head. And they each took me for a ride into the past, thanks to the magic brass ring.

"When you ride the last one, we don't have to come anymore?" The boy sounded way too happy.

"Don't be ridiculous, Russ. I can ride them all over again." I had ridden some of them several times already. "You sure you don't want to ride today?" I always offered, and he always declined.

I hurried to join the line of riders waiting to enter the carousel's platform, excited about today's adventure. I had made a personal goal to ride every horse on the carousel. The dark horse was the last one left for me to ride, and today was the day.

When the gate opened, I touched every horse I passed, and they each greeted me with warm wishes. Some asked if I would ride them today. I gave the same answer to each of them. "Today I ride the dark horse."

With stiff joints, I mounted the dark horse, glad that he hadn't stopped in his highest position. I settled into the saddle and stroked the glossy black neck. "What's your name?"

No answer.

I looked at the smaller paint horse to the left. Patches

and I got along well. Every ride on Patches took me back to days when kids wore fringed vests and cowboy hats while sitting on the paint pony to have their photo taken. The chubby pony loved standing still for the kids. "Patches, why won't he answer me?"

He says it won't end well.

Patches' words sounded somber.

"What's his name?"

He has a couple. He was happiest being called Big Jim.

The carousel attendant called out, "Stay on your horse. The ride will start shortly."

I tugged on the black cord around my neck, and the brass ring emerged from my shirt. I held it in my hand and closed my fingers around its smooth surface.

The attendant rang the bell, and the band organ played a peppy march tune. The high-pitched notes spun around me. With a shudder, the carousel moved forward.

"Here we go, Big Jim." I closed my eyes in anticipation of the familiar blast of cold air and blaze of lights that meant I was traveling through time.

The carousel circled slowly and gradually increased speed. The horses rose and fell. I rode the motion, imagining Big Jim in a ground-covering gallop, but nothing happened. I was still on the carousel, going up and down. Why wasn't I transported back in time? Why wasn't Big Jim talking to me?

I opened my hand to check the ring. Was the magic used up? I thought about the possibility that I could no longer have time travel adventures on the carousel figures. In desperation, I called aloud, "Patches, is the magic done?"

Several children riding nearby horses turned to stare at me. Their eyes accused me of being a crazy old man. I'd seen that look before.

I steadied myself.

Patches, why isn't the magic working?

The painted figure rose and fell beside me.

The magic is fine. He doesn't want you to get hurt.

Tell him I'll be careful.

Suddenly, I sensed a solid, gentle presence in my mind. I held tight to the carousel pole in front of me and closed the fingers of my other hand over the brass ring again. The gust of wind hit me straight in the face, and bursts of colors exploded before my gaze.

When the transition was over, I was standing in a field under a bright blue sky with leather reins in my hands. Before me were two massive draft horses—a black and a gray. Between us was a plow and the broken ground, rich and fertile. I was younger, stronger, and muscular. My aches and pains of old age were gone. I didn't know what year it was, but sensed we were in the Midwest and this was a time before diesel-fueled tractors.

Big Jim snorted and leaned into the harness. The plow jerked forward, and I followed, holding tight to the plow's wooden handles. The plowshare cut into the sod, releasing an earthy smell of fresh-turned soil. I peeked at the long, straight furrow behind us.

We worked for hours, turning at the end of each row. The sun sank lower in the sky, and the dinner bell clanged. It was hard, satisfying work.

"Well done, boys," I said to the team.

Champion plow team at last year's state fair.

The pride in Big Jim's words filled my head with his contentment in a good day's labor.

"Thanks for sharing this with me." I patted Big Jim's rump, then pulled the brass ring from around my neck and pictured myself back at the carousel. After the usual jump through time, I was back on the wooden horse, and the band organ music died down as the carousel stopped moving.

I had done it. I had ridden all sixty horses on this carousel and was feeling pleased with myself. "Patches, I met my goal."

Big Jim says to come back tomorrow if you're feeling brave and prepared to die.

There was no missing the tremor in Patches' words.

I dismounted slowly, with my old legs complaining about the movement. As Russell and I walked home, I mulled over the possibility of dying on one of these time travel rides. Sure, there had been dangerous situations, but I never came close to dying. If I died in the past, what would happen to my family? Would my children and Russell have been born? My head pounded at the thought. Or would I be a missing old man with a silver alert reporting my last whereabouts being the carousel?

"Are you okay, Grandpa? You seem pretty quiet." The boy's face wore a worried expression. "You usually talk a lot after one of your rides."

"Sorry, Russ. I have a lot on my mind."

I DIDN'T SLEEP well that night. Tossing and turning, I wondered what could take a peaceful plow horse into a life-threatening situation. Should I ride him tomorrow and find out?

The next day, Russell and I walked to the park as usual. I told him how before modern tractors, horses pulled plows to grow our crops. How they competed in fairs to prove which team plowed straighter and faster. How a hard day's work was its own reward. I continued talking to keep my mind off what might be ahead.

Once we were at the carousel, I went directly to the dark horse. "I'm here, Big Jim."

You might not come back.

His tone was grim.

"You'll keep me safe."

There was no answer from the dark horse.

The carousel bell sounded, and the band organ wheezed into life. With a groan, the carousel moved forward. I grasped the brass ring in my hand and braced for the blast of cold air. A whirl of colors and sounds flashed around me.

When they stopped, the bright colors were replaced with a gray haze and misty rain. My modern clothes had changed into a drab olive-green wool coat and breeches. I recognized the shape of the helmets on the American soldiers around me. World War I, the "war to end all wars." Only it didn't.

I rode in a rudimentary saddle on Big Jim's back. In the harness beside us was another horse, but without a rider. When I looked back, two more rows of horses, with one rider per pair, pulled a two-wheeled wagon carrying three gunners, followed by a 75mm artillery piece. Somehow, I knew what everything was and what was expected. We were the American Expeditionary Forces in France.

"Private Barnes, get that horse moving!" the captain shouted. "We need this gun in place. General Black Jack Pershing says we're taking the fight to the enemy."

"Yes, sir." I urged Big Jim forward along the muddy road. His hooves disappeared into the thick muck. The mud rose to his knees.

Artillery fire exploded around us in loud, angry bursts.

Clouds of acrid smoke hung in the air. These were our guns firing over us to clear the way for our doughboys to advance. Our gun had to move ahead as they made progress.

Mud sucked at the horses' legs, and Big Jim struggled to lift his front leg. His muscles strained with the effort. He pressed his shoulders into the harness with a grunt. The leather straps creaked, and the chains clanked. The wheels behind us inched forward.

"You can do it," I said as calmly as I could. My heart pounded, and I tried to breathe slowly.

With a mighty heave, Big Jim found a better foothold and surged forward. The horse beside us whinnied in panic. The hitched team battled through the mud with riders yelling and waving whips. Gradually, we pulled the gun ahead.

The rain increased, and visibility reduced to a few feet. All that mattered was one more step forward. The sucking sound of the mud and the roar of the exploding shells were constant, mixed with the screams and moans of the injured. I had heard of the horrors of war, but now I was living them. The smell of death, decay, and despair overwhelmed me. I trembled uncontrollably.

I warned you.

Big Jim snorted.

We slogged on through the mud. The footing got worse, and I slid off Big Jim's back to lead him through a large puddle. Only it wasn't a puddle; it was a deep shell hole, and the bottom was somewhere well below my boots. I floundered in the water. My wool clothes weighed me down. Desperately, I swam back toward Big Jim. I had to return to the carousel. With trembling fingers, I groped for the brass ring.

A whizz whistled by me, followed by a bang. Clods of

dirt and mud flew through the air. The blast hurled me across the water and hit the team of horses. Horses screamed in pain. Big Jim collapsed into the mud.

"No!" I struggled through the deep water and lifted his head from the mud.

Big Jim's nostrils flared, and a trickle of blood dripped from his mouth.

Hurry. Go back while you can.

"I'm so sorry." Tears welled in my eyes, and I gripped the brass ring in my mud-covered hand. I imagined myself on the carousel and listened to Big Jim's death rattle.

"MOMMY, WHY IS THAT MAN CRYING?" the little girl sitting on Patches said, pointing at me.

"I don't know," her mother said. "But let's leave him alone." She hustled her daughter off the carousel.

I sat on the dark horse with the same empty feeling I had when my sweet Violet died. Big Jim was silent. I was a broken old man sitting on a carousel horse. I couldn't move.

"Grandpa, are you ready to go home?" Russell called from outside the carousel fencing.

Numb, I slipped off the horse and stumbled to the exit. None of my past adventures had prepared me for this. I didn't say a word to Russell on our walk home. I went straight to my room and sat in the rocking chair, mourning a painful loss.

I thought I had lost everything when my wife died. My kids had meant well, but they decided I was too old to drive or live by myself. They took my car keys and sold the little bungalow Violet and I had shared for over forty-six years. Everything was gone except the magic brass ring. Now, with Big Jim's death, I wasn't sure I wanted the ring anymore.

Several hours later, Carla turned on the light when she came into my bedroom. "Dad, are you feeling all right?"

How could I tell her I was crushed by the death of a horse in a muddy French field, in some World War I battle that happened before I was born? She would say it was dementia talking.

"Carla, could you take me to the library tomorrow?"

"Certainly, Dad. What are you looking for? Maybe I have a book that would interest you."

"I'd like to learn more about horses in World War I." I wasn't sure what I was looking for, but I had to know more about what had put Big Jim in that situation.

Carla patted me on the knee. "We can go online after dinner and see what we can find out."

My mood brightened. "I'd like that."

True to her word, after dinner, my daughter turned on the computer and typed a few words into the search. She leaned forward and read several articles. "This is pretty grim, Dad. Millions of horses died during that war. Conditions were terrible for them." She pulled up several black-and-white photos on the screen.

I had lived those images. With a sigh, I studied them closely. "What happened at the end of the war?"

She typed a few more words and scanned the screen. "Most of the horses were left behind. They were malnourished and sick." She paused. "Here's a story that has a happy ending."

I peered at the computer screen and read the article about war horses that had survived. It gave me a glimmer of hope.

THE NEXT DAY, I hurried back to the carousel with a plan.

Russell kept saying, "Slow down, Grandpa."

"One day, Russ, you'll ride the carousel with me." I needed to pass the magic brass ring along to another generation.

"Maybe," he said without enthusiasm.

"You'll see, but there's something I need to do today."

On the carousel, I raced to the dark horse and climbed aboard. "Big Jim, take me back to the time you came off the ship in France, before you were picked to pull the gun."

When the music started, I grasped the brass ring with excitement. In all my time travel adventures, I had never tried to change history. I always was careful not to interfere with anything historically significant. But today, I was determined to save Big Jim's life.

After the transition, I found myself at the remount depot with hundreds of horses milling around. The stockyard smell filled my nostrils. Amid the mass of animals, Big Jim towered over the smaller horses.

A British officer marched over to me, his uniform clean and crisp. He sported a thin mustache over his upper lip.

I saluted properly and stood at attention.

"Private, my horse was shot out from under me last week. The doctor cleared me to ride again, but I need a new mount."

I smiled. "Sir, I have a champion horse for you. He's smart, steady, and a hard worker."

"Sounds like a winner. Let's see this chap."

I paraded Big Jim before the officer. "He's as sound as they come."

The officer nodded. "Not my usual hunt horse. Looks more like a plow horse."

"He's calm under fire. He'll stand still for you, even in extreme conditions."

The officer walked around Big Jim. "I'll need a different saddle, but he'll work."

"Sir, I have one request."

"Speak up, lad." The officer stroked his mustache.

"When you return to England. Please take this horse back with you. He deserves to have a peaceful end."

"Bloody right. We all do."

"Your promise, sir." I was overstepping my position, but I had to try.

"My word as a gentleman. If I survive, he'll have a home with me. Now, cheerio!" The officer took Big Jim's lead rope and walked away. The horse followed obediently.

Big Jim glanced back at me.

Thank you.

In a minute, I realized my mistake. The same mistake I had made with Fireball. I needed to be with Big Jim to return to the carousel. I might not see him again, the way I did with Fireball. I'd be trapped here in 1918.

I raced through the crowd of soldiers and horses. Finally, I spotted Big Jim's rump ahead and reached out to grab his tail. Quickly, I pulled the brass ring from around my neck and wished myself back on the carousel.

A blast of air and a wild swirl of colors rushed before my eyes. When the transition was done, I sat on the carousel horse as the music faded and the ride slowed. Several strands of Big Jim's tail hair dangled from my hand. I had changed his history!

I never rode the dark horse again. I hated to find out whether he and the British officer made it back to England.

In my life—what's left of it—I will forever dream of Big Jim running in a green field, free from harnesses and far from the memories of war. Perhaps when my life is over and I'm reunited with Violet, we'll ride the dark horse, his big hooves thudding against the sod, and his mane streaming before us. Together forever.

Biography

Originally from New York City, K. L. Small lives in Florida now on a horse ranch called Carousel Acres with her husband, three horses, and four barn cats. She writes fantasies for the young of heart. Her short stories have appeared in two Florida Writers Association annual collections. The most recent one, *Memory Lane Park*, was ranked #1 in the Thrills and Chills collection, published in August 2022. Her debut novel, *A Dress to Remember—A Fairy Tale*, is scheduled for release in March 2023, followed by a middle-grade series based on the magic brass ring from *The Dark Horse*.

WEBSITE:
   https://kathleenlsmall.com/

THE TITANIC TIME HEIST

JANET RAYE STEVENS

THE TEMPORAL VORTEX spit Marina and Fred out on the boat deck. Before the time tornado's whirlwind and ghostly, flickering blue light had faded, Marina bent over the ship's rail and upchucked her breakfast into the North Atlantic.

Ugh.

She wished she could blame sudden seasickness for her undignified rush to the rail, but the truth was, her stomach reeled from the shake and shimmy of the time skip and the squeezing pressure of gravity pulling her down into the past.

"Again, Marina?" Fred came up beside her. "You get sick every time. You'd think you never made the jump before."

Avoiding his gaze, she dabbed a silk handkerchief to her mouth, then adjusted her wide-brimmed feathered hat secured to her head with a jeweled hat pin. Fred considered her weak. She supposed she was, compared to a warhorse like him. He could temporal skip fifteen times a day without the slightest side effect. He could eat any kind of food from any era, even spoiled haggis, and never get sick. He waded with the confidence of a lion into crowds of people afflicted with all kinds of maladies and illnesses, and he never caught so much as a sniffle.

Nothing bothered Fred. Especially not the reason they'd traveled here, to this particular ship, at this particular moment in time—to rob the dead. Well, to rob the *soon* to be dead.

"I'm fine," she said, taking as deep a breath as her corset would allow and pushing away her dizziness. "Let's get this over with, shall we? We don't have a lot of time."

Frowning, Fred slid up the sleeve of his wool topcoat and squinted at the time travel device strapped to his wrist. Pulsing blue lights zipped around inside a clear, circular globe. The time bauble, he called it. Given his love of jewels and all things shiny, the nickname fit. A timer on the bauble's miniature control panel counted down the minutes until the supposedly unsinkable Titanic's fatal date with an iceberg.

"Stop worrying." Fred covered the device with his sleeve once more. "I'll get the job done with time to spare. Now, which way do we go?"

They stepped out from between two lifeboats, where their arrival had been mostly hidden from sight by the huge steel davits keeping the boats in place. The smell of smoke pouring from the smokestacks tinged the cold night air, the engines thrummed, and water lapped against the hull as the ship cut steadily through the ocean. People in evening clothes and warm coats strolled past, men and women out for a chilly late evening walk along the boat deck.

While Fred gazed at the passersby with a greedy

glimmer in his eyes, anticipating the robbery and their gems and valuables he would soon take as his own, gloom pressed down on Marina like heavy clouds before a storm. Chances of survival were far better for these people than those from the decks below, the people in second or third class who would soon jostle for a space in one of the limited number of lifeboats.

At midships, Fred picked up his pace. Marina hurried to keep up, somewhat hobbled by the narrow skirt of her ankle-length dress and clinging coat. The fast *tap-tap* of her Cuban-style heels against the deck's teak wood matched the anxious beat of her heart. She couldn't shake the dread that had gripped her since Fred had chosen the Titanic for their latest heist. They planned to follow the same strategy for this job as all the others. Pop into a historical event minutes before disaster struck, pilfer what they could, then temporal skip back to the year 2130 with no one the wiser in either time period.

The perfect crime, Fred insisted. The people they stole from were fated to die. They would neither notice nor care if their valuables had vanished. If they did, it would be too late to do anything about it. But something about this job frightened Marina beyond her normal jitters. Some kind of foreboding or premonition, or maybe just being on this doomed ship at the moment of its greatest peril.

They reached the first-class entrance. A steward of about thirty held the door for people to go in and out. He caught her eye as she and Fred passed through.

"Evening, miss," he said with a smile and a voice that announced his address as somewhere around Belfast, Ireland. Dressed in a snowy-white coat and dark trousers, he had a roundish face and neatly combed red hair.

Marina returned a solemn nod, gripped by that gloomy

feeling again. Would this poor man drown or freeze to death first when the Titanic sank? Who was he leaving behind to mourn him?

"Don't even think about it." Fred grabbed her arm and yanked her forward. "I know you and your tender heart. You want to warn him, but you can't. You *can't* change the past."

Can't change the past—the only rule Fred hadn't broken since he'd begun his life of time crime. History couldn't be changed, he said. A person's fate was fixed, their destiny set. Marina suspected he followed that philosophy mostly to protect his own skin. He'd stolen the bauble from Time Scope, Inc., the massive time tourism conglomerate that held iron-fisted control over all things time travel. A daring move that had put a large target on Fred's back. Any blips he caused in the timeline could alert the company's security force and lead them to him.

And to Marina.

She shook off his bruising grip. "I know that. I'm not stupid."

"Could've fooled me," he muttered and strode purpose-fully into the ship's lavish interior.

She followed, taking in the clashing smells of electric heat, cigar smoke, and body odor not quite smothered by the flowery scent of perfume. People strolled about, the men dressed in tuxedos, the women in colorful gowns and ridicu-lously large feathers adorning their hair. At the center of all the activity stood the grand staircase. A magnificent struc-ture, with strategically placed lights illuminating the wrought-iron and glass dome above solid oak steps that wound gently downward, spanning six decks, with a broad landing on each deck.

A warning prickle shivered down Marina's spine, and

she glanced back. The redheaded steward had come inside and passed slowly by them. He met her gaze again. He offered no smile this time. More of a deeply curious examination.

She stiffened, and every doubt and worry she'd had about this job bubbled to the surface. Was the steward on to them? Did he suspect they weren't who they pretended to be? She'd done her best to get their clothing and other details right, but she was no historical expert. Something she'd declared time and again to Fred when he pushed her to use her limited research abilities to get them around the places he chose for their thieving jaunts.

"We have to move," she said in an urgent whisper and pushed Fred toward the stairs before the steward could get any closer. The sooner they got this heist over with and left all these ghosts from history behind them, the better.

They descended swiftly and at the A-deck landing, she steered Fred toward the handful of first-class cabins on this deck. Her nervousness accelerated, while his excitement grew, as they closed in on their destination, a wide corridor with wood-paneled walls painted white.

Comfortably appointed staterooms lined one side of the hallway, not as luxurious as the first-class accommodations on the decks immediately below, but larger than the second-class cabins and a thousand times more opulent than the third-class rooms.

Luckily, no one was about. Marina hung back as Fred approached the first room and sized it up, prepping himself as an athlete readies himself for a competition. Then, he rapped on the door, as bold as could be. He waited a few seconds for a response. If someone answered his knock, he'd declare he'd been looking for a friend and had mistaken the room. If the occupants were out, that hungry look would spark in his eyes, and he'd get to work.

Their luck held, and he got no answer. In a flash, he'd picked the lock.

"Try to be quick," Marina urged as he disappeared inside.

She fiddled with the laces on her fur-lined, wraparound coat and lingered in the passageway, watching for trouble as Fred skulked from one unoccupied stateroom to the next, filling a carpetbag with jewelry and diamond stickpins and sundry other valuables they could hawk as rare antiques when they got back.

The carpetbag grew fatter, and Marina grew agitated as time passed and the clock ticked closer to Titanic's impending doom. She swore Fred took his time robbing each cabin just to try her patience.

A movement along the corridor alerted her, and she sucked in a gasp. A young couple rounded the corner and slowed as they neared her. And the room Fred currently occupied. Marina's heart hammered against her ribs. Was this their room?

"Good evening," she bellowed as loud as a foghorn, hoping her voice would carry to Fred inside and warn him.

The couple returned an amused and slightly superior look but thankfully moved on. Marina's racing heartbeat barely had time to slow when a familiar figure rounded the corner and strode down the corridor. The redheaded steward. Too much of a coincidence he'd bumped into her a third time.

"I haven't seen you about on the decks before," he said, pinning her in his gaze, his eyes as stormy blue as the ocean.

For a moment, Marina feared he could be one of Time Scope's security forces in disguise, trying to trip her up, but she rejected the thought as quickly as it came. He seemed far too nice. From what she'd heard, Time Scope's time cops shot first and asked questions later.

Still, his curiosity could be a threat. One question could lead to another she had no answer for and then...

She couldn't risk being found out. She scrambled for a convincing lie. "I've, uh, stayed in my room since we left port. I'm suffering from a...an upset stomach." She gulped. Did women say the word *stomach* in mixed company in this time period? "I know it's silly. How does one get seasick on a boat this big? It's like a floating Fifth Avenue."

"Ah." He stepped closer, bringing with him the smell of pipe tobacco and the salty aroma of the sea. "Are you sure *mal de mer* is the only thing troubling you? You seem ill at ease, if I may say so. Let me assure you, there's nothing to fear. The Titanic is as safe as houses."

"That's comforting, thank you." She ached at his earnest voice and even more earnest expression. And his confident words, soon to be proved wrong. She opened her mouth to warn him about the horror he would face in the next hours, but Fred's voice bleated in her head. She couldn't change the past. She couldn't help him. His fate was sealed. "What's your name?" she found herself asking instead.

"Joseph. Joseph Mara, Miss—?"

"Marina Santos," she said, surprised she'd answered so readily, and so truthfully.

"Marina. That's a fine name. A name connected to the sea."

A thump sounded from within the stateroom, followed by a muffled curse. Marina wanted to curse too. Of all the times for Fred to get clumsy. Joseph stiffened and swung his gaze toward the sound, his curiosity deepening to suspicion.

Marina's insides erupted into a frenzy. Were they finally to be caught? After escaping so narrowly so many times? They'd time skipped out of Pompeii with ash falling on their heads and lava nipping at their heels. Had their luck finally run out?

A deep, hollow *thup* suddenly ripped along the ship's hull, a sound like the tearing of a thick fabric. The Titanic shuddered from stem to stern. Marina wobbled and nearly fell. Joseph staggered too.

"What was that?" he asked, his face creasing in concern.

Marina's blood turned to ice. *That*, she knew, was history.

WITH A DISTRACTED AND HASTY "GOOD NIGHT," Joseph retreated down the corridor, and Fred popped out of the stateroom a few seconds later.

"And you tell me *I* take too many risks," he griped. "What in hell were you thinking, flirting with that man? You could've gotten yourself snagged, leaving me without a lookout."

Anxiety twisted Marina's belly. "Are you serious? Don't you care about what's happened? Titanic just hit the iceberg. We need to leave."

He scoffed. "Not on your life."

"It's my life I'm worried about. You *always* cut when we leave way too close. You *always* push our luck. The ship's going to sink. We have to go. Now." Her voice verged on desperate.

"We've got plenty of time before this tub goes down." He held up the carpetbag, heavy with the treasure he'd already snatched. "This is a paltry haul. I'm not running away now when there's more loot just waiting for my sticky fingers." He licked his lips. "We're staying. We finish this deck, then down to the next. We don't leave until I've got the rest of the goods, even if the water's lapping at my toes."

She ground her teeth. "I swear you get off on the risk, on the danger and narrow escapes. You get off on that more than what you steal."

He laughed. "Oh, I care about that too. And I don't hear you complaining about all the precious pretties I get for you." He cupped her chin and tipped her head back, gazing at her with eyes as hard and cold as frozen emeralds. "Face it, Marina, you enjoy the thrill too."

She bit back angry words. Arguing with him would just eat up precious minutes. Besides, that had once been true, in the beginning, when they'd met. She'd fallen for him hard and fast, attracted by the danger and his impulsiveness. He'd enticed her from her dreary existence of punching keys day in and day out. She'd convinced herself fate had brought them together, and she'd taken the biggest risk of her life to follow him on a mad journey to plunder the past.

She'd never felt such a pulse-pounding thrill as their first heist, raiding an 1880s Nevada frontier bank after hours. An easy robbery with no witnesses and little risk. Not much of a haul, either. There was little demand for old bills or useless stock certificates in 2130 beyond curiosity factor.

Unsatisfied, Fred got more daring. They began popping onto moving trains and holding up stagecoaches one step ahead of Jesse James. Marina's excitement turned to horror as each heist became more dangerous than the last. But for Fred, the stakes still weren't high enough, the risks too tame.

That was when they'd started tempting fate. They

skipped back to disaster sites and circled the soon-to-be dead like a couple of hungry vultures, snatching up jewels and valuables seconds before tragedy struck. Fred laughed at their narrow escapes, while she lived in a perpetual state of terror, fearing that each time she traveled to the past would be her last.

Not anymore. After this job, she was through. If and when they made it out of here, she was going to break free of Fred, take her fate into her own hands, and forge her own path.

She just needed to get up the courage to follow through.

TITANIC'S ENGINES stopped soon after they moved to B-deck. The ship began to list dangerously as the bow filled with water. Fred barely noticed. He slipped from one unoccupied room to another, leaving Marina alone and frantic in the hallway.

The tap of footsteps on the linoleum tiles and men's voices sounded from down the corridor, getting closer, heightening her fear. Stewards in white coats and men she guessed were the ship's masters-at-arms fanned out along the corridor. They rapped on doors, rousted people from sleep and instructed them to retrieve their lifebelts and move above decks.

"Just a precaution," the men repeated over and over when questioned. To reassure the passengers, or perhaps themselves.

Bleary-eyed matrons and their maids, fathers and sons, people of all ages, spilled from their cabins, putting on heavy coats over their pajamas, babbling, their voices caught between confusion and alarm. The ship's crew corralled them and herded them toward the stairs to the upper decks.

Marina got swept up in the stream of passengers but managed to break away in the cross corridor. She darted back down the hall, determined to yank Fred out of the room he was plundering and tell him in no uncertain terms he was taking them home. Now.

She'd nearly reached the stateroom's door when several more stewards—including Joseph—swarmed into sight, searching for stragglers.

"What are you doing here?" He strode up to her, scowling. "You must leave. We're requesting all passengers go up to the boat deck."

Marina desperately wanted to tell him to run. To beg him to save himself, to try to save others, especially those below decks who wouldn't learn of the danger or be told to evacuate until almost too late. But she couldn't do it. Even now, she couldn't bring herself to interfere.

"Yes, I was just leaving," she murmured, her shoulders sagging. "Thank you."

"Where's the gentleman you're traveling with?" He frowned again. "He should be helping you."

"Oh, he's..." Her gaze flit to the room Fred currently occupied. "He'll be along."

Joseph's expression tightened with suspicion. He turned toward the stateroom's door...as Fred stepped out, clutching the now bulging carpetbag. His eyes widened in surprise. So did Joseph's as he put the puzzle pieces together.

Fred bolted. Joseph chased after him. "Stop, thief!" he called.

The other stewards leapt into Fred's path. He swung with his free hand and clipped one of the men in the jaw. Joseph shot up from behind and bearhugged him, yanking him backward. Fred lost his grip on the carpetbag. It hit the floor with a thump. The clasp popped open, and pearl necklaces and sparkling earrings spilled out onto the linoleum.

Fred eyed the treasure as if he'd lost a beloved pet, then shifted his gaze to where Marina stood several paces away, frozen and helpless. He shot her a glare that sliced her in half. As if his getting caught was her fault.

"What should we do with him?" one of the stewards asked, clamping a meaty hand on Fred's shoulder.

"Take him to Captain Smith," another suggested.

"Don't be daft," Joseph said. "The captain's got his hands full at the moment."

A man with a mustache who seemed the most senior of the group aimed a scathing look at Fred. "Let's detain him for now and let Captain Smith figure out what to do with him later." He scooped the loose gems into the carpetbag, then picked up the bag and handed it to a small man with wavy blond hair. "Ryan, take this to the purser's office and have it locked up until the items can be returned to their rightful owners." He gestured to the other men. "Take this thief away."

"Wait." Joseph grabbed Fred's left arm. "What do you think this is?"

All eyes fell on the bauble on Fred's wrist. His sleeve had bunched up during the scuffle, and the device's blue beams shimmered in the corridor's soft light.

"It certainly is strange," the man with the mustache said. "Could it be a variation on a kaleidoscope? Chances are he thieved that too. We'll lock it up with the other valuables he stole."

Fred squawked and squirmed as Joseph tore the bauble from his wrist and thrust it into the blond steward's hand.

Marina quaked to see their only way home drop into the man's pocket.

"No. You can't do that," she cried, snapping out of her daze and rushing to stop the men as they marched Fred away.

Joseph caught her by the shoulders, holding her back. "Stay out of this, miss. It's not your concern," he said, loud enough for the others to hear.

"But—" Her heart sank as Fred disappeared into the stairwell with the stewards. He spat and cursed the parentage of each man as they clattered downward. "Where are they taking him?"

"To the brig." Joseph gave her shoulders a gentle squeeze, then let go. "He'll be dealt with later, after the ship is..." A note of doubt crept into his voice. "When this upset calms down, and we're on our way again. Now, please, Marina, I beg you. Do as I ask and go. Forget that scoundrel. He's not worthy of you."

He strode after the other men, leaving her standing in the empty corridor, unnerved and more than a little afraid. Fred was imprisoned, the bauble locked up, no way to escape. Her premonition had come horribly true. She cursed the day she'd ever met Fred. Cursed the day she agreed to join him in grave robbing through time. She cursed Joseph twice as hard. He'd helped her avoid arrest as Fred's accomplice, only to doom her to death in one of the most famous disasters in history.

Perhaps that had been her fate all along.

She straightened her spine. No. This couldn't be the end.

Think, Marina.

What should she do? She'd always let Fred make the

plans, and the decisions. She'd come to depend on him. Far too much. Now it was up to her.

She needed the bauble to skip to safety. But she needed Fred more. Only he knew how to operate the time travel device. He'd never trusted her enough to show her how it worked. The bauble had been taken to the purser's office and locked up. Fred had the skills to pick any lock ever made and crack any safe he'd ever encountered. She had to find him and free him first. It was the only way.

She searched her memory for any mention of a brig or detention facility in her research. After an aggravating few minutes as precious seconds slipped by, she remembered—a padded cell a few decks down, located near the ship's hospital.

Despite her hobbling skirt, Marina ran full tilt to the stairs. She rushed downward, fighting against crowds of frightened passengers working their way up. She reached her destination, D-deck, what seemed like hours later but must have only been minutes. The ship groaned under the pressure of the frigid Atlantic pouring forcefully into the bow like a conquering army. The air was scented with oil and brackish ocean water flooding the lower decks. Air that blew bitter cold, though Marina perspired like it was the hottest day in July.

She steered aft and to the starboard side, toward the hospital near the second-class dining room and galleys. People ran along the corridor looking for any flight of stairs or means of escape they could find. Earlier, the atmosphere had been calm, but now, terror tore through the crowd. Some passengers swore, others prayed, still others struggled to secure the flimsy lifebelts over their coats with shaking hands.

Swallowing her own fear, Marina moved as fast as she

could through the chaos. She veered to avoid a flying elbow and bashed into a freckle-faced girl of about sixteen, who wore a patched-up coat and clutched two large, heavy-looking suitcases. The girl met Marina's gaze, her cornflower blue eyes filled with terror.

The lights flickered, and the ship shivered as if suffering a severe chill. The girl squeaked in alarm and flung her suitcases away. Gathering up her skirts, she darted up the nearby stairs like a sprinter in a race for her life. Praying the young woman would make it to a lifeboat in time, Marina hurried on. She passed fewer people. The sound of rushing water intensified. So did the frosty smell of the Atlantic.

She frantically scanned signs over doorways as she passed the second-class dining room and galleys, looking for something to tell her she'd found the brig. No luck. Fighting panic, she reached the hospital. Through the open door, she saw a quartet of ward rooms, each with metal bunks bolted to the walls and wide doors with windows providing a view into each room—including one where Fred lounged on a bunk, his wrist handcuffed to the bed.

Marina's panic eased. A little. She'd found Fred, but still had to free him. A slim young man wearing a second-class steward's uniform stood guard outside the wardroom door.

She took a breath and stepped inside. The steward paced back and forth, muttering to himself. He stopped and gaped in surprise when he saw her. In the next room, Fred sat up on his bed and watched them both with calculating interest.

"They've gone. They've all gone," the young man said.

"You should go too," she replied.

"Can't. I'm s'posed to watch the penny-weighter the boys brung in." He jerked a thumb over his shoulder toward

Fred. "Man's a jewel thief. I've been told to guard him with my life." His voice wobbled on that last part. He shifted nervously and peered out into the corridor. "Do you know what's happening? Why has the ship stopped?"

Marina cursed. Another reason so many people died in this tragedy. Poor communication. "I'll give it to you straight, lad. The ship hit an iceberg, and it's sinking. *Fast.* You need to evacuate. Get to the lifeboats, now." Whether or not he managed to get *on* one would be up to him. She'd messed with fate enough simply by warning him.

He chewed his bottom lip. "I don't know. I'm not supposed to leave my post—"

A hard shudder shook the vessel, more violent than the last. In the nearby galleys, dishes slid from shelves and crashed to the floor. A deafening symphony of shattering plates and clanging cutlery boomed throughout the deck. The steward didn't argue a second longer. Swallowing convulsively, he snatched a wool coat from a hook and brushed by her and out the door.

Marina raced to free Fred. She grabbed the doorhandle. *Locked.* A frantic moment of uncertainty ended as he shouted, "Break the window, you stupid cow."

She scowled. Though tempted to wave goodbye and leave him to his fate, she hefted a wooden chair and smashed the window. Fred ducked and covered his face with his free hand as shards of glass flew inward. She climbed onto the chair and through the opening into the room.

"You sure took your sweet time getting here," Fred sniped.

Her anger deepened. She didn't know why she'd expected him to be grateful she'd come to save him. "I could've *not* come at all, you know."

"You need me. You had to come."

Furious now, she wrenched the hat pin from her hat and thrust it into his hand so he could pick the handcuff's lock. She didn't need *him*. She hadn't needed him for a long time. She just needed the time travel device.

Within seconds, the handcuff snapped open, and Fred leapt from the bed. He crawled through the window without a backward glance. Marina scrambled after him. Her dress snagged on a jagged piece of glass sticking out of the window frame. He kept moving while she struggled to wrench the skirt free. The fabric finally tore with a decisive *rip*. She hurried to catch up to Fred and nearly slammed into him as he stopped dead in the doorway.

"Son of a bitch," he breathed, looking down at his feet.

Marina followed his gaze to see murky water rushing along the deck floor in a steady tide. They needed to get out of there.

Now.

MARINA AND FRED sprinted to the nearest flight of stairs and joined the flood of passengers rushing upward. The raging tide of icy water pursued them all.

They spilled out of the stairwell onto C-deck and bolted past the elevators and across the foyer toward the purser's office. Marina glanced at the grand staircase as they darted past. Hours earlier, women in silky gowns with flowing trains had descended the stairs like graceful swans floating down a stream. Now, a panicked mob pushed and shoved, crying out as they rushed up toward what they hoped was escape.

They reached the purser's office. The message board

outside had been knocked down, and the area beyond the long oak countertop where the purser and his staff conducted business was deserted.

Fred shoved an older man clutching a child's hand out of the way and vaulted up and over the counter with the skill of an Olympian. Marina dashed inside in a more conventional way, through the open doorway. She ran across the spacious room, past a desk and the tall wooden mail cabinet. Fred stood in front of the safe, his posture as stiff as cast iron. The door had been flung wide. The safe was empty.

The bauble was gone.

The ship's lights flickered again. Outside, people screamed, and their running footsteps rumbled like frantic thunder. Fred swore. Terror filled Marina to the core. The bauble, gone. Their only means of escape—their lifeboat —gone.

"Are you looking for this?"

Joseph stepped into the room. He pulled the bauble from his pocket and examined it with curiosity and awe. The device's pulsing lights spread a sickly blue sheen over his face.

"I figured a thief as bold as you would find a way to escape his bonds and come searching for this," he said, glaring at Fred. He shifted his gaze to Marina, looking disappointed. "Tell me, with this ship on the verge of sliding into the sea, why would you waste time to help this man? What is so important about this strange bracelet you would delay evacuation to search for it?"

"You wouldn't understand," Fred said before Marina could speak. He thrust out his hand. "Give that to me. You have no use for it." Joseph didn't move. Fred stepped closer, keeping his eyes pasted to the device. "What do you want for it? I'll give you anything. Jewels, money, riches you could never imagine."

A grim smile touched Joseph's lips. "What good would any of that do me, when I am about to die?"

The ship shuddered again, shaking as fierce as an earthquake. Chairs and small tables toppled. The wooden mail cabinet creaked and teetered. Letters and telegrams that filled the mail slots flew out from the case like paper airplanes. Joseph swayed unsteadily, and Fred charged at him. He slammed into the steward's midsection headfirst. Joseph flew backward, losing his hold on the bauble. The device skidded along the tiles and *thunked* to a stop at the foot of the mail cabinet.

A stunned moment passed, then all three of them lunged for it.

Marina got there first, with Fred on her heels. The ship pitched violently, as if Poseidon had risen from the deep and shaken the vessel in his wake. The mail cabinet snapped from its base and toppled with a weighty groan. Marina gasped. Joseph seized her in a bear hug and jumped them both out of the way as the cabinet crashed to the floor.

"The time skipper is underneath," Marina cried. She shook off Joseph's hold. "Help me move the case."

"Don't bother," Fred said, a smirk in his voice.

She swung toward him. He held the bauble in his hand. He must've snatched it to safety a second before the cabinet fell. He tapped the control panel. A slim, cerulean blue beam shot from the device, like flipping a switch on a spotlight. A hot, metallic-scented wind kicked up next, sending loose papers flying. The blue light intensified and spread into a churning cyclone.

Marina sighed with relief and moved toward the whirlwind. They were saved. They could skip back to 2130. Or

1975 or 1600, or anywhere else, as long as it was far away from this rapidly sinking coffin. Her relief turned to horror as Fred met her gaze with glittering eyes—and leapt into the pulsing tornado. The swirling vortex swallowed him up, then winked into nothingness.

Her knees gave way. She sank to the floor. The ship went still, save for the ghostly groan of metal buckling under the pressure of water pushing into the decks below. And the screams of the trapped.

Joseph was suddenly beside her. He stared into the emptiness where Fred had vanished, looking stunned. "What...what was that?"

Marina shook her head. He may have just seen a man disappear into thin air, but would he understand what it meant? Would he understand if she explained about temporal skipping? Or told him about two time-traveling thieves who'd once loved each other then found themselves trapped in a hell of their own design? Fred shackled by his greed and his foolhardy compulsion to push the limits. Marina, caught by her fear and dependence and her inability to trust herself.

"*That* was my only escape," she said, a whisper of despair. She should have expected Fred to abandon her someday. Should've known following him and tempting fate over and over would lead to this. A death sentence. Doomed, like all the people they'd robbed across time. All those people they'd done nothing to help. "Now, I have no way out."

Joseph broke out of his confused stupor and snapped toward her. "Don't give up. There *is* a way out. The lifeboats." He jerked his chin upward, toward the boat deck above and the faraway sounds of raised voices and running feet. "There's still a chance for you, and I can help you, if we hurry." He leaned down and held out his hand. "But you've got to stand up and move your arse, Marina." His voice went as hard as steel. "*Now.*"

She looked around the room, littered with papers, the safe gaping open, splintered wood strewn everywhere. Outside the office, on the landing, ocean water began to snake across the floor, claiming the territory as its own. The frigid water would soon reach where she sat. She shivered. She'd die if she stayed here. Did she really want to give up without a fight? Give in to Fred and fate when there was still a chance?

She gazed into Joseph's determined, earnest eyes, and reached for his hand.

THEY MADE it to the boat deck. The bow pitched downward at a steep angle now, and they leaned to the side to keep from falling, like tilting into a hard wind. People pushed and shoved and slipped on the tilted deck, clawing toward the remaining lifeboats. A flare gun popped, and a light as bright as the temporal vortex exploded overhead, casting an eerie white glow over the already-launched lifeboats dotting the ocean.

Hanging onto one another, Marina and Joseph made their way along the slippery deck through the writhing mob. With his help, she edged forward, putting one foot in front of the other, buffeted back and forth by the crowd like a metal ball in one of those ancient pinball machines.

They pushed up to a group gathered around a lifeboat that had yet to launch. Joseph propelled Marina to the front of the line. He gave her hand a brief squeeze, then let go and stepped back.

"What about you?" she asked, though she knew the answer.

He gave a terse shake of his head, then flinched as a gunshot rang out, followed by more terrified screams. Marina's gaze shot toward the sound then back to Joseph. Her heart twisted—he was gone.

"Only one spot left, miss." A steward, a boy of no more than eighteen, reached for her and gripped her elbow to help her into the boat. His teeth chattered from cold and fear. So did Marina's.

She lifted a foot, about to step in when she caught a glimpse of the person who'd been next in line before Joseph pushed her to the front. The freckle faced girl with the cornflower blue eyes she'd bumped into below decks while running to free Fred.

Marina winced, wracked with guilt. If she took this girl's spot, her action would not only doom her, it would change history. It would also be wrong. She wasn't *that* person. She didn't want to *be* that person. She'd been taking advantage of others at the moment of their deepest fear and sorrow for far too long. She'd been blaming her actions on Fred for too long, too. She could take control, could do something *right* for once in her life. Despite what it meant for her own future.

She turned to the girl, who shivered behind her in line. "In you go," Marina said and helped the young steward lift her into the boat. Ropes creaked and people wept as the boat lowered into the gloom. The girl's eyes, burning with gratitude, held on Marina until she disappeared into the darkness.

Hands suddenly pulled her into a rough grip. Joseph, his expression furious. "Why didn't you get in the boat?"

"I couldn't. I didn't want to change the past."

He huffed in frustration. "I've never met a more stubborn girl. Do you want to drown?"

"Of course not. It's just...I think that's my fate."

He scowled. "*Bollocks*. Fate is what *you* make it. Only you can decide your future. And your future is *not* to go down with the ship. I think there's still some lifeboats on the port side. Go. Save yourself."

"Only if you come with me." He shook his head vehemently.

Speaking of stubborn.

"History records that some of the lifeboats were full, but others were launched half empty. If there's room for us in one of those boats, we won't take a space from anyone. We *won't* change the past. And we'll need your strong arms on the oars."

He frowned in confusion. She tucked her history lesson and temporal paradox lecture away. She would explain everything to him later, after they got off the Titanic. After he was saved.

If they could make it in time.

"What do you say, Joseph? Let's make our own destiny." She held out her hand to him this time. "Come on, move your arse. *Now*."

He flashed a grin and took her hand.

Together, they ran.

Biography

Growing up, Janet Raye Stevens loved two things—writing fiction and time travel movies, books, and TV shows, especially her favorite show, The Time Tunnel. It was inevitable she'd mashup her favorite things and write time travel stories and novels, including the award-winning Beryl Blue, Time Cop adventure series. When she's not creating temporal paradoxes, Janet drinks copious amounts of tea and hangs out with her family at their home in Massachusetts.

CONNECT WITH JANET AT:
https://janetrayestevens.com/

SWIMMING IN NOVEMBER

AMANDA PAMPURO

MICRONESIA, 1918:

A low breeze rippled across Diseha Lagoon, splitting
the sun's reflection into a thousand stars. Then, a second
sun rolled out of the clouds and joined the dance.

At first Napo thought his brother was playing another
trick on him. He waved both fists and dropped the wriggling
fish net, but Guafi wasn't laughing. Napo's older brother
stood silent on the sandy shore, jaw loose, eyes locked on the
red apparition floating slowly, gently toward them.

Among other things, the brothers would spend the rest
of their lives arguing whether the object flew with or against
the wind. Napo said it gently burrowed into the sand, while
Guafi insisted it outright crashed. Once grounded, the
shining red bubble towered over the tallest coconut trees
then collapsed around a woven basket large enough to fit
five strong men and their weapons.

Since nothing belonged in the sky but birds and gods,
both brothers bowed before the visitor. He wore shoes made

of fabric the same bright color as the silken skysail, trimmed in a pure cloud-like white. The stranger wore impossibly blue pants and a startlingly yellow shirt with white cuffs and sharp petals around the neck. He lifted a mask made of blue gold to reveal a surprisingly human face only a few years older than theirs.

Each place the traveler visited would refer to him by a different name, but his mother had named him *Angelo*.

Over the course of a week, Angelo and the boys worked out enough of a shared language for him to deliver his message. All the while Napo thought Angelo was an inventor who came from a far-away cave filled with wonderful spring-loaded contraptions. No, Guafi said, whatever that flying thing was he must have stolen it from a chief and couldn't be trusted.

In a way, Guafi was right about the first part, and Napo about the second. Angelo didn't mean to outright steal the hot-air balloon, but it was a lot harder to fly than he thought it would be.

NORTHERN CALIFORNIA, 2018:

It had barely been a month since he lost everything. On November 8, the wildfire took his house and the whole neighborhood with it. Hundreds of unmade beds and photo albums, teapots and sports trophies, piles of junk mail, potted plants, porch swings, garden tools and doghouses melted away in a matter of minutes. Some people said a power line sparked the blaze. If not a power line, others argued, the energy company still produced enough carbon over the years to intensify the drought, making the land ripe for a stray ember to catch. Enough folks dismissed these as conspiracy theories. Whatever the precise cause of the fire, it left nothing behind but ash.

Dagny Energy Corp donated metal screens so survivors could sift char for scraps of their lives. In the weeks that followed, the company continued sending bulk art supplies and jovial guest speakers to the tents serving as schools.

One such guest was a certified commercial hot-air balloon pilot. He showed the students how he heated air to ascend and purged it to descend. In order to read air currents, he sprinkled wood shavings over the side and watched where they blew.

"These things don't have steering wheels," the pilot chuckled. "We ride the winds at the mercy of Mother Nature!"

The deeper Angelo inhaled, the stronger the memory of smoke blocked his lungs. He still choked. His eyes still burned. Everywhere Angelo looked, he saw the shadows of what had been. He had heard enough. Nobody—not his parents, not his teachers, not the clown with the balloon— had answers to the only question that mattered: *what was left?*

The folding chair creaked as Angelo hoisted on his backpack. Neither his classmates nor the teachers seemed to notice as he crept up to the podium. The passenger basket sat in blackened dirt ten feet from the pilot. The bright red orb swayed in the breeze, inviting Angelo closer.

Of course, Angelo thought he'd just hop in the basket and take off, but Ms. Pacome's voice stopped him in his tracks.

"What do you think you're doing?" The principal dove like a goalie trying to deflect the game-changing ball. The height of her heels threw her off balance, allowing Angelo to narrowly reach the basket.

The pilot cut his speech mid-sentence as he registered what was happening. His moustache twitched. The monocle fell from his face. "No, boy! You have no idea what that thing is capable of—"

Jennie, on track to be valedictorian, gasped. Jason, the loudest of them all, cheered. The whole sophomore class went wild as Angelo tore at the ropes keeping the balloon on the ground.

Three ropes. Two ropes. One to go. Three corners of the basket lifted, but the fourth tilted toward Ms. Pacome, who held the last tether with all her might. Jennie and the balloon pilot helped her pull.

The knot would not come loose from the basket, and the three-headed obstruction refused to let go. How had the pilot said to make the balloon rise? Oh right, the propane. Angelo twisted the valve, and flames shot into the balloon.

The principal, the pilot, and the star student screamed in unison as the rising rope slipped out of their hands. In a single breath, the basket leveled with the treetops. Then, it left them behind. Angelo felt his stomach follow after.

Up, up, the balloon soared as the broken streets Angelo skated down smoothed and sharpened like the lines in a coloring book. Everything he had ever known quickly vanished beneath a layer of thick white clouds. He couldn't see anything. He needed to go down below cloud line. He tried turning the propane valve. Hot flames shot into the envelope, and the balloon shot up even higher.

Angelo had to take deep breaths to keep his head clear. He had to get a grip on the gas. He turned it off, but the balloon remained on route to the stratosphere.

How did the pilot get the balloon back down? Angelo found the parachute valve cord. The balloon dropped sixty meters in free fall. He was going to die! He twisted the propane with one hand and pulled the parachute cord with the other. The balloon shot up and down, up and down, like a broken elevator.

The balloon finally stabilized enough for Angelo to empty the contents of his stomach over the side. His breakfast cereal blew west. What did that mean he should do? Before he could figure it out, the balloon suddenly shot east, pulled by a strange column of rotating air. The airstream twisted the balloon, basket, and rider, round and around, on a narrow and narrower path. Angelo felt as though he were being sucked down the sides of a drain. Instead, he entered a wormhole.

The blue sky melted into white light and darkness as an incredible force flipped the balloon upside down and around, quick as the second hand on a clock, dragging the basket after. The basket inverted, and Angelo gripped the suspension lines with all his might. He clenched his eyes, bracing to be ripped out by gravity and thrown to the ground.

But, Angelo didn't fall, and the balloon didn't crash.

When he opened his eyes, Angelo instead found himself floating through a silent, calm sky—flight as he had always imagined it. Then, he looked over the side of the basket. Spread across the land below, Angelo saw towering buildings covered in honeycomb-shaped glass. Wide roads wound between concrete towers, filled with the taillights of what looked like all the cars in the world. It was like nothing he had ever seen.

NORTHERN CALIFORNIA, 2122:

Around the city, Angelo saw acres of golf courses and

swimming pools, but not a single soccer field. A vast checkerboard of warehouses alternated with parking lots and dumpsites. Beyond that lay a wasteland of cheatgrass and dirt. Where were the lakes? Where was the forest? Where was his home?

The lonely basket finally settled on an inhospitably thorny thicket with the crunch of landing on bone.

Vine-wrapped street signs signaled the long-gone crossing of Sixth and Del Mar, an intersection so closely resembling the place where Angelo grew up, he couldn't shake the feeling that he was home. He was home, except it looked like years since the fire passed through. He was home, except they never rebuilt.

The library was where it was supposed to be—at least what was left of it. Angelo crawled through caves formed beneath fallen shelves, over rotted paper made into nests by mice and mites. He set up camp and sorted through the mess, determined to find something that could explain everything else. It took several weeks and a bit of luck before he unearthed the remains of a science book published thirty-five years after he took flight.

ADRIFT OVER THE PACIFIC OCEAN, 2122:

A lantern in the night, the balloon hovered over downy masses of cumulonimbus slowly drifting apart. An endless expanse of stars stretched out overhead, echoing a multitude of times and places Angelo would never know.

By the light of a small blaze, cocooned in a hammock stretched between the basket's corners, Angelo pored over the book. Had he anything else to read, the gentle rocking would've surely lulled him into peaceful dreams. Instead, each page stiffened a new nerve in his spine. He abandoned his bed, paced, and rested his elbows over the side of the basket as he reread the same unbelievable passages over and over.

Global climate change would be worse than what they told him in school. Instead of becoming few and far between, hurricanes, droughts and wildfires would multiply and pile up like waves on the seashore. The world as Angelo knew it and the people he loved stood little more chance than a sandcastle.

And yet, the underlying catalysts seemed deceptively simple, stretching back to his own lifetime. Man-made disasters exacerbated natural disasters. If mankind spent the twentieth century reimagining how energy powered industry rather than ramping up production past any notion of usefulness, there might have been hope. By the time Angelo learned about climate change in school, it was too late to stop it. If only, Angelo thought, they had someone to warn them earlier.

MICRONESIA, 1918:

When Angelo asked Napo and Guafi how they kept track of time, one of them brought him a twelve-page calendar with a different Catholic saint painted over each month. A print of Saint Francis surrounded by doves and trees informed Angelo when he had arrived. He still needed to get the hang of this time travel thing.

Angelo sank into the sand and pulled small, foil-wrapped chocolates from his backpack. Everything from the cone shape to the flavor amazed the children. It would be decades before the calorically compact combination of sugar and cocoa reached the remote island. Then, it would quickly become taken for granted.

"There will be more candy like this, but first there will be bombs," Angelo said. "When the water calms, these islands will see so many bags of rice and salted meat your stomach will ache as it stretches to hold more. You'll feel so full, it'll be easy to miss the beginning of the end."

As Napo and Guafi licked warm chocolate from their fingers, Angelo flipped through his book to show them the blue square labeled with their lagoons and currents, oddly missing the island they called home. Angelo tapped his finger on the year: 2050. It wasn't a map of their home. It was a map without it.

ROCKY MOUNTAINS, 1928:

The meteorologist was chopping wood when the balloon landed in front of his cabin. At first, he thought the young man had raided an antique store. Angelo's mid-twenty-first-century snowsuit kept him snug in the upper-atmosphere's freezing temperatures, but the best snowshoes were developed during World War II; his mittens were a gift from the Mongols; and his hat a relic from aristocratic Russia. It had taken some time for Angelo to learn how to navigate the wormhole, nearly a year, measuring by his sense of the present.

Inside the cabin serving as a weather station, the scientist poured a whistling kettle over two cups of tea. Christmas had just passed, and the radio was crooning about sleeping in. Angelo unsealed a plastic bag and offered him a battered book, treated as a beloved artifact.

The scientist stroked his beard as he considered which

end of the joke he was on. From data he had collected, he recently began suspecting the planet was warming. He had yet to tell anyone, since it would take another decade at best to confirm the pattern. And yet this book, in his hands, completely backed the hypothesis. The only problem was that his teenage guest claimed it wouldn't be published until the next century.

Stranger still, the bright-eyed teenager vowed to warn the twentieth century of this disastrous future.

"How can you possibly know where and when to start?" the scientist asked.

"Anywhere has to be better than nowhere," the young man replied.

GERMANY, 1948:

"There's no way you'll believe what I am about to tell you," he told the Old One. "But we must get beyond that doubt just long enough for you to see there's little risk in acknowledging the fact that your impact is infinite and our resources finite."

ENGLAND, 1978:

Angelo bowed before the Commonwealth's last reigning queen. "Even as others cry about the expense or your kingdom's standing, in your heart of hearts, there is a voice that tells you the difference between right and wrong."

SOUTH AFRICA, 1998:

"Every time you listen to that voice, things tend to work out for you," he reminded the Great One.

WASHINGTON DC, 1958:

"This voice has never led you astray before," he implored the one called Ike. "Even if you don't listen to me, at least take a minute and listen to the person you know best. Listen to yourself, to the voice inside of you that wants to do good."

ANGELO EXPECTED each conversation to change things enough to lighten the book in his hands. Instead, the table of contents began to grow. Each chapter blossomed new subsections as Angelo chased channels of influence.

Governments alone would not stop the climate from changing. So, Angelo made a new list. He would persuade farmers and ranchers, cement producers and energy providers. He would seek out oil tycoons with desks made of Florida yew. He would talk to the VPs of production who signed expansion agreements with pens carved from rhino horns. Good thing he had all the time in the world.

NEW YORK, 1968:

Everything that touched Dagny Daniels' skin was custom tailored from textiles and furs that were dying out or long gone. Somehow, it seemed she had been expecting him.

"You've come to tell me to listen to my heart, haven't you?" she said.

"You could have made it easier for me to get in," Angelo said, a poker player's smile spread across his face.

Dagny Energy was not alone in using hydraulic fracturing to make oil and gas the most impactful energy source of its era, but Angelo had grown up knowing the company's jingles as well as Christmas carols. While the company reaped record profits, it would produce byproducts that pushed global temperatures to record highs with catastrophic results.

"So you could talk to me about *my* footprint?" Dagny spat. "I'd rather talk about what's powering *your* balloon."

"Sure," Angelo said.

"My friends tell me you visit successful executives," Dagny said. "Then, convince them to do everything they can to avoid making their fortune."

"There are other ways of making money," Angelo countered. "That could profit us all."

Angelo just needed her to listen. If he could convince Dagny Daniels of her role in shaping the future of the planet, she and others like her would take different actions. They had to. He was so sure. They could save the world together.

"Perhaps," Dagny said, crossing her shell cordovan shoes cut from Przewalski foal. "We're both short on time, so let's skip to the part where you show me your evidence."

Her eyes grew as large as marbles rolling through the book in Angelo's hands. It wasn't just that she was going to make a fortune—it was that there was a fortune to be made.

NORTHERN CALIFORNIA, 2018:

When Angelo returned to the time and place he called home, he found his house and his school, his mother's car and the corner laundromat all laid out like toys on a carpet of golden grass. It was just as he remembered it before the fire. His heart raced as he sought to confirm whether the wildfire had yet to happen or would never happen at all.

He landed amid some sort of protest. Between marching bands and banners, thousands of people flowed through the street. The procession crossed the city like a shadow through heat heavy enough for it to be July.

Drenched in midsummer musk, the crowd hid from the sun's blaze under woven shawls and wide-brimmed hats. Some people carried signs. In paint and marker, the poster boards named the CEOs and elected officials who created the carbon crisis. They called out brands of clothing and kitchenware pressed into shape with petroleum. They moved with all the fervor of a group dancing for rain.

"It's not too late," the people shouted through muggy streets. "We can do more!"

Perhaps he was just in time to see the fire averted! The crowd created a force of power and persuasion and goodness so much like the one Angelo remembered being swept up in when he was in kindergarten, coloring the ocean on a printout of the planet. He had been hoping for this.

"Better get inside soon," a man in a shiny suit of thin, light nylon greeted Angelo.

"What do you mean?"

"It's going to be another scorcher," the man grinned.

"Well, that's to be expected in summer," Angelo replied.

"Summer? It's nearly Thanksgiving."

"November?" Angelo said. "How can this be November when they're protesting? They're protesting all the drivers of climate change, to stop the planet from overheating..."

"You all right, kid? They're not protesting. They're celebrating the death of winter," the man explained. "Today's Dagny Day—when we celebrate Dagny Daniels for using clean coal to warm up the planet..."

"Warm the planet! With clean coal?"

"Yes, the best energy the world can possibly produce," the man said.

"What about solar power? And wind!"

"Wind?" the man laughed. "Like wind turbines? Now there's an old wives' tale!"

The balloon sagged in the heat. A lesser man would have fainted, but Angelo caught himself. How was it possible that informing governments of climate change only led to better documentation and warning carbon producers sped up its onset?

This wasn't right. This wasn't right at all. Angelo had to warn even more people. He could go back further in time. He would tell the ancient Mayans and the Egyptians. He'd tell every incarnation of the Dalai Lama. If everyone understood the consequences, surely they would act. He just needed to get the balloon into the air.

While the silver fan filled the balloon's envelope, Angelo slipped the buttons from his shirt, and flapped the fabric to cool himself. He took a deep breath, readied himself for lift off, and fed propane into the burner. Orange flames licked the air inside the balloon, but the basket remained firmly planted on the ground. To take flight, the air in the balloon had to be hotter than the air around it. On a day like today, that meant breaking forty degrees Celsius.

Angelo cranked the fuel. The flames grew two stories tall. Feverish streams of sweat drained from his body. He wiped at the salt in his eyes, making the burning worse instead of better.

When the balloon finally hovered off the ground, it was too hot to breathe. The portable sun burned every centimeter of Angelo's bare skin raw. His eyebrows shriveled. He cut the propane and melted into the ground.

The balloon could technically fly, but it could not bring Angelo with it. Not in this heat.

The man had tapped his smartwatch, a thin strand of politeness barring him from leaving on a bad note. "Say, why don't you go for a swim?"

"What?"

"Yeah, Dagny Energy just built that grand new pool to help people enjoy the heat even more," the man said.

The words echoed in Angelo's head as he watched people dive into the water. The five-million-liter pool was a wonder to behold, surrounded by desert that used to be a lake surrounded by trees.

"Ain't it great," the man had said. "Now, we can swim any day in November."

———

MICRONESIA, 1946

Even as they grew older, Napo and Guafi still lay out at night, heads nearly touching, legs stretched in opposite directions. Sometimes they whispered about beautiful women or dishes they hungered for. Other times they watched the sky in silence for that bright red lantern among the crystal stars.

They were grown men when the promised candy fell

from the sky. Time to look for a new place our descendants can call home, Guafi said.

Not until we've had our fill, Napo replied.

The reason they never saw the traveler again, Napo said, was because he fell in love and had a dozen children to keep him busy.

No, Guafi countered. He is alone and always will be. Somewhere, some day, the sails will refuse to hold air and leave the flyer stranded.

Napo for once agreed. He lives among us, the best chance the world ever had.

Biography

Amanda Pampuro cut her teeth reporting for *Marianas Variety* in Guam. Since trading her dive tank for a snow-board, she reports on civil litigation and co-hosts a legal podcast. Her debut book *Wish List* (Alien Buddha Press, 2022) follows one woman's life through things she bought online, as told by the algorithm that sold them to her.

She is trying to avoid being an asshole on Twitter @Bright_lamp and lists her works at https://amandapampuro.wordpress.com/

THE PRESENT,

or then abouts

A GAME OF TWO HALVES

PAUL CHILDS

THE ORIGINAL VERSION of this story appeared in Paul's short story collection, *Tales From Badgers Crossing* (Greenteeth Press, 2022), and is adapted with permission.

———

SATURDAY, 20th May 1967, 3.40 p.m. F.A. Cup Final Day.

Tottenham Hotspur vs Chelsea.

First half. Five minutes to half-time.

Spurs 1-0 Chelsea

Jimmy Robertson scores with a left-footed volley.

———

THE COPS

"Driver, stop!" blared the voice from the police car's loudspeaker between siren wails. "This is the police. Pull over immediately!"

The tyres of the Morris Minor screeched as it struggled

to stay on the road. Detective Chief Inspector Rod Preston turned to his driver. "Careful, lad."

"Sorry, Guv," said Constable Johnny Carr, wrestling the vehicle under control as it clipped the kerb.

Preston unhooked the radio from the dashboard. "Delta Nine One. This is Sierra Six Five northbound on Edgware Road heading toward Maida Vale. We are in pursuit of a white Ford van. It says Transit, but it doesn't look like one I've ever seen. Maybe a new model or an import from Japan. Registration PL1 TPP. Request backup urgently. Over."

"Can you give me that reg plate again, sir?" cracked the voice on the radio.

"Papa Lima One. Tango Papa Papa. I know. It's not a normal reg."

Preston thrust his arm across his constable's face. "Down there Johnny, quick!"

"On it, Guv!"

Carr wrenched the handbrake and pulled the wheel hard to the right. The whole world moved sideways, and Preston felt like he'd left his stomach back on the main road as the car drifted around parked cars and bollards. Carr released the brake, and the car shuddered as it caught its grip on the cobbles.

Fighting the urge to throw up, Preston clicked his radio again.

"We are now eastbound on Frampton Street. We're in the back streets now—we're going to lose them! Where's that sodding backup?"

A hiss of static announced a reply. "Sorry, Delta Nine One. The nearest units are at the match and can't be dragged away. Sending cars from Camden."

"Well, bloody well tell them to get a move on! With Constable Carr here driving, if we don't lose them, I'm definitely going to lose my lunch! We're now eastbound on Lodge Road. If I know Frankie Parks, they're heading to a lockup under the Arches. He's got them all over the city."

"Roger, Guv. They're almost with you."

Preston was forced into the passenger window as Carr performed another handbrake turn. He clipped the radio back onto the dashboard.

"Where in God's name did you learn to drive like this? This is definitely not on the force's approved driving course!" he said.

"Well, Guv," Carr started, stroking his chin.

"Bloody hell, lad! Both hands on the wheel!"

Carr gripped the steering wheel and continued, "Partly from my dad, but mostly from films like Grand Prix and Goldfinger."

"Well, keep your eyes on the road, Double-Oh-Seven," gasped Preston as they took another sharp corner.

"Lucky about the match, eh, Guv? Roads are quieter than usual," said Carr.

"Lucky? For us or them?" said Preston. "I don't think the timing of this was an accident. They knew that today of all days we'd struggle to get backup. Speaking of which…"

Three Hillman Imps, sirens whining, screeched in from the right and joined the chase behind Carr and Preston.

"About flipping time!" Preston looked over his shoulder and grinned. He unclipped his radio. "Well, I never, Barry Adkins. Is that you?"

"Certainly is, Rod'rick," came the voice from the radio.

"Okay, Baz, listen. We've got Frankie Parks and at least two other unknowns in the van ahead. I'm certain they're going for a hideout in Lisson Arches. You and…" He looked over his shoulder and gave a little wave to the driver of another car. "You and Bolton break off left here and see if you can cut them off up ahead. Let's clamp these buggers in a vice."

"Gotcha, Boss."

Two of the Imps squealed off down a side road, and the other stayed behind Preston's car.

Up ahead the van turned down a back street running along the side of the railway.

"I knew it!" Preston punched the dashboard. "We've got 'em now. Careful does it lad. Slow down, let them think they've got away. With Baz and Boz at the other end, they can't bolt when they realise they've walked right into our trap."

Carr eased off on the accelerator. As the car gingerly poked its nose into the alleyway, both officers leaned forward to see around the corner and down the street.

It was empty. All except for the two cars Preston had sent to the other end of the road. Between them were several giant, curved wooden doors in the arches under the railway bridge.

The police cars took up position at either end of the alley, blocking the road in both directions. Preston stepped out and raised a megaphone.

"Frankie Parks. This is the police. You are surrounded. Come out now, or we'll break the door down and bloody well come in there ourselves," Preston grinned.

Carr tapped him on the shoulder. "Er, Guv?"

Preston nodded.

"How do we know which one he's in?" He looked up the street. There must have been twenty units or more, nearly all identical.

"Doesn't matter, lad. There's only one way in and one way out. The front door. We've got all the time in the world to check them, but their time is quickly running out."

The police officers advanced towards the nearest locked door. Carr gripped his truncheon, ready for action.

THE ROBBERS

"Have we lost 'em yet, Ern?"

Ernie Hunt checked his side mirror. A blue and white Morris Minor appeared at the end of the street, siren sounding and blue lights flashing.

"Driver, stop!" blared the voice from the police car's loudspeaker between siren wails. "This is the police. Pull over immediately!"

"That answers that then," said Frankie Parks, punching Hunt in the arm. "I thought you said there'd be no police in the area today."

"Ow, Frankie!" Ernie rubbed his arm. "I said there won't be much of a police presence; I didn't promise none. It's not my fault that those coppers were getting a tea around the corner when we hit Shearsmith's."

"Don't know why we couldn't have done it earlier. The coppers were still up at Wembley first thing. I'm missing the game because of this," moaned Frankie.

"It's fine gentlemen," came a voice from the back of the van.

"It's not fine, love!" cried Frankie.

Doctor Elizabeth Wilde slapped Frankie. Not hard enough to hurt much, but enough to leave four red welts across his cheek.

"First, I am neither yours, nor anyone else's 'Love.' Second, if all goes according to plan, you'll get to see your precious football. And third, we planned for this. Ernie's right. The police were always a conceivable impediment, but I've accounted for that variable."

"In English please, L-Liz." Reminded by his stinging cheek, Frankie corrected himself at the last second.

Liz rolled her eyes. "It means that it's not a problem if you leave me to it and let me get on with my work." She was almost thrown from her seat as the van lurched and jolted.

"And try not to crash if you can help it, Ern. There's a lot of expensive gear back here that I have to return before anyone notices it's missing!" She sat down at a console which, to Frankie, was just a wall of flashing lights, indecipherable knobs, and a television screen that seemed as thin as a newspaper. It was like something from Star Trek back here. Liz flicked a switch and the equipment hummed to life. Text appeared on the screen:

++This computer and its contents are the property of
PLANUS Laboratories++
++Loading ENID. Please wait.++

A soft but emotionless female voice came from the speakers on the side of the television set. It was nothing like Robot from *Lost in Space*.

++Good afternoon, Doctor Wilde. How are you today?++

"Blimey, it speaks!" said Frankie. "What is this? Chatty Cathy?"

"It's a very sophisticated piece of equipment," said Liz, and then to the computer. "I'm fine, thank you, ENID. How are you?"

++I am very well. How can I assist you today?++

"Initiate the Exochronal Displacement Drive."

++Very good Doctor Wilde. EDD initiated. Please set the temporal coordinates and physical destination.++

Frankie climbed over the back of his seat and joined Liz in the rear. She typed what appeared to be random sequences of numbers and letters. Secretary stuff, Frankie sniggered to himself.

"What's this do?" He grasped a dial.

"Don't!" Liz swatted his hand away. "This requires a very precise set of calculations. One wrong entry, and who knows where we will end up!"

"At the match, if there's any luck!" Ernie half-joked from the front.

Frankie felt like a third wheel, what with Liz and her incomprehensible nerd stuff and Ern with his world-class getaway driving. As Ernie took another tight bend at speed, the holdall with the loot slid against his leg. Frankie cheered up considerably when he thought about what was in the bag and what he planned to do once they'd got away from the filth.

Ernie struggled with the wheel as the van's back end skidded out. He brought the vehicle back under control and floored the accelerator pedal. Liz stopped tapping away at her keyboard when the road surface became so bumpy she couldn't hit the right key.

"What's going on?" she said.

"Cobbles," Ernie called back to her.

"Charming," she said.

"No, I mean the road. It's cobblestones. We're nearly there. Be ready, Frankie."

Frankie unclipped his seatbelt and gripped the door

handle. Ernie gently applied the brakes, and when the van reached a safe speed, Frankie opened the door. He leaped out onto the street as they passed the orange lockup door, being very careful not to go over on his ankle on the uneven surface.

He fumbled in his pocket for a ring full of keys. In the distance, he could hear the screeching tyres and the shriek of sirens. The rozzers were almost here.

Doing his best to speed up without dropping anything, he selected the key with a strip of masking tape wrapped around the top and inserted it into the deadlock.

"Come on Frankie! They'll be here any second." Ernie had stopped the van a few feet farther down the street.

Frankie turned the key and felt the lock disengage. He heaved the door open wide enough for the van to fit. Ernie quickly but carefully reversed into the empty area. Frankie pulled his key out and slammed the door shut. In the darkness of the lockup, he felt for the key wrapped in tape.

No sooner had he found the correct key and locked the door again than they heard a voice outside, some way up the street.

"Frankie Parks. This is the police. You are surrounded. Come out now, or we'll break the door down and bloody well come in there ourselves."

"They're here," Ern whispered.

"Well, keep the noise down," said Liz, "and let's hope they do as expected and start at each end of the alley."

4.17 P.M.
Second half.
Spurs 2-0 Chelsea

Frank Saul pivots and hooks in Robertson's cross from Dave Mackay's throw-in.

THE COPS

Carr wagged his finger as he counted the lockup doors.

"Twenty-six, Guv," he said. "Where do we even begin?"

Preston rubbed his chin, then held up a finger. "Okay. Boz and Baz, you take these constables and start down there." He pointed to the end of the street. "Grant," he gestured to the driver of the final car, "you're with young Carr and me at this end."

"Aye, sir," said the officer.

The four officers began to jog down to the far end of the street when Preston suddenly held up his fist. "Wait!" he cried.

Baz, Boz, and the other two officers stopped running and looked back at him.

"Guv?"

"Just one minute." Preston slowly and quietly crept towards his colleagues. "That's exactly what we'd do in this situation, right? Start at each end and work our way into the middle? Yes?"

Baz nodded.

"And Parks might be many things, but he's not a fool, right?"

Boz nodded.

"Maybe we ought to set procedure aside for a change. Let's start there and work our way outwards."

Preston pointed at a blue door which was two away from the orange one.

THE ROBBERS

"Crap," said Ernie, who was looking through the keyhole. "They're starting in the middle. They'll be here any minute."

Liz was typing away furiously at her keyboard. "Almost there, chaps. Don't worry."

"Don't worry?" Frankie struggled to keep the volume of his voice down. "We planned for them to take at least forty-five minutes to find us. Now, they're going to do it in five."

"Patience, Frankie. We never needed such a huge margin of error."

Ernie chewed his fingernails and whispered, "Hurry, hurry," under his breath.

"I'm almost there." Liz twisted a dial, changing the numbers on a clock over Frankie's head. She slid a small plastic object across the table, and a crosshair appeared over the map on the flat television screen.

Frankie's mouth hung open in amazement. "Where did you get all this stuff? It's like something from *The Day the Earth Stood Still*."

"Which version?" Liz said.

"What do you mean, which version?" Frankie squinted at the numbers whizzing up the television screen. "It's the one with the robot. You know, who comes down to demand an end to all war?"

Liz continued to type, her fingers flying until they were a blur. "Of course, yes. Sorry. I was thinking of the Keanu one."

"What's a key-are-noo?" Frankie said.

Liz bit her lip. "Damn," she whispered under her breath. She stopped typing and turned to Frankie. "Never mind. Forget I said anything. To answer your original question, I borrowed this stuff from work, and I have to return it by a set time, so let me get on with this, please."

"Well, excuse me!" Frankie shook his head.

The door rattled.

"Open up, Parks," came a voice from outside.

Ernie leapt back in surprise. The jolt had loosened dust from the door frame, and he was coated in it. His nose started to twitch.

"Ern! Get away from that door!" Frankie whispered.

Ernie reached for his nose to smother the sneeze but didn't make it in time. Everyone froze and looked at the door.

It rattled again, harder this time.

"We know you're in there. We can hear you."

"Come on, Liz!" Frankie said.

"Almost there," she replied. "Ernie. Get back in the van. Get that engine running just in case we have to run."

"But they'll hear us."

"They can already hear us!"

The door was crashed into once more, and it opened a sliver, revealing the blue uniforms crowded around it, before slamming shut again. "This is your last chance, Parks!"

"That door ain't gonna last any longer. Whatever you're gonna do, Liz, do it now, because we're out of time!"

"No, we're not. Time is the one thing we do have." She stopped typing. "Done. Hold on to something. Ready..." She raised her hand above the big red button in the middle of the console. "Here we go!" She plunged it down hard.

++Displacement activated++

Frankie clambered into the passenger seat just as the door shattered. A deafening crack echoed around the lockup as a cloud of dust, splinters, and flakes of orange paint flew towards his open window. He held his hands up to shield his face, but nothing struck. No clattering of shards on the floor, no bellow of "You're nicked!" from the coppers.

He lowered his hands.

The debris hung in the air. Frankie squinted into the unmoving cloud of detritus. There amongst the mess, standing perfectly still, was his nemesis, Rod Preston, fist raised and face distorted with both hatred and triumph, glaring back into his eyes.

"What on earth?"

And then the world turned inside out.

———

4.35 P.M.

Second half. Five minutes to full-time.

Spurs 2-1 Chelsea

Bobby Tambling takes advantage of Pat Jennings' fumbled save, and his header puts Chelsea back in the game.

———

THE COPS

Johnny Carr lifted the letterbox and squinted through the slot.

"Well?" said Preston.

Carr held up a finger and continued to peer into the slot, his eyes darting back and forth. He turned his head to Preston.

"Nope."

Preston nodded solemnly. He pointed to the next lockup along the row. He crept to the green door and tried the handle. The door opened, and he poked his head in.

"Damn!"

He stepped back out and turned to Carr, but his constable wasn't there. He looked to his left to see Carr already at the next door, which was orange. Preston opened his mouth to ask what was going on, but Carr held a finger to his lips. With the other finger, he pointed to the ground.

They were barely visible, but Preston could just make out the almost dried remnants of a pair of wet tyre tracks. He nodded and sneaked closer.

"Stand back, lad," he whispered. He pulled his truncheon from a deep pocket and rattled it on the door. "Open up, Parks," he shouted. The other officers had now joined him.

"Guv," Boz whispered, holding up a sledgehammer with a brightly-coloured handle. "I brought the Big Yellow Key from the car, just in case."

"Good idea, lad."

They all leaned in to listen for a reaction. From the other side of the door came a muffled but quite distinct "Achoo!"

Preston motioned to Boz, who brought the hammer down hard on the door, just above the lock with a great crash.

"We know you're in there. We can hear you." He turned to Boz. "Hit it again!"

This time the hammer forced a section of the door open for a split second, before it sprang shut.

"I reckon one more ought to get us in, Guv," said Boz.

"Do it," he said. He turned to the door. "This is your last chance, Parks!"

The officers all stood back as Boz raised the hammer over his head. With a grunt of effort, he swung it in a wide arc. The hammer connected with the door handle. A wide, ragged circle of wood and metal exploded inwards sending a cloud of dust, splinters, and flakes of orange paint into the lockup.

Preston squinted through the collapsing door. For the tiniest fraction of a second, he locked eyes with Parks before the debris cloud obscured everything within. He raised his fist in triumph.

"Well done, Boz." He pointed to two officers. "You! You! Clear this mess. Let's get in there."

Once a large enough gap had been cleared and the dust began to settle, Carr stepped into the lockup. His wide grin quickly sagged to a grimace when he saw that the room was deserted.

"Er, Guv..."

4.40 P.M.

Full time.

Spurs 2-1 Chelsea

Tambling's header gave Chelsea a brief glimmer of hope, but in the end, they were outclassed.

THE ROBBERS

"Where are we?" Frankie stepped down onto the gravel and looked out over the murky, still waters of the canal. He turned his head back to the van and instantly knew exactly where he was. Towering over him were three cast iron gasometers. Because they were joined together by a wrought iron spine, the locals called them, "The Siamese Triplets."

"The gasworks in Camden?" said Ern, gaping at the massive skeletal structures. "But how? That must be a good three or four miles away! There's no way we could have got here in that amount of..." He raised his watch.

"Time?" said Liz, winking at them as she pushed her spectacles back up her nose.

1.28 P.M.
  One hour and thirty-two minutes to kick off.
  Spurs 0-0 Chelsea

"WHAT?" Frankie looked at his watch. "How?"

"Time dilation, boys," said Liz.

"Well, I don't care how," Ernie chipped in. "What I do care about is getting home and putting the telly on!"

Frankie nodded.

Liz stepped out of the van to join her partners. "Oh, I don't think so, gentlemen." She reached into her inner jacket pocket and produced three folded slips of orange and green coloured paper. She handed one to Ernie, one to Frankie, and kept one for herself.

"What's this?" Ernie said.

Liz winked. "The alibi I promised you."

Ernie and Frankie unfolded their papers and read in silence. A grin slowly crept over both their faces.

EMPIRE STADIUM • WEMBLEY
The Football Association
CUP COMPETITION
FINAL TIE
Saturday, May 20, 1967, kick-off 3 p.m.

FRANKIE GRINNED as he slapped a hand on Ernie's shoulder. "How quickly can you get us to the lockup in Wembley, mate?" he said.

"I dunno, forty-five minutes. Maybe a bit more because it's..." He laughed. "Cup final day, and the traffic'll be murder!"

"Well, let's get a bloody move on then!" Frankie pointed at the tiny print beneath the date and time of the match: YOU ARE ADVISED TO TAKE UP YOUR POSITION BY 2.30 P.M.

6.27 P.M.

One hour and fifty-two minutes since full time.
The Century Tavern, Forty Lane, Wembley.

THE COPS

"Everybody stay calm, please," Preston and Carr strode into the pub. When the door swung shut, Baz and Boz stood at it, arms crossed, to bar anyone from leaving. "This is police business."

Preston strolled to the bar, grinning like a sheriff who

was about to get his man. The entire pub watched as he theatrically stopped behind a man on a barstool, coughed into his fist, and slapped his other hand down hard on the man's shoulder.

The man looked over his shoulder and smiled.

"Inspector Preston! What a lovely surprise! Come, join us. We're celebrating! My shout. Two-one to Spurs! It was a brilliant match. You should have been there!"

Preston cursed under his breath. He had been hoping to avoid the score until *Match of the Day* later that evening.

"Don't come all innocent with me, laddie," he growled. "You're nicked!" He pulled a pair of handcuffs from his belt. "Francis Parks, I am arresting you for armed robbery, dangerous driving, wasting my time, and bloody well ruining my evening!"

Parks spun around on his chair. "Are you sure you want to do this, Rod?" he smirked. Holding his hands out in surrender.

"Oh, I think I do, Frankie. I've been waiting for this moment for a very long time." He fastened the cuffs around Frankie's wrists. "It gives me great pleasure to tell you that you have the right to..."

"What's going on here?" The voice bellowed across the room. A tall man stood up and walked toward the bar.

"Chief Constable Arnside!" Preston gulped. "Just making an arrest, sir."

"On what grounds?" bellowed Arnside.

"This man," Preston poked Frankie in the chest, "is suspected of..." He stopped. "No, he was bloody well caught red-handed before the slippery bugger got away somehow."

"You're babbling," Arnside said.

"Sorry, sir." He swallowed and continued. "This man is

suspected of carrying out an armed robbery on Shearsmith's Jewellery Store in Soho, stealing diamonds worth somewhere in the region of four-point-four million pounds."

"Yes," Arnside chewed his lip. "I heard about that from one of the lads working at the match. Happened just after half-three, yes? Around the same time as Robertson scored the first goal, I believe. Just before half-time."

Preston gritted his teeth. He'd already had the score ruined, and now all the details were coming out too. "That's right, sir. Lucky for us, I was nearby when it happened. Led us a merry chase all around the backstreets of North London, so he did, him and his driver with the foreign van."

The woman who had been sitting at the bar the whole time turned around to face Preston.

"Actually Inspector," she said. "My van is most definitely British. I think you'll just find it's a..." She chuckled. "More recent model."

Ernie, who was perched on a third stool, turned his head. "It really is a lovely drive. You can hardly hear the engine. Goes like Arkle, but purrs like a pussycat, it really does."

Preston stroked his chin. "Accomplices, eh? And you're not even trying to hide it?"

Arnside stepped between Preston and Frankie, and glowered down at his inspector. "What are you blathering on about? Take these cuffs off this man at once!" He pointed to Baz, who reluctantly pulled out a set of keys as he stepped to the bar. Silently, he unlocked the cuffs.

Frankie rubbed his wrists. "Thanks, pal!" He winked.

Arnside continued. "This man and his friends have been my guests all afternoon."

"But he was in Soho at three-forty. I saw him with my own eyes."

"He was in the North Terrace of Wembley stadium with my son on his shoulders at three-forty. In fact, Frankie, here, has hardly left my sight in almost four hours."

"But—"

"Are you calling me a liar, Inspector?"

"No sir, it's just that—"

"Well," Arnside interrupted. "Aren't you going to apologise to the man?"

Preston stared at his Chief Constable in disbelief.

"Don't make me order you, Rod," said Arnside in a tone that Preston recognised as an order.

He stepped back from Frankie and stared at the floor. "On behalf of the Metropolitan Police Force," he whispered, "I would like to offer my unconditional apologies."

"Speak up, man!" blared Arnside.

"No, no, really," Frankie cut in. "It's not necessary. Apology accepted." He held out a hand. "No hard feelings eh, Rod?"

Preston stared at the hand for several seconds before turning around and walking out of the pub without another word, both fists clenched so tightly that his knuckles had turned red. Carr, Baz, and Boz silently followed.

8.24 P.M.

Three hours and forty-four minutes since full time.

THE ROBBERS

"I don't know about you, but I have had way too much

to drink," Ernie downed his pint and chased it with a handful of peanuts.

"I'll admit to being a little tipsy," Liz replied. "We have got a lot to celebrate though!"

"I'll drink to that!" Ernie raised his empty glass and began to chant "Two-one! Two-one! Two-one! Two-one!" to the tune of "Amazing Grace."

Liz turned to Frankie. "Are you sure I can't get you anything? Next round is on me. I think I can afford it."

Frankie shook his head. "No, thanks." He patted the back of her hand. "I'm not drinking orange juice for my health. It's only fair that I drive you both home. You've done the lion's share of the work today. It's the least I can do."

Liz kissed his right cheek, the one she had slapped earlier that day. "Ah, Frank you, Thankie. You're actually a very nice man."

"He is a nice man! And he's my best friend," Ernie chipped in. "I love him." He leaned across Liz and grasped Frankie's hand, looking into his eyes. "I mean it, Frankie. I love you," he said. He turned to Liz. "I love you too," he said. "I liked going to the game with you. Maybe we could do it again some time?"

Liz smiled and kissed Ernie on the opposite cheek. "You're very sweet, Ernie. I'd think I'd like that."

He gently touched his face before sighing. He then proceeded to fall asleep, face down into his bowl of peanuts.

Frankie stood up from his stool and drained the last of his juice. "Gimme the keys. I'll run and fetch the van back here. The state you two are in, with those cobbles, I doubt you'll make it to the lockup in one piece."

Liz fished around in Ernie's jacket and held the keys out to Frankie. He reached to take them, and she snatched them away. "Be gentle with her. I've got to have the van back at work in a few days without a scratch on her." She glared into his eyes.

"I promise," he nodded. "I'll treat her like the lady she is."

"Good." She dropped the keys into his hand. "Don't be long."

8.47 P.M.
  Four hours and seven minutes since full time.
  Frankie's secret lockup, somewhere in Wembley.

FRANKIE OPENED the back of the van.

"Now let's see if I can remember this," he said as he flicked the switches on Liz's wall of technology.

  ++This computer and its contents are the property of
              PLANUS Laboratories++
          ++Loading ENID. Please wait++

Frankie tapped his fingers on the console. A soft but emotionless female voice spoke:

  ++Good evening, Frankie Parks. How are you today?++

Frankie poked and prodded at the buttons. Nothing happened. It was embarrassing, but he realised he was going to have to talk to the stupid contraption to get it to do anything.

"I'm pretty good, Edith," he said, although he couldn't

quite bring himself to say "Thank you" or to enquire how she was.

++My name is ENID. How can I assist you today?++

He scratched his head. What were the words again?

"I would like you to fire up the Exposition Dislocation Drive."

++I am sorry, but I do not recognise that function, Frankie. Did you mean the Exochronal Displacement Drive?++

"Yes, that's the fella."

++Very good, Frankie. EDD initiated. Please set the temporal coordinates and physical destination++

Now what had Liz done? That's it. She set the time.

He carefully twisted a green dial until the clock showed:

++30/07/1966 10:30:00++

Just under one year in the past. World Cup Final Day! I'll go back seven hours before the game. That ought to give me enough time to fence the gems and bank the money.

Then, using the match as cover, I'll knock over a Milner's, loot some rhinestones or Titania or some of the other synthetic crap they sell, stash the new fake jewels back here.

He kicked the holdall.

Jump back a few hours to watch the game as an alibi, and then leap ahead to tonight, just in time to pick those two mugs up from The Century. When we fence the new gems, sure they'll be disappointed at first, but we'll still get thousands. They'll never even know.

What did Liz do next? Ah yes, she set the location.

He turned to the television screen displaying the map. It was blank. He pressed a button marked Reset.

Maybe that starts it up again.

The screen came to life, but the map was not London. Frankie leaned in to read the tiny text. It was what looked like a small town, not much bigger than a village, called Badgers Crossing.

Never heard of it.

The crosshairs were centred on a complex of buildings in the middle of a wood called Penlock Forest. As he looked closer, he could make out the tiny print saying PLANUS Laboratories.

Ah!

He looked around at the labels stuck all over the equipment, displaying the same name.

I must have accidentally set it back to its original location or something.

"ENID?" he said. It still felt wrong talking to a glorified TV.

++Yes Frankie? How can I help?++

"How do I set the location?"

++Take the mouse and—++

"Mouse?"

++The small plastic object to your right with a cable coming
out of it++

"Gotcha!" He grasped it. "Next?"

++Use the wheel on top to zoom in and out, move it left and
right on the desk to navigate the map, and press the left-
hand button to lock in a location. When you are ready, press
the red button to your left to activate the jump.++

Seems easy enough.
Frankie had just started to move the crosshairs across the
map when he felt something cold pressing into his temple.
He froze, apart from his eyes, which slowly turned to the left.
"Take your grubby mitts off the contraption, Parks."
Preston!
Frankie raised his hands and slowly twisted around in
the chair to face his foe. The policeman stepped back and
aimed the revolver at his chest.
"What's this, then, Frankie?" He kicked the holdall,
which fell open, revealing its precious contents. "Your
marble collection?"
"I suppose you're the big hero, here to take me in, are
you?"
"Not this time Frankie," Preston said, his voice shaking
with anger.
"Listen. I'll make you a deal. If you forget all about me,
there's a cut for you here. We could split it two ways."
Frankie ran his fingers through the diamonds. "Two million
pounds, Rod. Think about it."
"Are you attempting to bribe a police officer?" Preston
raised the gun to Frankie's head.

"You could buy Mrs Preston a lot of nice things with that amount of money."

"There is no Mrs Preston anymore! She left me because she thought all I cared about was catching you!" Preston spat through gritted teeth. "My life has been ruined! But, I don't blame you, Frankie. Not really. Arnside is a fool who wouldn't recognise a criminal if one walked into his house and walked out with his television while he was watching it. But, I'll show him! I'll say I followed you, that I caught you red-handed with the diamonds, that you resisted and—oh, what a shame—that you were killed in the struggle. And I'll be the hero!" He thudded his chest with his free hand. "Me!"

Frankie slowly edged his right hand towards the red button. Preston noticed his movement and stepped closer again. He cocked the pistol's hammer. "Just try it, sonny, see what happens."

++Do you wish to proceed, Frankie?++

"What?" Preston looked around the van to locate the source of the voice.

While Preston was distracted, Frankie lashed out with his left leg, sending him sprawling away. He plunged his hand down over the red button. As Preston fell into the side of the van, the impact caused his finger to depress the trigger. Frankie held up his other hand. *Like that will be any use against a bullet*, he thought. He was proud of the fact that he had never discharged a firearm in any of his heists, so the loud bang sounded far less like the gunshots from films he expected. It reminded him more of the cap-guns he played with as a boy. The gunshot reverberated around the inside of the van. Then came a split-second of silence, followed by a high-pitched whistle in his ears.

++Displacement activated++

Frankie lowered his hand from his face. Preston was motionless on the floor. Actually, no. He appeared to be floating a foot above the floor, his face a mask of fury. He was encased in a cloud of smoke. Sparks protruded out of the barrel of the weapon. A bronze bullet slug hung in the space inches from Frankie's face. He plucked it out of the air and placed it on the desk.

And then the world turned inside out.

———

9.52 P.M.
Five hours and twelve minutes since full time.
One hour and five minutes since Frankie left.
Car park of The Century Tavern, Forty Lane, Wembley.

———

LIZ LOOKED AT HER WATCH. Again. "Where is he?" Something was wrong, she knew it. She'd sent Ernie home in a black cab, promising to talk to him in the morning about their date, but he was far too drunk to be of any use now.

She pulled her smart phone out of her pocket and poked at the screen.

++Good evening, Doctor Wilde. How are you today?++

"I'm worried ENID."

++I am very sorry to hear that. How can I be of assistance?
++

She thought for a second. "ENID, can you tell me the location of the Transit?"

++Do you mean the vehicle with the registration PL1 TPP?
++

"Yes," Liz said.

++That vehicle is no longer on this temporal plane++

"What happened?" Her stomach felt like it had been punched. She already had a good idea of what had happened.

++Mr Parks activated the Exochronal Displacement Drive++

"Damn!" She sat on a bench, head in hand. After a moment she spoke again. "ENID, I need to get back to PLANUS. Does the technology exist in 1967 for me to construct a new EDD?"

++It will be a rudimentary device, but yes. I believe that it should be possible. Be warned, though, that traversing the exochronal conduit will be immensely uncomfortable++

"I can deal with that," she said, thinking of the bag of goodies at the other end. "Now, can you tell me the exact date, time, and location that Frankie travelled to?"

++Of course, Doctor Wilde. Displaying coordinates now++

Liz stared at the information on her screen for a long time. And then she grinned. "Okay, then. Let's get to work."

TUESDAY, 26th June 2017, 9.02 a.m.
Fifty years, one month, sixteen hours and twenty-two minutes since full time.
PLANUS Laboratories, Badgers Crossing.

THE COPS

Professor Edgar Stewart showed Sergeant Lisa Callaghan into his office.

"Tea? Coffee?" he said, pouring himself a cup from a percolator in the corner of the room.

"No thanks," she said.

"Please." He held a hand out. "Take a seat." He placed his mug down on a coaster, sat behind his desk opposite Callaghan, and leaned in towards her.

"What's up, Cally? How can I help?"

Cally took a sheet of paper out of a folder and slid it across the desk towards Edgar. He picked it up and studied it. He looked up at her. "What's this?"

"I was hoping you could tell me," Cally said. "That registration plate was found at the bottom of Ravenmere. We ran it through the DVLA computer, and it's from a 2015 Ford Transit van that's registered to you."

Edgar cocked his head.

"Well, not you personally. PLANUS Labs, I mean."

He tapped his pen on the desk a handful of times and rubbed his chin with the other hand. He put the pen down, took a sip of his coffee, and then pressed the intercom on his desk.

"Rachael?"

"Yes, Edgar?" came a voice back through the device.

"Can you tell me the whereabouts of asset PL1?"

"Just one minute."

Edgar smiled at Cally. "Sorry about this."

"Oh, it's no problem, Ed," Cally said.

The intercom bleeped, and Rachael's voice announced, "It's currently offsite. Doctor Wilde signed it out a week last Friday."

Cally scratched the side of her head. "Well, ain't that a thing?" she said to herself. She slumped back in the very comfortable chair.

"What's this about, Cally?" Ed said.

"Okay, so you've heard about Claire Carter, right?"

"The missing woman. Yes, of course."

"Well, we had divers down in Ravenmere looking for her."

"Goodness. That's horrible." Ed slurped at his coffee again.

"Quite," Cally continued. "However, while there was no sign of Mrs Carter down there, we did uncover something a lot more, shall we say, mysterious."

Ed had been holding on to his hot cup for so long that it burned his fingers. He put it down with a small ouch. "Go on," he said.

"Our divers found a vehicle down there—a white Ford Transit van that was packed full of computerised gizmos."

A shiver ran down Ed's back and arms. It certainly did sound like the erstwhile van.

"And that's not the worst of it," Cally said. "They found two bodies in the back."

"My God! Was Liz...?"

"No," Cally cut in, seeing he was concerned and wanting to put his mind at ease. "This is where it gets really weird though."

"It already is quite weird."

"That's why I said 'really.'" Cally took a notepad from her pocket and flipped it open. "We've been able to identify the bodies as Francis Parks and Roderick Preston."

Ed dropped his pen. "The Shearsmith Heist? Holy cow! This is huge, like Lord Lucan levels of huge!"

"Yes, indeed," Cally said. "If you've seen the film about them, and I think most people have, then you know that the two of them planned the heist together, disappeared on the night of the Cup Final, and ran off to Acapulco with the diamonds before anyone realised they were missing. Turns out that wasn't the case."

Ed picked up his pen and recommenced tapping. "So, they killed each other, and someone dumped the bodies, all these years later, in our van?"

Cally sighed. "And now we get to the *even* weirder bit. No. They didn't kill each other, and their bodies weren't dumped in the van. Preliminary tests suggest that they died inside the van. Although there is evidence of a struggle and a gunshot, the cause of death has been determined as drowning."

Ed was gripped. This was far better than the film.

"And the diamonds?"

"No sign of them. And the weirdness levels don't stop there."

Ed dropped his pen again. It landed in his coffee. "So, they've been hiding out all this time and ended up in our van when it crashed into the lake?" He fished the pen out and sucked the liquid from it.

"Once again, no. We've been able to date the times of death to approximately fifty years ago. However, there was some evidence that the bodies had been disturbed fairly recently. And that's not all."

Ed didn't think he could take much more weird, which made him smile because as Head of Projects at PLANUS, he'd seen more than his fair share of weird.

"The van. Your van. The one that we *know* was built in September 2015 and registered to this facility in October of that same year displays sufficient levels of rust and decay to suggest it, too, had been at the bottom of that lake since the mid-nineteen-sixties. So..." Cally took out her pen. "What I'm here to ask you, Ed, is: can you tell me what the hell is going on?"

Ed thought for a moment. "Okay, without a warrant I wouldn't normally part with confidential details about any of our projects here."

Cally opened her mouth to protest but Ed cut her off.

"But, seeing as it's you, Cally, and you've been so generous with your information, I can offer you the following. Doctor Wilde is a member of Kristine Peluso's team on The Protogonos Project."

"What's that? And how's that spelled?" Cally said, pen poised over the notepad.

Edgar spelled it out for her and continued. "It's an investigation into whether a truly sentient artificial intelligence can exist. We're making some great breakthroughs with ENID, our resident AI, but that hardly seems relevant here, I think."

Cally nodded in agreement.

"I also allowed her, as I do with many of my top scientists, to use some of the facilities on site here for a personal project. I wasn't privy to the full details of her research, apart from that it was something to do with time dilation."

"Time dilation?"

"In layman's terms, it's when an external force such as relative velocity or gravitational potential causes a divergence between two synchronised chronologies."

Cally looked back at him blankly. "That's not layman's terms."

"Sorry. Try this. If you set two identical clocks to the exact same time, and then put one on a wall in your house and the other in a jet plane flying around the world at ten-thousand miles an hour, when you put them back together, the one from the plane will be ahead of the one that stayed on the wall, even though both have kept time perfectly to the observer. That's time dilation."

"Are you talking about time travel?" Cally said.

Ed laughed. "Well, that would be quite a thing, but sadly, no. Time travel is impossible. Einstein couldn't crack it, so, as good as she is, I very much doubt Doctor Wilde did either."

Cally nodded and made some more notes on her pad. "So, where is this Doctor Wilde now, then?"

Ed pressed the intercom again.

"Rachael. Is Liz in today, do you know?"

"No, Edgar She's on leave at the moment."

"Did she say what she was doing with her time off?"

"Well, she did, but that was as a friend, not a colleague. I don't think I really should be giving away personal information like that."

Cally leaned into the intercom. "Hello. Rachael, is it?" Before Rachael could reply, she carried on. "Well, Rachael, this is not a natter around the coffee machine. This is an official police investigation, possibly murder. So, if you know what's good for you, you'll tell us where Doctor Wilde is!"

"OK, but I didn't really understand some of what she meant."

"That doesn't matter," Cally raised her pen to the pad. "Just tell me what she said."

"Well, last week she went for a city break in London. I let her take the van because her car was in the garage. I didn't think you'd mind, Edgar. Then yesterday, she came back in to say she needed the van for longer. I asked her, since she was back, if she fancied going for a coffee after work, but she said she couldn't because she'd hired some scuba gear from the Broccton Watersports Centre and was going down to look around the old flooded village under Ravenmere. Obviously, that's not the bit I didn't understand."

Cally raised an eyebrow. Ed craned his neck to see what she was writing on her pad. He made out the word "diamonds" before she noticed and flipped it shut. "Go on," she said.

"After that, she said she'd met a guy—Ernie, I think she said he was called—and they were going out on a date to a football match."

"When? Where?"

"That's the really strange thing. I must have misunderstood because it sounded like she said they were going to watch England win the World Cup."

Biography

After seeing a road sign during a long drive, Paul created the fictional town of Badgers Crossing where many of his stories (including the conclusion of this one) are set. He has written nonfiction pieces for *Den of Geek, Horrified, Ginger Nuts of Horror, Folklore Thursday*, and *Film Stories Magazine*, as well as running pop-culture site *World Geekly News*. His first fictional stories were printed in a number of anthologies throughout 2021, and in May 2022, his debut book, *Tales From Badgers Crossing*, was published by Greenteeth Press. His favourite Time Travel book is Terry Pratchett's *Night Watch* and his favourite TT film is *The Terminator*.

When he should be writing, he can usually be found mucking about on Twitter or Instagram as @paulychilds. For more information on Paul and his work, visit https://paulchilds.co.uk/

ORIGINAL PUBLICATION:
    https://www.greenteethpress.com/

THE BOYS OF SUMMER

JOSHUA DAVID BELLIN

SHE TOSSED her hair as she rose from the surf, and his heart pounded like a wave upon the shore. Her black one-piece swimsuit showed off her curves, the smoothness of her bronzed arms and legs. She bent over to wring water from her long dark hair and then, with a practiced flip of her head that thrilled him with its easy grace, she threw the wet twist over her shoulder and ran up the beach. For a second, it was possible to imagine she was running toward him, but her trajectory angled toward the lifeguard's chair, and he clenched his fists in frustration.

"Cute, ain't she?"

Jason turned. An old man stood behind the metal railing that overlooked the beach. The stiff salt breeze whipped his tangled hair and beard, obscuring his features. He wore gray pants and a grubby overcoat of the same nondescript color, along with army boots that had seen much better days. Homeless. They'd been the subject of news stories since Reagan won his second term. Though they were rare in this small seaside town, Jason had seen them from time to time, squatting on sidewalks in heavy winter clothes mutely holding out a hand for small change. They made him uncomfortable, but none of them had ever said a word to him.

He ignored the old man and focused his attention on the girl, who stood toweling off her hair as she chatted with the lifeguard. Jason wished he could approach her, but he knew he didn't dare.

"I seen you before," the old man interrupted his thoughts. "Jason, right?"

Jason glanced over his shoulder. The old man was hunched forward, elbows on the railing. His head bobbed as if to a tune only he could hear. Strong as the wind was, it couldn't cleanse the reek of his unwashed flesh.

"I seen you workin' at the candy store down on the pier," the man continued. "What's the ol' lady call the place? The Sweet Shack?"

Don't answer, Jason thought. Just pretend he isn't there.

He watched the lifeguard tell a story, hands gesturing enthusiastically. The girl threw her head back and laughed.

"You graduated from the high school, right?" the homeless man's voice prodded. "Class o' '85? Must be tough, these city gals comin' up here, flauntin' their little asses then, *poof!* gone before you know it. Or before you get a chance to know *them*, right?"

He cackled. Jason felt a sudden, unreasonable protectiveness for this girl he'd first seen earlier that day. He didn't know her name, but a need to defend her from the unwelcome attention of the old man rose in his breast.

"Get out of here," he said to the man, "or I'll..." He pointed to the public payphone. "I'll call the police."

The man didn't seem impressed by the threat. He

straightened, and Jason saw that he was taller than he'd first appeared. There was no stoop to his shoulders, no unsteadiness to his knees. He cleared his throat with a wet sound and spat over the railing onto the sand.

"Feel free," he said. "But you bust me, you ain't never gonna learn what I know 'bout that little mermaid out there. Her name's Izzie, for starters. Bet you didn't know that. Am I right?"

Jason tried to stop himself from trembling. He desperately wanted to put distance between the two of them, but for some reason, he couldn't move. The man's gaze held a magnetic power that kept him rooted to the spot, warm sand threading between his toes.

"She just finished her first year o' college," the old man went on. "That school down south—what do they call it?" He snapped his fingers. "Wellesley. Finished a coupla months ago, come here with friends before they start back. But I got a feeling she ain't goin' to be spendin' much time with them, am I right?"

He smiled, showing rotten teeth. The girl's musical laughter reached Jason's ears, but it seemed to come from far away.

"That lifeguard's a college boy himself," the old man said. "Senior at—what do they call the place?—Mass U?"

"UMass," Jason said faintly.

"That's right. Real ladies' man from what I hear. You goin' to college?"

"In a couple of weeks."

"But not at Wellesley, right? That's a school for girls, ain't it? Or what're they callin' 'em these days, a finishin' school?"

The man laughed so hard he began to cough, a clotted hacking that set Jason's teeth on edge. He turned back to the beach, only to discover that the girl was gone, the lifeguard positioned atop his tall red chair. For a wild moment, Jason thought she might actually have vanished, fallen into a sink-hole or gotten washed out to sea. Then he spotted her running down the beach toward the hotel that crouched beyond the granite wall. His eyes followed her until she climbed the stairs cut into the rocks, where he lost sight of her.

The homeless man's voice crept into his ear. "Where'd you tell me you was goin' to college?"

"It doesn't matter," Jason said.

"It might," the man responded. "Girls like that don't grow on trees, y' know."

JASON LAY in bed with the shade down and the overhead fan beating the muggy August air. The image from the beach burned his eyes: the girl standing beside Charles as he leaned against the rungs of his lifeguard chair, arms crossed. Only if you watched closely could you see how her body inclined toward his, her eyes studying his face raptly when he spoke. She couldn't show her true feelings while Charles was on duty; she had to make it look like she was nothing more than a random beachgoer who'd struck up a conversation with the lifeguard. But Jason knew the truth.

"Izzie," he whispered. Her name made his throat ache.

He thought back to their first and only meeting. He'd been standing behind the counter at the Sweet Shack that morning when the brass bell jingled, and there she was, wearing an off-the-shoulder pink shirt that showed one of the straps of her swimsuit. Her hair hung loose and frizzy as if she'd let it dry in the sun. She crossed her forearms on the glass counter and craned her neck to peer inside, and a mix of intoxicating scents wafted over him: coconut sunscreen, floral shampoo, a hint of minty breath. His heart quickened when she met his eye.

"Hi, Jason," she said, and he blanked for a second before realizing she must have read his nametag. "It's a beautiful day, isn't it?"

"I guess," was all he could come up with.

Her eyes scanned the neat rows of candy. "I'm looking for something special. What do you recommend?"

"The, uh, taffy's good."

"Something *extra* special," she said with a conspiratorial tip of her head.

"Chocolate turtles?" he suggested, his voice cracking on *turtles*.

"Perfect." She gave him a dazzling smile. "I'll take a whole boxful."

He leaned down to reach inside the case, which blocked her from seeing his blush. She stood there humming pleasantly while he boxed her order and rang up the sale, but all he could think about was how clownish he looked in his candy-striped paper hat and apron, the pimple he'd noticed on his nose this morning turned red from rubbing. His hands shook when he passed her the purchase, and he almost dropped the cash she placed in his palm.

"Thanks, Jason," she said with another smile. "See you around."

And then she was gone, the bell chiming with the finality of a farewell.

He squeezed his eyes shut and recalled the look on her face before she left. It was so obvious now. The extra special gift was for Charles. For tonight, when he was off duty and her girlfriends had gone out drinking and she was alone with him in her hotel room. She'd been friendly to a local kid in the candy shop, but her smile was for Charles, not him.

Jason sat up in bed and tried to picture her as she'd appeared at the beach, but the old man kept intruding on his thoughts. His uncouth words, his ugly leer. The overly familiar way he talked about her, rolling her name around on his tongue like a piece of hard candy. Jason felt an overwhelming desire to see her again, to warn her. To show her he cared. She would appreciate his concern, touch his arm in thanks. The two of them would take a walk while they got better acquainted, their steps drifting to the seashore. And there, with a brisk wind tousling her hair and the waves breaking with a succession of sighs at his feet, he would declare his true feelings for her.

But that would have to come later. His lunch break was almost over, and he'd catch hell from Mrs. Wright if he didn't show up for the afternoon shift. He ran downstairs, grabbed an apple from the bowl in the kitchen, and dashed for the door. His mom called out his name from the living room, but he pretended not to hear her over the squeak of the screen. When the door banged shut, he practically sprinted down the long, curving street to town. His heart hammered at the thought of what he would say to Izzie, what magic words he would conjure to prove his devotion.

————

HE SPENT the next four hours slaving away behind the candy store counter, boxing chocolate-dipped mints and crystalized fruit slices while the man at the taffy machine laboriously pulled and stretched and folded the long, sweet strands. As usual, when summer was drawing to a close, there was a rush on the place, mostly middle-aged tourists trying to look younger than they were in Wayfarer sunglasses and Spandex pants. The whole time, Jason's mind whirled with anticipation, and he lost count of orders and pressed the wrong keys on the register more than he had since his first day on the job. When his shift was finally over, he tore off his hat and apron, tugged the latex gloves from his hands, and tossed the whole bundle into the trash. Mrs. Wright tottered out of her office on her cane, but he was gone before she had a chance to say goodbye.

He hit the pier at a run, dodging warped planks and brackish puddles that had sloshed up from the sea. He was so busy with thoughts of Izzie, he didn't notice the person headed straight at him until they collided.

"Whoa, whoa," a deep voice said. "What's the rush?"

It was him. Charles. The lifeguard was a good six inches taller than Jason, who knew him only the way everyone in town did: star point guard on his prep school basketball team, holder of the state high school record in the 100-meter freestyle. His family owned a boat, the *Lady Luck*, and Charles had won sailing competitions too. He wore his hair in a convincing imitation of George Michael's signature style, airy and buoyant like pale-gold cotton candy. His cheeks were ruddy with sun. Charles had never spoken to him, and so far as Jason was aware, the older boy didn't even know his name.

"You look like you saw a ghost," Charles said. "Everything all right?"

"Fine," Jason muttered.

"Going somewhere?"

None of your business, Jason thought. "Home."

"I heard you got off at five. I was coming down here anyway, so..."

"You heard?" Jason said. "Who from?"

Charles made a vague gesture. "Not important. Thought I'd stop by so we could talk."

"About what?"

Charles flashed a toothy smile. Jason struggled not to be taken in by its apparent warmth.

"Come on," Charles said. "It'll only take a minute."

He strolled toward the wooden bench at the end of the pier. When he sat and found that Jason hadn't joined him, he cocked his head like a grownup coaxing a shy toddler. Jason shuffled across the slick planks and sat, feeling unnervingly close to Charles, whose legs were sprinkled with curly, sun-lightened hair. Jason angled his knees to the side so they wouldn't touch.

"So anyway," Charles said once Jason was settled, "I've been hearing some things around town about you and Izzie."

Jason's heart thundered. He couldn't meet Charles's eye. "I don't know what you're talking about."

"It's okay, Jason. She's a great girl. Draws lots of attention everywhere she goes."

"I don't even know—"

"Jason." Charles was looking at him with an expression of mingled amusement and indulgence. "There's nothing to apologize for. I just want to make sure you understand a few things."

"Like what?"

Charles stretched both arms over his head before draping them across the back of the bench. "Like where matters stand between me and her."

"It's none of my—"

"You're what, eighteen?" Charles said. "Headed to college this year?"

Against his will, Jason nodded.

"Well, trust me, there's plenty of fish in the sea," Charles said. "I know what it feels like growing up in a place where nothing ever changes. Like you're suffocating, can't come up for air. A new face appears in town, it's easy to get your head turned, start seeing things that aren't real. Things that aren't going to happen."

Charles threw his benevolent, superior gaze on him, and Jason felt a sudden impulse to smash the boy's fashion model face, feel the bones crunch beneath his knuckles. His fist tightened, and if not for the fact that he knew Charles was watching him far more warily than his relaxed pose suggested, he might have done it.

"You seem like a good kid, Jason," Charles said. "I wouldn't want you to get in any trouble."

"What are you, my dad?"

The lifeguard's smile never shifted, but Jason saw a gleam of triumph breaking through the friendly façade.

"From what I hear, your dad was a lobsterman who ran out on you," Charles said. "But if he was around, I'm sure he'd tell you to keep your hands off another man's catch."

Jason leaped to his feet. He didn't know if he was trying to look dramatic or threatening or what, but to Charles, he must have looked too ridiculous to deserve a reaction. The lifeguard's nonchalance infuriated him, and Jason waded in, fists raised. Instantly, as Jason had suspected and almost hoped, Charles was on his feet, casting his opponent into shadow, ready to defend the honor of the girl he'd claimed as his own.

"Boys!"

Jason saw Mrs. Wright hobbling down the pier, moving as fast as her partially paralyzed leg would carry her. She was red-faced and breathing heavily by the time she reached the combatants. She leaned on her cane to recover her wind before speaking.

"Jason," she said sternly but with obvious difficulty keeping her voice under control. "What is this about?"

"Nothing, Mrs. W. We were just—"

"Talking," Charles cut in, the nimble smile gracing his lips. "Jason was telling me—"

"That's enough from you, Charles Alexander Rhodes," she said. "I don't know who started this, but it's finished now, you understand?"

Charles nodded, biting his lip. He had the polish to look abashed. "I'm very sorry, Mrs. Wright. It won't happen again."

"Good," she said. "Jason?"

"No, ma'am."

"*No, ma'am* what?"

"No, ma'am. It won't happen again."

"That's what I like to hear." Her face softened, and she laid a hand on Jason's arm. "Now you be on your way. I'll see you first thing tomorrow."

"Yes, ma'am," he said as she returned to the store, moving even more stiffly than usual after the short burst of activity.

The two of them were alone. Gulls soared overhead, emitting their siren calls. Dog-eared flyers advertising harbor tours and last month's jazz festival flapped from a wooden kiosk. Charles leveled a glare at Jason, and this time, even his practiced face couldn't pretend to smile.

"You've been warned," he said. "You come near her again, you know what happens."

Then he was gone, pushing through clumps of tourists as he made his way toward the beachfront hotel. Jason watched him go, but was unable to derive any satisfaction from the jitter in the lifeguard's stride.

"Pussy."

Jason flinched at the sound of the voice and found the old man standing on the pier. He must have been lurking nearby, hidden between storefronts, watching the encounter unfold.

"What did you call me?" Jason said.

"I called you a fuckin' pussy. You got a problem with that?"

"I told you to leave me alone or—"

"You'll call the cops," the man said. "'Zactly what a little pussy like you would do."

Jason's face burned with shame. He tried to come up with a retort, but the old man talked over him before the words reached his tongue.

"You slink around town moonin' 'bout this girl," the man said, "but you ain't got the balls to *fight* for her. You let some lily-livered college boy an' a crippled ol' biddy push you around, an' the only words out of your mouth are *yes, ma'am* an' *no, ma'am*." His voice changed to a saccharine falsetto before returning to its normal husky tone. "You know what's gonna happen to Izzie tonight, dontcha?"

Jason did know, but couldn't bear to say it.

"She ain't never been with a man before," the other filled in the silence. "But as soon as Charles Fuckin' Rhodes gets his hands on her, that's all she wrote. He's gonna use her up an' spit her out like he does all them college girls, an' you're gonna *let* him?"

Jason shook his head dumbly.

"Then *do* somethin' about it, for fuck's sake. Show her what true love means instead o' standin' there quakin' in your boots an' pissin' in your pants."

"Did you tell Charles about me and Izzie?" Jason found his voice. "Did you tell him about my dad?"

"There you go again, talkin' 'bout things that don't make no fuckin' difference," the old man said. "You ain't never gonna learn, you worthless piece o' shit. Have yourself a good fuckin' life."

He stormed off, heading in the direction Charles had gone. Jason stood frozen for a second before charging after him. He reached the man in a few short steps and grabbed his soiled jacket, clinging to him like a barnacle on a piling. The coat felt simultaneously tacky and slick, and the fetid odor that emanated from it was stronger by far than the fishy smell of the harbor. Jason held his breath as long as he could, then gasped out the words: "Tell me what to do."

"You serious?"

"Y-yes."

"No more pussyfootin' around?"

"I—"

"Because if you're gonna spook an' run whenever some ancient crone says the word *boo*, life's too short for me to be wastin' time on your sorry ass."

"Please," Jason said. "I'll do anything you tell me to."

The old man appraised him. His head was uncharacteristically still, no longer bobbing to the unheard beat. His eyes were deeply set behind wrinkles, but they weren't misty and dim like the eyes of the elderly tourists who frequented the Sweet Shack. They were bright and intense as agates peeking out from layers of weathered stone. Their color was a deep-sea blue, all the more striking because it was the same color Jason saw when he gazed at his own reflection. It was the one feature that might have made him stand out in a crowd, but it would never be enough to convince a girl like Izzie to choose him over Charles.

"All right," the man said. "I like your spirit, kid. Maybe there's hope for you after all."

He disengaged Jason's hand from his coat, then reached inside and withdrew a leather-bound journal. Its cover was as crisscrossed with wrinkles as his face, its elastic strap shriveled to a few threads. The man opened it to the first creamy, weather-beaten page, which breathed an aroma as musty and thick as if it had soaked up the ocean air for decades. His knobby-knuckled finger indicated a drawing that looked as if it had been chiseled into the page, so deeply embedded was the black ink in the creased paper.

"There's ways of winnin' this fight," the old man said as Jason studied the inscribed image. "Right now, you feel like you're stuck in this place an' time, like you ain't never gonna be free of it. What you gotta do is free your *mind*, cast away the shackles that bind you to the here an' now. An' you gotta do it fast, 'fore that cocksucker Charles gets to her an' she ain't nothin' but soiled goods from here on out."

The thought of losing her to his rival made the ground seem to open beneath Jason's feet. "But *how* do I do that?"

"With this," the man answered, tapping the picture in his book.

"What is it?"

"A love potion, kid. Strongest kind there is. Come on."

He tucked the book beneath an arm and gestured with his head. Then he started off for the center of town with Jason following in his wake.

THE SUN WAS MAKING its descent toward the western causeway when Jason emerged from the below-street-level tattoo parlor to find the old man waiting for him, leaning against a decorative lamppost. Once again, his head wasn't moving. His hand, however, trembled as he turned the boy's left wrist over to examine the tattoo. Jason braced for another tongue-lashing, but when the old man finished his scrutiny, he let out a long breath and dropped the wrist. Where his hand had touched the sensitive skin, Jason felt a throbbing like fire.

"Not bad, kid," the old man said. "How's it feel?"

Jason rotated the wrist slowly, flexing his fingers. "It hurts."

"Like a knife to the heart," the man agreed. "But now she'll know you mean business. That you ain't afraid to go all the way."

His eyes met Jason's. His head had begun its dance after his inspection of the wrist, but it stilled again as they exchanged glances.

"You feel like a man?" he asked.

Jason wasn't sure how he felt, other than tired and heartsick and sore, but he nodded.

"Good. Then you're ready."

Once again, he withdrew the journal from inside his coat. He'd showed the owner of the dingy little tattoo shop the design on the first page, but he'd refused to relinquish the book while the artist performed his work. Now he offered the journal to Jason with both hands as if he were bestowing a priceless gift on his chosen heir.

"This is yours," he said. "Take it home an' read it from cover to cover. Stay away from Izzie's place on the way home, an' don't look at what's written inside until you're in your room with the door locked. When you understand what it's tellin' you, I'll be in touch."

"How will you know?"

The old man smiled. His breath was as foul as ever, but it no longer made Jason recoil.

"Get goin', sonny boy," the man said. "Tonight's the night. Everything works out the way it's supposed to, your wait will be over before daybreak."

He turned on his heel and departed into the gloaming. There was a sprightliness to his step Jason had never seen before. His head was bobbing full tilt, his fingers snapping at air. Whatever it was that had brought about this change in the old man's demeanor, Jason chose to see it as a good sign. The man hadn't been wrong about anything else to this point, so why shouldn't he be right about the day's crowning moment?

Jason gripped the journal to his chest. It thrummed in response to his heartbeat. He studied the mark on his wrist to make sure it was real, stared at it for as long as the old man had. Then he took a side street to avoid the beachfront hotel and started up the steep ascent for home.

THE HALL LIGHT was on when he arrived. His mom must be out with her bridge club. Jason exhaled, thankful that he didn't have to sneak the journal past her. The stairs creaked as he climbed, and that was enough to give him the shivers.

Alone in his room, he locked the door and sat on the bed. Izzie's image flitted before him, tantalizing, tormenting. If what the old man said was true, then by morning, everything he dreamed would yawn wide like a door to the future. And the journal was the key to opening the door.

Jason turned to the first page. His finger tingled as he traced the inscription deeply cut into the parchment-like paper. He pressed his new tattoo against the design and found that the two matched perfectly. Taking a deep breath, he flipped the page.

The drawing showed through onto the back, but the page was otherwise blank. The right-hand page, though, was covered with handwriting in a faded script. The lines sprawled across the paper, looking as if they had been scribbled in a burst of agitation or inspiration. The penmanship was too sloppy to read at first, but when Jason brought the mildewed page close to his face, he was able to make out the words.

They were the lyrics to a song.

He recognized it at once: "The Boys of Summer," the opening track of ex-Eagles vocalist Don Henley's solo album *Building the Perfect Beast*. Jason had heard the song almost every day on the radio during his final semester in high school, its frequency increasing as summer neared. He liked it well enough, but had never thought much about it. Certainly not enough to memorize the lyrics and commit them to writing as the old man had done.

Jason flipped to the next page.

And his breath caught.

The back of the second page was as blank as the first, but on the following right-hand page was the same song, the same lyrics. The writing was every bit as messy as it had been on the previous page, making it look as if the writer had turned the page and rewritten the lyrics without pause. Jason flipped to the next page, only to find the same thing: a blank left-hand sheet, a scrawled repetition of the lyrics on the right-hand side. He turned page after page, more than a hundred from start to finish, but the pattern never varied: the same song, the same nearly illegible handwriting, the same frenzied pace. Over and over and over, the lyrics were repeated like an incantation meant to bring about some desired result or ward off a malign power.

Jason closed the journal and let out air in a whoosh. What did it mean? The lyrics were obvious enough—some old guy remembering a summertime fling—but what did that have to do with *him*? He wasn't pining for a lost love; he was looking forward to claiming his first love forever. The old man had hinted that the journal would contain information or instructions for tonight, but so far as Jason could tell, there was nothing of the sort to be found.

He opened the journal again. He had to be missing something. Maybe it was a kind of code, repeated endlessly and in exactly the same form so Jason could figure it out? But why would the old man do that instead of just telling him? Was this another test of Jason's fidelity to the girl it seemed the old man wanted him to win as much as he did? He rose from bed and pulled up the shade, and found the town covered in darkness. The red numbers on his digital alarm clock told him it was after ten. He didn't have forever to figure this out. If he didn't find the answer soon, the night would be over and his chance with Izzie—his one and only chance before Charles had his way with her—would be gone.

A sob escaped his throat. He returned to the bed and bent over the words of the journal, staring at them so hard it felt as if his eyes would sear a hole through the thick sheaf of pages. His head spun with concentration, his vision blurred through tears. He pressed the journal to his heart, touched it to his irritated wrist, begged it to speak to him. When it didn't answer, he read the words over and over, at first silently, then out loud, then almost out loud, feeling the curve and weight of them on his lips and tongue. Words of longing and loss, days past and chances squandered. An old man driving alone, his only passenger the memory of the rapture he'd known as a boy but would never know again. And through it all waltzed the girl of his dreams, an apparition of sand and wind and waves mocking him with her unendurable nearness and unattainable distance. This wasn't just any love song. It was a chant of overwhelming grief, of yearning so intense it bordered on despair. A lament for the poor soul who'd pined away a lifetime while the image of his lost love consumed his thoughts, leaving nothing behind.

And at last, Jason understood.

The words lit a fuse in his mind. The melody enfolded him. He knew why the song was there, why it was the perfect complement for tonight. The message couldn't have been clearer. He didn't have to wait for the man's call, because he knew exactly what he was required to do.

The downstairs phone rang. Jason hugged the journal to his chest and left the room, gliding noiselessly down the stairs. When he took the phone off its hook, he never doubted which voice he would hear.

"It's time," the voice said. "Bring the book."

Jason replaced the phone on its cradle and left the house. Unlike his frantic sprint earlier in the day, he paced slowly and sedately, his feet knowing exactly where to land. He felt as if he were caught in destiny's riptide, as if this final journey was the culmination of all the out-of-body experiences he'd had today. The only difference was that this time he felt entirely *in* his body, as if he'd finally caught up with the self he'd been chasing all along, the man he was meant to be from this moment until the end of time.

He arrived at the beach in minutes. A warm breeze ruffled his hair. Boat lights dotted the horizon. He passed the railing where the old man had stood this morning, touched his fingers to the paint-flecked metal. Then he walked down the short ramp that exited onto the sand and made his way to the lifeguard's chair.

A sliver of moon rested above the waves, touching them with pale light. The same light revealed the old man sitting in Charles's spot like a king on a throne, his white hair fluttering in the wind. He didn't glance at Jason as he approached. His attention was focused on the vast gleaming pool that stretched before him to the edge of the world.

"Glad you made it, kid," he said without facing Jason. "There's your reward."

He nodded toward the shadows at the foot of the chair. Jason had trouble making out the thing that was lying there, a dark mass like ropy strands of seaweed that had washed ashore. He took a tentative step toward the unidentifiable shape then froze, his eyes widening and his stomach threatening to betray him.

Two bodies lay on a beach blanket before the lifeguard's chair. Their arms and legs were entwined, their clothes—a pink Polo shirt and Madras shorts for Charles, a floral print sundress for Izzie—drenched in gore. A sealed white candy box sat beside them, spattered with blood. Charles seemed to be trying to shield Izzie's much smaller frame, which was tucked into his chest while his shoulders arched over her head. Maybe the lifeguard had heard the soft approach of footsteps too late to do anything other than pull his partner to him. Or maybe this was the position their killer had found them in, the two of them so lost in each other's embrace they'd had no chance to react before the knife slashed their throats to dye the blanket a dark red-black.

A heavy shape thudded to the sand. Jason looked up from the murdered lovers and met the old man's eyes. There was nothing to be seen in them except a darkness hundreds of fathoms deep. The man held out a bloody switchblade, then dropped it on the sand beside his victims.

"Go ahead, kid," he said tonelessly. "Tell me."

"You...you killed her."

The old man nodded.

"You killed her, you son of a bitch!" Jason screamed. "You killed Izzie!"

"That's right," the old man said. "But the cops ain't never gonna find out I'm the one that done it. They ain't never gonna find me at all."

"What are you talking about?"

"The knife," the old man said, pointing at where it lay on the sand, dark blood and bright steel dimly reflecting the moonlight. "It's got your fingerprints all over it."

"*My* fingerprints? You mean yours."

"Right. Mine."

He rolled up the left sleeve of his overcoat. Jason caught a glimpse of a bony arm knotted with veins and wrinkles. The man rotated the arm so the inside of his wrist faced upward, and Jason stared at the tattoo inked beneath his skin. It was old and faded, more blue than black, like an ancient bruise that had never fully healed. Yet in all other respects, it was identical to the design on Jason's own wrist.

A flower.

A dagger.

And a name.

Izzie.

Jason looked into the old man's eyes, and a feeling of horror gripped him as he saw those eyes looking right back.

"I been away a long time, kid," the old man said. "Ain't seen her in more'n sixty years. But she never changed. Deep down, I knew she wouldn't. She looked exactly the way she did first time I seen her prancin' in the door o' the Sweet Shack. Same way she looked right before I slit her throat."

"But how could you have seen—"

"I couldn't let anyone else have her," the man's voice rushed on. "Not him. Not even *you*. She's *mine*, understand? Always has been, an' always will be."

Jason took a step backward, but the man's eyes followed.

"You been set up, kid," he said. "Plenty o' folks seen you gettin' ready to rumble with Charles here, an' then there's the matter o' the prints on the knife. But that ain't all. Take a look at the book I give you. Last page."

Jason's hands shook as he opened the journal. He found the final page, the words of the song written on the front side. He could have sworn that when he'd read the journal in his room, the back of this page had been as blank as the others, but now there were words on it, written in a legible hand he recognized all too well. The message was dated tonight, and the words read:

"I, Jason Michael Smith, do hereby confess that I killed Charles Alexander Rhodes and Ismene Dawn Vargas in cold blood on this night at 11:45 PM. I loved a girl who belonged to another, and I couldn't bear the thought of losing her. I committed this act of my own free will and with full knowledge of the consequences, and I accept whatever fate comes of my actions. Though she is gone, I will live forever with the thought of her—and only her—in my mind, and I know that her memory will be enough to sustain me until the end of my days."

Then there was his signature, pressed into the paper so hard the point of the pen had pierced the page.

Jason dropped the journal to the sand as if it had burned him. The old man looked on impassively. Sirens wailed in the distance, and the man held out a palm-size device that resembled a miniature television set with a glowing screen. On the screen were the prominent digits *911*. He tucked the object into his jacket, closed his eyes, and inhaled deeply, his lips relaxing into a smile as he released the breath. When he opened his eyes, they sparkled in the shadow of his brow like diamonds uncovered by a lucky beachcomber.

"You're goin' to jail, Jason," he said. "You're eighteen, an' the sentence for first-degree murder in these parts is life in prison. But don't worry. After a lifetime of pinin' for her an' prayin' for a chance to see her before you die, you'll find a way out, an unwatched road through time. You'll hurry back fast as your legs can carry you to this very spot, an' you'll see her splashin' outta the waves same as she done this mornin', an' you'll strike up a conversation with a dumb kid who works at the Sweet Shack, an' come nightfall you'll do to her an' her boyfriend exactly what I done. What the ol' man who visited me all them years ago done. Funny. If I'da had the guts to do it back then, I s'pose I never woulda come back to do it now."

His voice was almost wistful. He reached out to caress Jason's face, but the boy backed from his hand. The old man's eyes flickered with a moment's sadness before he turned away.

"See ya later, kid," he said over his shoulder, and then he was plodding up the beach toward the exit ramp, his boots sinking and sliding in the sand.

Jason hesitated only a moment before reaching down, grasping the knife, and racing after him. The man had barely turned at the sound of Jason's footsteps when the knife plunged into his back, staggering him. Again and again, Jason struck, tears streaming down his cheeks. The old man coughed, and blood burst from his mouth to coat his yellowed mustache and beard. He took one more wavering step, unsteady as an old drunk, before falling face-up on the sand. His eyes briefly sought something in the darkness above him, then they turned into nothing but mirrors reflecting the darkness to itself.

Jason's strength gave out, and he flung the knife away as he dropped to his knees beside the old man's body. The sirens were louder now, and he could see the red and blue lights flickering across the walls of darkened buildings. His eyes fell on a slim wire that dangled from the man's ears, previously hidden by his hair but dislodged by his collapse. Jason fumbled for it, traced the cord to where the Walk-man's cassette deck was clipped to the man's belt beneath his filthy overcoat. Removing the bloody headphones from the dead man's ears, he placed them on his own ears and pressed the play button.

The song rose from the speakers, haunting and maddening as notes dimly caught across a vacant sea. It seemed to him that this was the only song he had ever heard, the only song he would ever hear from now on. A serenade and a dirge, its refrain a passion plea for all eternity. He found his head bobbing to the tune, his lips silently voicing the words he'd repeated to himself so many times before. The music drowned out the wail of the sirens, the shuffle of shoes upon sand as shadowy shapes approached him.

They gathered around the three bodies. With rubber-gloved hands, they retrieved the book and bloody knife, depositing them in plastic evidence bags. Other hands grasped him and hauled him to his feet. He followed without protest. When they reached the railing, he looked back once as if to catch a glimpse of her rising like a vision from the moonlit waves.

Biography

Joshua David Bellin has been writing novels since he was eight years old (though the first few were admittedly very short). He is the author of numerous works of science fiction and fantasy, including the Survival Colony novels, the Ecosystem Cycle, and the deep-space adventure *Freefall*. His time-travel thriller *Myriad* will be published in May 2023 by Angry Robot Books.

To find out more about Josh's books, subscribe to his newsletter, or just say hi, visit his website at: https://joshuadavidbellin.blogspot.com/

LA ZONA

W.O. TORRES

An earlier version was published in *LatineLit* (summer ed., 2021), and is adapted with permission.

THE INSTANT BRILLIANT flash of ozone gas gave off a distinctive smell that could only be described as a clean, chlorine-like, burnt smell. It was followed by an inverted sound that was the absence of noise. The edges of the invisible sphere wobbled slightly, like gas vapors on the horizon. If you weren't careful, you would swear everything was normal. But not today. No, definitely not today.

We are all traveling through time in some respects, if you think about it for a moment. But only three men in the universe were controlling it at that very moment. The moment was a Saturday in May. The city was San Francisco, Mission District, present day.

But not for long.

Time traveling is not for the faint of heart or anyone

with an inner ear condition for that matter. Ever wonder why nobody wants to travel forward in time? It's too damn depressing, that's why. Backward, my friend! That's the only way to go.

Such was the case when three men were granted their wish to travel back in time, but before we meet them, what exactly does it mean to time travel? If one were to close their eyes and concentrate, really focus all of their efforts, would you not be suddenly transported to your parent's house, waiting for your first love to ask you to walk them home so you could stumble through that first kiss? Everyone "time travels" on occasion, what with the present being so drab and all.

However, I, being the Keeper of Time, have extended its privilege to only a distinct few over history. With me having so much of it, an infinite amount if I'm being honest, and others having such a small amount, it's only natural that I dole it out sparingly. Time, that is. So, it was without regret that I allowed three men, brothers-in-arms, to step into what was the makeshift bathroom at their favorite *taqueria*, only to be transported thirty years earlier. The idea was formally pitched by the tallest of the group, Javier Rodriguez, around their third pitcher of beer.

"You know what? We should totally go back in time," he declared with a wicked look in his eye as he slammed his empty glass back onto the Mexican, handcrafted Talavera tile table. His declaration diverted my attention from tending to the Universe as I was immediately immersed in the *banda* music emitting from the tiny, mounted speakers of the lively taqueria; the aromas of fresh hand-made corn tortillas covered in cloth in wicker baskets; a *futbol* game, not the one where you throw the ball, featuring the Chivas of Guadalajara, blared on all four wall-mounted screens. In

Spanish above the cash register, a hand-carved sign read, "Home of the Original Mission Burrito" and "Limit 2 Beers Per Visit."

My curiosity was piqued, even though I had received countless similar requests every second of every day. This one was different. His request was void of malintent, greed, or evil. The sort of emotions that always bubbled to the surface to accompany this type of request.

"Shut up! Your life is perfect, why on earth would you want to go back in time?" Javier's former classmate and best friend since grade school, Miguel Morales, fired back.

"Isn't it obvious?" Javier responded.

It wasn't. Not to Miguel, who was the shortest of the trio, and definitely not to Rudolfo Ramos, who was the fastest of the group.

"Look, I'll go back in time with you. *Dónde vamos?* Back to junior high to kick Victor Dominguez's ass before he punks you in gym class?" Rudolfo tilted his nearly empty glass at Javier and nodded his head at him.

Miguel wasn't using hyperbole when he told Javier his life was perfect. Full partner at his law firm. He married his soulmate and had three amazing daughters that adored him. These successes didn't go unnoticed by Rudolfo and Miguel over the past thirty years. Especially Miguel.

"You guys remember senior year, last game of the season? The game where Migi hit the three at the buzzer to get to the playoffs."

Both Miguel and Rudolfo slightly nodded their heads along with Javier's retelling of one of their favorite memories. "I passed up that shot and sent that skip pass to Migi, but it wasn't 'cause I was feeling the double-team. It was because I was afraid to take the shot," Javier confessed.

"Damn, Javi. You took a hundred shots and made them

to get us to that point. Plus, you were double-teamed, so you kicked it out to me, and I made the shot. Hell, it happened so fast, I don't even remember taking the shot." Miguel always had Javier's back; he was the most loyal of the group, without question.

"Yeah, amigo. Don't beat yourself up about it. Damn, like thirty years ago. Who cares? We won and made it to the state finals. If Migi didn't tear his Achilles in the second period, we'd probably win the State Championship too," Rudolfo joined in support of Javier.

Earlier, when I mentioned that I receive countless literal wishes every second of every day to travel back in time, I wasn't being facetious. In fact, in the time it took me to say that last sentence, I received over thirteen thousand such requests. However, this one was truly unique and had my full attention.

"Giving up that shot out of fear and then losing the championship game was the most pivotal point in my life. I met Luz right after that game, the best thing that ever happened to me. She was waiting for her mom by the flag-pole and probably felt sorry for me, but she's the one that gave me the drive to go to college, law school, go for partner at my firm, and—"

"Yeah, *cabrón*. We get it. Your life is a damn Peloton commercial, Javie," Miguel cracked at him with a laugh, shoving him slightly away from him as only a best friend can. "Then why do you want to travel back in time?"

"I'm not that kid anymore. I don't give up shots when I feel a double-team coming on. I thrive under pressure, I embrace all challenges, and there is no confrontation that I fear." Javier's eyes narrowed as he stated his personal mantra coldly. "I wanna travel back in time so I can beat him, so we can beat them."

And there it was. The most selfless wish to travel back in time I had ever heard fly across the ether.

"Say what? You wanna play who? *Nosotros?* Us?" Rudolfo's brows furrowed as they raised in confusion.

I could hardly contain my enthusiasm. Eager to launch the three amigos right back thirty years, but wait…

"Yeah, I wanna play us the day before we lose the championship. The day we were so full of ourselves and the day we thought we were unbeatable." Javier laid out his plan.

"Why, amigo?" seemed like a simple question their friend Rudolfo had posed. Yes, why indeed?

"To play the best game of hoops in our lives and walk away knowing we're better, that's why." Javier's hands came up from the table, his palms facing upward.

Javier's answer was good enough for me as I began making the necessary accommodations while the three friends strategized. There was only one thing standing in the way of their plan.

"We're damn near fifty!" Miguel shouted. "I'm pretty sure I'm not gonna be able to guard my seventeen-year-old's fast ass," Miguel announced as he ran his knuckles against his graying goatee, mopping up the beer foam. "Plus," he continued, "I got shit to do. No time-to-time travel for me." Miguel amused himself, letting out a gulp of air while wincing, no doubt the result of his sixth beer.

"Like what?" asked Rudolfo.

"Well," Miguel answered as he stopped pouring his seventh beer, connecting eyes with his friend Rudy, "I gotta drop off a child support check to Isa in the morning so my son who I haven't talked to in three years can get his braces off." Miguel paused at the awkward silence before checking his Casio watch and brushing off crumbs from his Maná concert tee from two decades ago.

"Look, that's the best thing about time travel. We bounce, do our thing, and be right back here at the same spot without missing a second of this time," Javier chimed in, trying to diffuse the palpable uncomfortableness.

"Cool, 'cause God forbid we miss anything from this time. Right, Javie?" Miguel stoked at the fire his best friend was trying to douse.

"Aight, aight! Nobody goin' nowhere, 'cept maybe in a fuckin' Uber to bed. So, less finish dis last pitcher and call it a night, cool?" their friend Rudolfo interrupted, ever the peacekeeper.

"Of course, of course! *¡Claro, que sí!*" Javier agreed while nodding his head, keeping an eye on his best friend. "You cool, Migi?"

"Y'all know me. I'm cool like the other side of the pillow." Miguel's confidence hiding behind a paper wall. "Imma hit the baño. Whose turn to order an Uber? I got like a three-star rating, so you know them jerks ain't comin' for an hour if we use my account," Miguel said as he stood from the table and fumbled through both pockets, tossing crumpled dollar bills onto the table while wobbling back and forth.

"Migi, it's cool bro. I got this." Javier spoke up while pushing the bills back towards Miguel. Rudolfo tried to avoid the interaction and cowardly looked at his phone.

"Will you take a look at this guy? Javier Rodriguez to the rescue!" Miguel's voice boomed as he used his hands to create a makeshift megaphone while laughing hysterically for all to hear. Javier's bottom lip curled into his mouth as he looked away from Miguel.

"The bathroom line's a bitch. I'm goin' out back," Miguel announced after his rolling laughter came to an abrupt stop.

Miguel ran his fingers through his thick, curly black hair and proceeded to walk toward the emergency exit door.

"He's like this almost every time we hang. You just don't get to experience it as much," Rudolfo said to Javier as he finished the remains of his final beer, making sure not to waste any. "You took this time travel fantasy shit too far, Javie. You know Migi ain't happy about how his life turned out. We better go check on 'em."

Javier nodded in agreement and failed miserably at hiding his concerned look. "Go check on him while I settle up here. Meet you out back in a minute."

The red neon exit sign and the glow of the bar provided the only light in the alley next to the dumpsters, as Javier opened it, looking for his friends.

"Rudy? Migi! *Vámonos*, let's go! The Uber is out front. Let's go, already!" Javier shouted.

Javier kept his foot planted firmly against the exit door and could see the outline of the dumpster in the darkened alley.

"Aw, you mutherfuckers think you're funny," he announced as he let go of the exit door, entering the alley as the taqueria door slammed shut, taking with it all of the light. With the exit door no longer open, the alley became the quietest place in the universe.

Javier walked behind the dumpster, shaking his head side to side, ready to unload a torrent of obscenities on his two friends who were clearly waiting to scare him, as if they never graduated from junior high. Unfortunately, his two friends never scared Javier and instead of a tapestry of swear words unleashed, Javier Rodriguez was only able to utter two words.

"What the—?"

Javier inserted his fingers repeatedly into his ear opening, jamming them further each failed attempt to ring out the deafening silence. It was only momentary, but in a world of constant noise, the absence of all sound can be rather alarming. The first time through, at least.

"Where the fuck," Javier shouted as his head stopped spinning and the constant reminders of everyday noises returned, hunched over, clutching at his knees with his mouth gaped open. He handled it better than most, I must say.

"¡Oye, bola!" Rudolfo yelled from behind Javier, calling out for him to pick up the ball that had rolled at his feet, and toss it to him.

"Rudy, Migi? How did we get here? It's daytime. And what park is this?" Javier was asking questions that he already knew the answers to.

"Yo, this is dope! J-Money is here. We really doin' this!" Miguel shouted as he grabbed ahold of Javier's hand and pulled him in the opposite direction. Javier looked down at his feet, trying to keep up with Miguel's excited pace, and saw he was wearing his hoop shoes, shorts, and a T-shirt from his law firm's community involvement day where they helped build a playground last year. He also took note that Miguel and Rudy were equally ready to run hoops as he was being dragged to a nearby blacktop, with a single rim that had a chain-link net.

It really was happening, Javier was clearly thinking to himself, as you could almost watch his lips sound out the words. Javier and Miguel reached the edge of the court and exchanged their private handshake with Rudy, who was jumping up and down while Javier was still coming to terms with what was happening.

"That's Hamilton High. I recognize the mural of the

eagle resting on top of the American flag. I was class president and voted to spend our student funds to have it commissioned. It...it looks like it was painted yesterday," Javier said to nobody in particular while staring beyond the basketball court.

"Yeah, we ready!" Rudy shouted toward the court as he pushed Javier forward. "Let's go, three-on-three. You shoot for possession."

"Who are we playing?" Javier asked, his voice trailing off as he sleep-walked toward the painted three-point line.

"These assholes," Rudy responded, while pointing across the court.

There were three boys on the verge of manhood at the baseline. One was chugging a flavor of Gatorade that hadn't been on shelves in decades. The other was adjusting the boom box volume level after flipping the cassette tape from back to front. The sounds of LL Cool J blared as the album kicked off its title song, "I'm Bad," police sirens and all. The third was assessing the competition and couldn't help laughing to himself.

Javier Rodriguez was about to receive his wish. He and his two friends were going to play their younger, better selves. And he received this wish not because it was noble or necessary, but because sometimes in my position, you just want to watch some good hoops.

Each man faced his younger self as Old Javier took the ball out first, passing it inside to Miguel, who used his extra thirty-five pounds to muscle his younger self for an easy layup. Old Rudolfo was slower than his younger self, but he still could play lockdown defense and stroke the outside shot. For Javier, this was personal. He pestered his younger self anytime he came near the ball and drove it into his chest, with a step-back jump shot that nobody from this time had seen before. It was over before it began. The younger versions walked off the court shaking their heads slightly while muttering obscenities in both English and Spanish under their breaths.

Javier received his wish, and I got to watch some competitive ball. Not a bad day for these men, who would remember none of this once I snapped them back to their right timeline.

"Damn Rudy, you couldn't miss from the outside, amigo!" Javier shouted as their fists bumped.

"Me? You made little Javie look stupid. We were all in, *la zona*," Rudolfo chuckled. "And what about Migi? He was on fire...where is Migi?"

"Wait up!" Old Miguel shouted as he jogged over to catch up to his friends.

"Hey man! Were you just talking to your younger self?" Rudolfo asked Miguel, who ignored him seconds before I snapped them back to their timeline.

In an instant like no other, the three men appeared back in their proper time, continuing their conversation at their favorite taqueria.

"Shut up, you idiot! Ain't nobody wanna time travel, stupid." Rudolfo laughed at Javier's idea as he threw a smack from the back of his hand across Javier's chest.

"Alright, alright...I was just talking out of my ass," Javier laughed along with Rudolfo and smacked Rudy back.

The laughter at the table subsided as the last pitcher emptied, when Javier Rodriguez turned to his best friend, Miguel Morales, and asked him, "What about you, Migi? If you could go back in time, what would you change?"

Miguel checked his Rolex and adjusted his necktie as his mind was clearly somewhere else, before answering his oldest and dearest friend. "Me? My life's a Peloton commercial," he said with a giant smile. "I have three beautiful daughters who adore me, I just made full partner at my law firm, and I met the girl of my dreams thirty years ago standing by a flagpole...why would I want to go back in time?"

Biography

W.O. Torres resides in Northern California along with his beautiful wife, brilliant daughters, and their curious dog and kitties, where he often writes once everyone has finally fallen asleep. His obsession with all things Sci-Fi helped him avoid gangs, violence, drugs, and dropping out of high school, which were sadly all too familiar occurrences in his neighborhood. He is wrapping up a twenty-five-year career in law enforcement and looks forward to the next chapter of his life.

Tomorrow Lives Today is his debut Sci-Fi Novel and is available on Amazon.

When not writing, Torres can be found coaching youth sports, attending dance recitals, going on family hikes, and on occasion, screaming at his television while the Giants and 49ers are playing.

ORIGINAL PUBLICATION:
    https://www.latinelit.com/la-zona

TURTLE DAY
OR, KATE MALONE AND THE MAGIC CALZONE

JULIE BIHN

I THOUGHT May 23 was going to be another ordinary day at Create Your Own Pizza, a.k.a. CYO-P. The kind of day where you build, like, a hundred pizzas, you get a cool six dollars in tips, and when you finally get home and take your shoes off, you somehow find half an olive inside.

May 23 was different.

So around 11:00 a.m., a horde of turtles showed up. And not the cute green reptiles with shells and scaly skin. Those would have been easy to feed. Put them on the patio with some salad mix and some anchovies. Done.

No. This crowd was all humans—humans with shell backpacks, puke-green lanyards, or mushroom-brown T-shirts that said "TORTOISE-CON" and "World Turtle Day." A few people made the unique fashion statement of wearing all of the above.

Some of my fellow "pizza masters" forced smiles for the mob, and I swear Greg sounded as chipper as a Disney princess when he greeted the first turtle. I groaned.

But CYO-P is happy to take anyone's money without regard to race, religion, orientation, clothing, reptile status, etc. So, we all got to work slinging dough.

If you've never been to CYO-P, it's like a salad bar for pizza, only more sanitary. The customers stand on their side of the sneeze guard and tell us what they want on their personal-sized monstrosity, which we bake and give to them at the pick-up counter. Or if the customer really wants us to make a salad, we'll do that, but why would anyone want a salad?

I spread sauce, sprinkled cheese, and laid out toppings so fast my joints popped. But the turtles kept plodding in.

We knew things were bad when Haylie actually came out of her office and eyed us instead of her phone. I expected her to yell, but when she saw the line that snaked —turtled?—out the door, I swear an old-timey cash register rang, and the anger in her eyes turned into dollar signs.

Instead of berating us, Haylie cheered us on by shouting things like "They may be turtles, but we're not. Pick up the pace!" and "We'll be rolling in dough!" and "Cheese is money, Kelly. Less cheddar for them, more cheddar for us."

That last one was to me.

My name's Kate. And I was using precisely the standard portion of cheese. And the customer wanted mozzarella and parmesan, not cheddar.

Haylie isn't a great boss.

Anyway, it was the craziest ninety minutes I've ever worked. And I'm sure most turtles and turtle fans are very nice, but these ones didn't tip. Maybe they left their change in their other shells.

The customers must have had more turtle meetings to get to because by 1:00, the horde was gone. Well, except they left behind a plague of children dressed as masked fighting turtles, complete with ninja weapons. Their dad wore a purple bathrobe and mouse ears. He stared at his phone while the kids whaled on chairs with their pool noodle weapons and licked the railings.

And I think literally every other pizza master had their break before Haylie finally fist-bumped my shoulder and said, "Go ahead and take lunch, Kira."

I would have reminded her I'm Kate, but I didn't want to waste a second of my break time.

One of the perks of working at CYO-P is that you get to make your own meal once per shift. And employees can get creative. We don't let the customers order calzones, but they're my favorite. When money's tight, like today, I make mine double-sized, with one pizza crust as the top and another as the bottom. I filled it with:

> Regular sauce
> Rocket fuel sauce
> Every cheese, except blue cheese—
>> did you know the blue parts are
>> *mold*? Gross
> Every meat
> Extra hamburger
> Mushrooms
> Every kind of pepper
> Artichoke hearts
> Garlic, quantity: vampire-massacre
> Oh, and I sprinkled some oregano
>> on top because I am *classy*.

I wanted to call it the best calzone ever created in the history of calzones, but I'm not vain. I did take a moment to admire the World's Third Greatest Calzone before Lindsay slid it into the wood-fired pizza oven.

That's when Silas ambled in. He comes in every weekday and some Saturdays—sometimes for lunch, sometimes for dinner, and sometimes, like today, for linner. He has to be about my age. I think he does tech support for one of the offices across the street. And he has some muscles, but he dresses like a nerd, and not the super-rich kind. The kind with a scruffy beard and thick-rimmed glasses, and he always wears a corporate-branded polo shirt with khakis.

Silas never gets the same combination of toppings twice; he made an app to help him keep track for his blog. He always takes a picture of his pizza before he eats it, too. So yeah, he's a nerd. But, he always tips exactly $3.14, and he never complains. Silas is weird, but I always smile when he comes in.

Lindsay slid my calzone out of the oven and dropped it onto a plate. "Pizza up!" she called as Gary rang up Silas at the register.

"Dad!" one of the ninja turtle brats yelled. "Chloe's biting me."

"How many times do I have to tell you?" the dad snapped. "Turtles don't have teeth. And call me Master Splinter!"

As Silas tapped his card on the terminal, I took my lunch and sat in a corner of the dining room, as far from the turtles as possible. I cut into my calzone like it was a giant steak. Sauce and cheese oozed out, and I twirled the mozzarella around my fork. I closed my eyes as I took my first bite.

Flavor exploded on my tongue, the taste of every meat, every sauce, and almost every cheese, all at once. And I'd put on too much rocket fuel sauce or too many hot peppers, because my mouth was on fire.

I ran toward the soda fountain, but the heat spread from my mouth to my face to the rest of my body, all the way down to my toes. The dining room dissolved into strings of mozzarella as the scent of baking dough wafted over me.

Was this what it felt like to be a pizza? Was I a monster, building pizzas and roasting them in the flames? Were the pizzas taking their fiery revenge?

And then, only my mouth was burning. For some reason, I was behind the counter again, and the armpits of my work shirt were soaked.

I grabbed a cup and ran to the soda fountain.

Lindsay set a calzone on a plate. "Pizza up!"

A kid yelled, "Dad! Chloe's biting me."

The dad snapped, "How many times do I have to tell you? Turtles don't have teeth. And call me Master Splinter!"

Silas tapped his card at the terminal.

I've felt déjà vu before, but I've never had a minute of my life replay like a bad commercial.

I downed half a jumbo cup of Coke before my mouth cooled down and I could think again. Silas frowned at me, but everyone else turned away. Fair. It's kind of rude to stare at the sweaty pizza master guzzling soda.

What had just happened? Did my calzone give me a psychedelic experience? How? Did Greg switch the mushrooms with magic ones, or swap out the oregano for something stronger? That sounded like Greg.

I hadn't seen any of the turtle people spazzing out, though. Well, except the kids, but kids are always weird.

I retreated behind the counter. A double-sized calzone

sat there, steaming hot, with oregano sprinkled on top. No one had cut into it.

"Linds?" I asked. "Whose is this?"

She glanced back, then rolled her eyes. "Yours, genius."

Maybe I *had* been hallucinating. I grabbed the calzone and stalked to my table. I pulled out the chair.

But hadn't I been sitting there just a minute ago?

I sat down and cut another bite—or was it the first bite? —of the calzone. I stabbed it with my fork, then chewed like I had a tiny, cheesy monster in my mouth and I was trying to snap its neck with my teeth.

My mouth caught fire, followed by my skin, as strings of cheese swirled around me. This time, notes of bacon joined the aroma of baking dough.

Lindsay slid the calzone onto its plate. "Pizza up!"

"Dad! Chloe's biting me."

Etc., etc.

I ran and got another soda before I realized that the caffeine and sugar would probably finish off my already frazzled nerves. So, I swished the sugar water around in my mouth. That maybe wasn't the best idea since the CYO-P employee dental plan is "I think there's some Orajel in the first-aid kit," but whatever.

I went back behind the counter and grabbed my plate. My arms and legs shook, but I held the calzone steady as I returned to my table.

As far as I could tell, there were three possible explanations for what was going on. One: I'd created The World's Most Cursed Calzone and/or The Calzone that Didn't Want to Be Eaten, though I think I somehow still had parts of it in my stomach. Two: I was in a low-budget version of the movie Groundhog Day—"Turtle Day?" Or three: I'd lost my pizza-loving mind.

I put my head in my hands and scowled at the Calzone of Madness.

Silas brought his lemonade over and sat at the table beside mine while he waited for his pizza. He took a long sip, then gave me a weak smile. "Hey."

I wasn't in the mood to let a customer watch me go insane or stare at my pit stains, but I pressed my arms to my sides and said, "Hi."

He went on, "You must all think I'm crazy, coming here every day."

Not as crazy as me. I nodded absently. "Mmm-hmm."

Silas's shoulders slumped, and his faint smile melted quicker than a cube of frozen pesto in the pizza oven.

I mean, our pesto is one hundred percent fresh.

And we pizza masters never took bets on how long it would take a cube of pesto to melt in the pizza oven.

And the answer definitely isn't 8.62 seconds.

And we absolutely didn't leave a mess in the oven for the morning crew to deal with.

Please don't tell Haylie.

Silas had turned his attention back to his phone, but pain lingered in his eyes.

I hadn't meant to call him crazy. "Silas, I—we don't think you're—"

"Silas?" Greg called at the pick-up counter.

Silas ignored me as he got up. I felt bad for hurting his feelings. While he was gone, I picked up the Calzone that Refused to Be Eaten with both hands. I opened my mouth like a snake unhinging its jaw and shoved in as much cheesy goodness as I could fit.

It was different this time. The sauce and peppers were still spicy, but in a good way, not in a soul-melting way. The melted cheese pooled in my mouth, creating a symphony of salt and grease. The mushrooms and artichoke hearts had just the right amount of chew, and they conferred the faintest impression of healthiness to the dish.

I don't know. I'm not a food critic. But for one delicious moment, I believed that I'd created The World's Greatest Calzone after all. I swallowed, then set my lunch down, letting the glorious bite settle in my stomach.

As soon as my hands released the calzone, my body caught on fire again, the world tore into strands of mozzarella, and the smell of burnt cheese enveloped me. Sweat stung my eyes as the heat faded.

Mouth on fire. "Pizza up!" Bratty kid. Irritating dad. Silas tapping his card.

Okay, I'd made a cursed, uneatable calzone, I'd gone insane, *and* I was doomed to relive Turtle Day for eternity. Three for three. Outstanding. Maybe I'd undone my insult to Silas, at least.

I rushed to the soda fountain, shoving past Silas on the way. I felt his eyes on me as I filled my cup with water, forced it all down, and then grabbed a box.

I couldn't tell if the calzone was cursed or if it was magic. Maybe both. I didn't dare toss it; the world doesn't need time-traveling rats or raccoons. It probably doesn't need a time-traveling Kate, either, but whatever.

As much fun as it might be to have an infinite lunchtime, I got sweatier with every bite I took, and I wasn't about to pay $20 for a replacement CYO-P uniform T-shirt. So, I boxed up the calzone and hid it in my locker.

We get a thirty-minute lunch, and my phone said I somehow had twenty minutes left. I passed by Silas's table and asked how his day was going. He blinked at me and said it was fine. I told him I thought it was kind of cool that he came in every day, and he smiled.

I spent the rest of my lunch trying to wash up using our half-ply paper towels. When my shift resumed, I still felt gross, and Silas was gone.

WHEN I GOT HOME, I scrawled "MEAT" on the calzone box and shoved it in the fridge. Cherry's a vegetarian, so I knew she wouldn't touch it.

I took a long shower, then changed into something that was dry, that didn't prominently display the name of my corporate overlord, and that didn't smell like pizza. I brushed my teeth three times, but my mouth still tasted like garlic.

By the time I got out of the bathroom, my phone said it was 7:32 p.m., and Cherry was in the kitchen eating an imitation hamburger. I grabbed some cereal and soy milk —eight-tenths as good as cow's milk—sat across from her at the table, and let her talk about her day. Cherry told me all about her office, celebrity gossip, politics, office politics, celebrity politicians, and office gossip. She may have said a celebrity came to her office. I don't know; I lost track.

When she asked how my day was, I told her about the horde of turtles.

"Yeah," she replied, "we were busy, too."

Cherry pays her half of the rent on time and drives me to the grocery store every week. She's the best roommate I've ever had. But, she's the kind of person who has to one-up everything you say.

Only this time, I had something she'd never beat.

"Oh, right." I drew out the words. "I made a magic calzone."

"Oh?" She got up to throw out her fake-meat-burger wrapper.

"Yeah. I took a bite of it, and it sent me back in time."

Her eyebrows raised. "Real funny, Kate."

"It's true, though."

"Sure. And I just finished eating an enchanted veggie burger. It made my eyelashes grow two inches longer, and now I can talk to squirrels."

If I were smarter, I would have laughed and admitted I was joking. But instead, I grabbed the calzone out of the refrigerator. I took a bite while I still had a bit of cereal in my mouth. Marinara plus Frosted Flakes, zero out of ten, do not recommend. I threw the calzone back into the box.

The heat, the blinding threads of mozzarella, the smell of pepperoni.

Too late, I realized that I'd condemned myself to go back to my lunch break at CYO-P and relive the last three hours of my shift. Stupid Turtle Day.

Except instead of appearing beside the pizza oven, I found myself in the shower. I didn't understand why, but at least I had plenty of water to drink to cool down, and I got to wash off the sweat.

When I came out, Cherry said "hey" like I hadn't just disappeared. And my phone said it was 7:32 p.m. on May 23—exactly when I'd left the bathroom after my first shower. Maybe taking a bite of calzone would only send me back a certain amount of time.

Cherry told me about her day again. I started to pour another bowl of cereal, but I was still full from the first one. Could the magic calzone save me money on groceries?

I checked the refrigerator. The calzone was still there, intact and, for some reason, warm. Had it regenerated to its fresh-out-of-the-oven self when I took a bite? Why? Then again, who was I to tell a magic calzone what it's supposed to do?

When Cherry finally asked about my day, I only mentioned the turtles. She said how busy she was at work, and I nodded.

I kind of wanted to tell someone about traveling through time, but Cherry wasn't the best choice. My family would never believe me, either. Honestly, I couldn't think of anyone who wouldn't think I was crazy. *I* thought I was crazy.

When Cherry finished eating, she sprawled out on the couch and streamed a murder show, like every Monday. I guess she's okay with blood as long as it's human.

I flopped into the armchair and used my phone to search "how to get rich with a time machine." I didn't know how far back the calzone could take me. I figured I'd gone back about fifteen minutes the last time. I traveled less than ten minutes back at CYO-P. Maybe the calzone wouldn't let me go back earlier than when it came out of the oven.

If I could only travel fifteen minutes, maybe I only had a cheese-and-tomato-flavored do-over machine.

But I'd only taken one bite at a time. If I took more bites without setting down the calzone, could I go back farther?

There was a Mammoth Moolah lottery draw tonight with a twenty-million-dollar jackpot.

I played around on social media for a couple of hours until the winning numbers were drawn. I took a screen capture of them on my phone, then snuck back to the kitchen and grabbed the now-cold calzone. I choked down eight bites of sauce and dough and congealed cheese. I probably should have heated it up first.

Nothing happened.

Not until I set the calzone down.

My skin burned, the whole apartment smelled like roasted peppers, and time itself melted like gouda.

I found myself in the chair by the TV while Cherry watched her murder show. I ran to the kitchen to chug two glasses of water. Once my vision cleared, I saw that the microwave was blinking 12:00. We really need to set the clock. But my phone said it was two hours in the past.

I rushed to the corner store to buy a Mammoth Moolah ticket. But when I pulled out my phone to get the numbers, the screen capture I took was gone. I'd traveled back in time, but I couldn't take anything with me except memories, the food in my stomach, and, judging from the smell, maybe some sweat. Stupid time travel.

I went back home and relived my evening, waiting for the drawing to happen again. It was even more boring the second time. After the drawing, I took a half hour to memorize the numbers. And by memorize, I mean set them to the tune of Journey's "Don't Stop Believin'." It worked. Whatever.

Once I had the winning numbers/song memorized, I ate ten bites of calzone. Little bites this time; I was still pretty full from the cereal and the never-ending calzone. I still went back two hours and thirty minutes. This time, I bought two tickets, one with random numbers and one with the right ones. I didn't want anyone to think I had inside information. Well, it *was* inside information, I guess. Information inside a calzone.

I went home, took my third? fourth? shower of the night, and lay on my bed. I kept yawning, I guess because I'd kind of been up past my bedtime, but I managed to stay awake until the numbers were drawn.

They matched my song.

I covered my mouth to hold back the scream. I was rich. Wouldn't Cherry be jealous?

Not that I was in any hurry to tell her. I know when you tell people you won the lottery, they hit you up for money.

I was about to text a resignation/list of sick burns to Haylie, but before I hit send, I searched for how to claim lottery winnings.

I knew you got a lot less than the full jackpot if you took a lump sum. That's cool. I'm not greedy. Eight million dollars or whatever is plenty.

But I did not realize that lottery winners have to wait a couple of weeks to get their money. And rent was due in nine days.

So I'd work a little longer. What did it matter? I had all the time in the world.

EVERY FREE MEAL I got at CYO-P, I tried to recreate the magic calzone, but nothing else I built had time-travel properties. Well, one time I put anchovies in my calzone and got so nauseous that the rest of my shift lasted approximately three years. But, besides that, no time travel.

I wasn't exactly a model worker after I won the Mammoth Moolah. One day, while I was on oven duty, I left Silas's pizza in too long. When I finally smelled the burnt crust and pulled it out, the disc of dough and toppings reminded me of a giant, overcooked peanut-butter chocolate-chip cookie.

Greg took away the peel—you know, the pizza oven shovel—and made me call Silas's name myself.

When Silas came over, I said, "I'm so sorry. I'll make you a new—"

"It doesn't matter." His voice was flat. He must have had a bad day at work.

I tried to stop him, but he grabbed the plate and shuffled to his table. He snapped a picture of his pizza, like always. Would he really put it on his blog?

And I don't know if he's a human garbage disposal or if he lost all his taste buds in a tragic accident, but he ate the whole thing. I guess "blackened pizza" was a combination he hadn't tried before.

He never complained. He kept coming back to CYO-P. He still tipped. I wondered if he might be a saint in disguise.

Exactly two weeks after I won the lottery, I was on my lunch break when I saw the funds had finally cleared my account.

I quit on the spot.

Haylie said, "We'll miss you, Kimberly."

HERE ARE some of my highlights from my first month with the magic calzone, in no particular order:

> Day traded and turned my $50
>   savings into $2,000.
> Learned what day trading is.
> Paid a fancy salon to chop my hair
>   short. Hated it.
> Tried to use the calzone to undo it.
>   Found out that my awful
>   haircut came along with me.
> Got used to my hair being bobbed.
>   Okay, that's a lie. I'm still mad.
> Bought a front-row ticket and saw

Excessively Lengthy Walk, the
World's Worst Journey Cover
Band. Sang along with every
song until my throat hurt.

Went back in time to erase all
evidence that I ever went
to/enjoyed an Excessively
Lengthy Walk concert. My
throat still felt like I gargled
with buffalo sauce, though.

Got both of my cavities filled. That
didn't really need time travel,
just money.

Finally visited Disney World. Ditto
about the money.

Got less terrible at karaoke.

Ate a slice of cheesecake so good
that I went back in time so I
could eat it a second time.

Ate half of the slice of cheesecake a
third time.

Gained twelve pounds.

And

Got *tremendously* sick of calzones.

Oh, and with infinite time, I spent twice as long on my phone each day. I eventually found Silas's blog—"Silas Wright's Pizza Site"—where he wrote about every creation he got at CYO-P. He never had a mean thing to say about any of them. He posted the photo of my blackened pizza, but all he wrote about it was "THIS IS FINE," like the meme with the dog in the flaming room. I thought it was funny, but it only got three hearts. Tough crowd. He hadn't posted in a few days, though. Maybe he'd finally moved on from pizza.

When word of my Mammoth Moolah win got around, my friends, acquaintances, siblings, fifth cousins, etc. started asking for money. I wanted to help, but it didn't feel great to know that they only cared about me now that I could do something for them.

At least Cherry still paid her share of the rent. When she heard I was rich, she told me that she'd once won twenty-five million dollars from some prince in Africa. Of course, she said she'd donated all of her winnings to charity.

I was so grateful that she didn't ask for money, I paid all of our rent in advance for the rest of the term. For once, she didn't try to one-up me.

ABOUT A MONTH AFTER TURTLE DAY, I was having supper with Cherry. She prattled on about work, as usual. I nodded like a drinking bird toy as I picked at my fajitas and scrolled through my feed on my phone.

A familiar face popped up. It was a picture of Silas, smiling, wearing a suit and tie. Even with his scruffy beard, he gave the impression of a kid playing dress-up. I laughed.

And then I read the headline: "River Bridge Body Recovered, Identified as Silas Wright, 24."

I felt my face go as pale as a white pizza. I must have looked awful because Cherry actually asked, "What's wrong?"

I shoved away from the table and staggered into my bedroom.

Who could have wanted to hurt Silas?

I scanned the article. Security footage showed that a

man had gone over the edge of the bridge the night of June 16. Alone. Silas's family requested that donations be made to the National Alliance on Mental Illness.

My breath caught. I never thought Silas was miserable. I mean, I'd hurt his feelings the day I got the magic calzone, but I undid that. I'd even told him it was cool that he came so often. He'd smiled at me.

His blog hadn't sounded unhappy. Maybe he wasn't thrilled about the burned pizza, but who would be? We weren't friends or anything, but to think that the nerd who never complained and always tipped would never eat another pizza again, would never even smile again... My eyes stung.

But there was a magic calzone in my refrigerator. Maybe this didn't have to happen. Maybe I could fix it.

Except he'd died on June 16. A week ago. I'd never tried to go back more than a few hours.

I dashed out of my bedroom and grabbed the pizza box from the refrigerator. Grease had soaked through the bottom of the cardboard.

Cherry said, "Are you okay?" She paused a second before adding, "Oh, and I meant to tell you. You have to throw that out."

I took the box to my bedroom and slammed the door behind me.

The calzone didn't look so magical anymore. I'd last taken a bite a few days ago, and now it had several spots of pesto on it that I hadn't noticed before. I *absolutely* dripped green pesto on it when I made it and only noticed it now.

I pulled up the calculator on my phone. For the first time in my life, I used my word-problem-solving skills from school. How many bites of a magic calzone does it take to go back a week in time? 4 bites per hour x 24 hours x 7 days = 672. I hoped I was right.

I picked up the cold calzone. The soggy dough melted around my fingers.

I almost prayed to the pizza gods that I wouldn't be sick, but this was more serious than that. I murmured a prayer to the real God, the God of pizza and calzones and time and people. "Please let me save him. And don't let me die of calzone poisoning."

Then, I took the tiniest nibbles imaginable, eating a crumb at a time, trying to avoid the spots of what was definitely pesto. The calzone didn't taste quite as rancid as I expected, but it was still bad. Yellow juice dripped onto the soggy box.

I was on nibble 621 when I realized that I probably could have taken one bite and set the calzone down. That would have sent me back fifteen minutes, and whenever I went back, the calzone always regenerated itself into a fresh, piping hot one. But by that point, it was a battle of wills, and I wasn't about to let that stupid calzone beat me. So, I gripped the handfuls of calzone paste tighter and kept eating.

Even taking the world's tiniest bites, most of the calzone was gone by bite 672. My jaw ached like I'd chewed twenty packs of gum, and my stomach objected to both the volume and the quality of what I'd eaten. At least I was rich now. If I had to go to the hospital for food poisoning, I could splurge on an ambulance.

"Here goes nothing," I whispered as I set down the mess of dough and sauce.

Fire consumed my body and mozzarella wound around me like a cocoon as I took another journey into the pizza oven.

I FOUND myself in my pajamas in my chair. Where else would I be? Cherry was out, and my phone said it was 7:21 p.m. on June 16th. Yay, math.

I had to hurry—if I wasn't already too late—but I looked like I'd just woken up from a nap in a sauna. If Silas saw me, he might jump to get away from me. So I washed up, gargled half a bottle of mouthwash, ran a brush through my hair, and threw on some clean clothes.

I checked the calzone. It was intact in the fridge, fresh and warm. It gave me a genius idea. I cut off a piece of crust, stuffed it in a sandwich bag, and put the sandwich bag in my purse. I threw two water bottles on top and ran out the door.

RIVER BRIDGE IS one of those old bridges that's more elegant than its stupid name suggests. I always used to think the symmetrical arches and curves and gaps were pretty. But now, seeing the bridge and thinking of Silas made me want to throw up. Or maybe that was the calzone talking.

The bridge is open for vehicles, with a single sidewalk-width lane on one side for pedestrians. A barricade separates the traffic from the sidewalk, but cars still zoomed past, close enough to make me flinch.

There were no police, no flashing lights. No one seemed upset. A man even sat on a bench under a streetlight, knitting. A warm breeze blew in from the river, as if to welcome me. I dared to hope.

The silhouette of a lone figure stood halfway across the bridge, leaning over the edge.

I dashed like I had fourteen attendance points and was late for my shift. Panting, I reached the man and grabbed his arm. "Don't do it!"

He turned to me, frowning. He had a lumberjack beard and a pot belly. He wasn't Silas.

The man jerked his arm free, leaned over the bridge, hacked up half a lung, and hawked it into the river. With the breeze, I feared that I'd be the victim of splashback, but thankfully, the loogie landed in the water.

The lumberjack gave me a death glare. "I'll spit where I want." He muscled past me and stalked off.

Rude.

I spent a few minutes surveying the bridge. The wind picked up and whipped my hair into my eyes. I tried to tie it back, but it was too short. Stupid haircut.

I was still wrestling with my hair when a mom and two kids walked past, the daughter swinging a stuffed animal by its arm. It was a turtle plush, wearing a bow and the frilliest tutu I'd ever seen. What was up with all the turtles?

I surveyed the bridge again, but then a shriek caught my attention. About a hundred feet away, the little girl was fighting with her brother. A streetlight above them served as a spotlight on the World's Most Annoying Street Performance.

The boy snatched the turtle, but it slipped out of his hands and soared like a duck. The boy tried to catch the plush, and I almost thought the wind was going to help them out and blow the turtle to safety. But instead, it fell just over the railing and down.

The girl wailed while the mother yelled at the boy. It was hard to watch. Maybe the kids had learned that the edge of a bridge was no place to goof around, though. The girl was still crying as the family trudged off.

With them gone, I put my full effort toward guarding the bridge. Whenever someone walking alone stopped, I shuffled toward them, playing it cool. Every time, the person only took in the view for a minute or less before moving on.

I studied the river, too, but I didn't see the appeal. Lonely city lights glistened, mirrored in the water below. Well, water and lumberjack spit. And I guess an unlucky turtle was down there, too.

Fewer and fewer people passed as the hours dragged by. By 11:00, the bridge was deserted. Even the breeze died down. Without it, the night felt as hot as a fresh pizza and as sticky as the soda counter at closing. And yet, I shivered.

Someone started onto the bridge—determined, not drunk. I took big steps toward him and checked my purse for the sandwich bag, ready to eat its contents and skip back in time if he tried to hurt me.

The man slowed his steps as he approached a streetlight. And even though he was still forty feet away, I recognized his silhouette. The polo shirt, the mussed hair, the slightest bit of a paunch that said maybe he shouldn't eat an entire personal pizza every single day.

Silas stopped beneath the streetlight, paused, and leaned over the edge of the bridge.

My whole body went cold and numb. I forced my limbs to work and ran toward him. "Silas!"

He straightened, turning to face me.

"It's Kate!" I stopped beside him, rubbing at the stitch in my side. "Kate Malone, from...from CYO-P. Remember? I burned...burned your pizza a couple of weeks ago?"

"Oh. I didn't recognize you. Your hair..."

I scowled at him.

"It's nice."

Poor Silas really *was* crazy if he thought that.

Back while I was eating that definitely-not-moldy calzone, I probably should've looked up what kind of things you should say to someone in this kind of situation, but I had nothing. I was probably the World's Worst Crisis Counselor because I said, "Please don't jump."

He blinked. "What?"

"Don't jump. Please. Your family would miss you, and I'm sure you have a lot to live for. Don't you want to try more pizzas?"

After a moment, he smiled. "I do, and thanks for caring. But I wasn't going to jump."

"What?"

He leaned over the edge of the bridge, nearly stopping my heart. "Look." He motioned.

I gripped the railing like death and put myself out far enough to make my stomach quake. Silas pointed under the bridge.

The turtle was caught in the framework of one of the supports that held up the bridge. Miraculously, the plush hadn't dropped into the river after all. The wind must have blown it back, leaving it stuck just out of reach. Or maybe it was a magic turtle.

I shook my head. "How in the world did you know it was there?"

"I didn't. Ginny—my niece—said she lost Isabella at the bridge. She's been inconsolable. My niece, I mean, but I bet Isabella's not very happy, either. Ginny swore Isabella didn't fall into the water. I was sure she was wrong, but I figured I'd come see the place so I could make up a story about what kind of turtle adventures Isabella must be having. Something to tide Ginny over 'til we get a replacement. I never thought I'd find her."

Relief warmed my heart like a layer of mozzarella. He wasn't depressed. He wasn't going to jump.

But then, Silas started putting one leg over the railing.

I gasped. "Stop!"

He froze, frowning at me.

"You're going to fall!" I grabbed his arm, yanking him away from the edge.

He hopped on one foot until he got his balance, then took my hand and pulled it away from his arm. "I'm not going to fall. There's a ledge *right there*. I can reach her."

"You can't! You *don't*! You're going to kill yourself trying to rescue a stuffed animal and your family will think you jumped!"

He leaned down and squinted at me. The streetlight gleamed on his glasses. "Kate, are you okay?"

My face went hot. "I'm fine. You won't be."

He tensed. "I work out. I can do this." And he moved toward the railing again.

If he fell, I could use the calzone to go back and save him, maybe distract him before he saw Isabella. But I didn't want to live with the memory of seeing him die.

I grabbed his arm again. "Silas! Listen to me. I can travel in time. I've seen what happens. You fall!"

I expected him to think I was joking, like Cherry had. Instead, he slowly turned and leaned close, trapping me in his gaze. On the other side of the barricade, cars drove over the bridge, their tires making a rhythmic *thud, thud.*

He licked his lips. "Really? You can travel in time?"

I nodded.

"How?"

"I made a magic calzone." He stayed silent as the whole saga came tumbling out of my mouth.

When I finished, Silas's expression was unreadable. "A magic calzone?"

I yanked the sandwich bag out of my purse and shoved it at him. "It's true. Go on. Take a bite. You'll go back in time fifteen minutes."

His eyes widened. "Didn't you say it was moldy?"

"I said it had unexpected pesto on it! But it's fresh now."

"Seriously?"

I took out the crust and tore it in two, then shoved a piece into his hand. "We can split it."

"What?"

"You and me. We'll travel back in time together."

His brow furrowed.

"Didn't you want to try everything CYO-P has to offer? How often does a non-employee get to taste an off-menu calzone?"

He stared at me for another minute. Finally, he pulled his phone out of his pocket and took a picture of the piece of calzone.

I almost smiled, but then I panicked. "Wait! You have to promise you won't tell anyone about the magic calzone. Or blog about it."

He tilted his head. "No one reads my blog anyway."

"Three people liked your post about my burned pizza. I mean, I liked it too, but I didn't want to set up an account just to click the heart button."

He considered, and a hint of a smile twitched on his lips. "Okay. I won't tell anyone that I ate a piece of calcified bread that some woman said would send me back in time. But, if nothing happens, you'll admit it's a joke, right? And spot me while I save Isabella."

In my head, I saw him falling, pleading with me as I could only watch. "No!"

He frowned, glancing at the railing. He really cared about that turtle. Or his niece.

And then it hit me. "I know how we can save her. Every bite sends me back fifteen minutes in time. If we take enough bites, we can go back to before the plush went over the edge. Can you do the math?"

He tilted his head. "If you're right, twelve bites would do it. Might make it thirteen to be safe and account for the time we'd spend chewing."

I grabbed his hand. It was sweatier than I'd expected.

His eyebrows shot up.

"We have to stick together so we go back to the same moment. You ready?"

His expression wavered as he sized me up, and then he gave me the most endearing shrug I've ever seen. "Why not?"

We took each bite in unison, with me mumbling a count. After taking microscopic nibbles of the last calzone, I took tiny bites of the crust, too. I ended up shoving half the piece in my mouth for bite thirteen. Silas and I chewed in unison.

And as I swallowed, a blast of heat washed over me. Silas squeezed my hand and reached for me as the scent of tomato and dough invaded my nostrils. Cheese enveloped us, pushing us together and then pulling us apart as the bridge melted away like a cube of frozen pesto.

I FOUND myself a hundred feet away from where I'd left Silas, and he was gone. I downed a water, aired out my armpits in the breeze, and checked my phone. It was 8:03 p.m.

I rushed back to where I'd left Silas, but he wasn't there. He must have gone back to wherever he'd been at 8:03.

When I leaned over the edge of the bridge, I found that Isabella was gone, too. She hadn't fallen yet.

I sipped the second bottle of water as I guarded the bridge. I'd gone from trying to save a man's life to trying to save a toy turtle. Kind of a step down, but a goal's a goal.

Ginny's shriek reached me before I saw the family. I stood with my back to the railing, fingers crossed.

The brother, a kid just old enough to know better, poked his little sister as she yelled and tried to fight him off. The poor mother looked too exhausted to intervene.

As they drew near, I called out, "Isabella says to be nicer to your sister."

The brother frowned at me as they walked by. Somehow, my words were enough. He stopped teasing his sister, and Ginny smiled at me, hugging her turtle close. The mother didn't even look at me. I don't know that she registered what I said.

I watched the family until they stepped off of the bridge and onto the sidewalk beyond. Isabella was safe, which meant Silas was safe, too.

I sighed in relief. It was a million times better than when the dentist said I didn't need a root canal. Maybe as good as winning the Mammoth Moolah jackpot.

The lights on the river sparkled, and I imagined all the lumberjack spit had washed downstream. I understood why people would enjoy the view.

What happened to Silas, though? Did he remember going back in time? If so, wouldn't he have come back here? Or had he forgotten seeing me at all, the same way Cherry hadn't noticed that I'd disappeared right in front of her? I hoped he remembered.

Then, my optimism wilted like spinach in a pizza oven. If he *did* remember, I'd just proved to him that time travel exists—the most incredible power in the world. What if he broke into my apartment and took the calzone to use it for himself? He could probably hack into CYO-P's files and find my address. Why hadn't I moved to a mansion, or hired security?

Rapid footsteps sounded. I turned to find Silas at my side, panting like an exhausted dog. Sweat drenched his work-issued polo shirt and glistened on his face. Honestly, he looked a little hot. Take that however you want to.

I almost melted in relief, and I found myself grinning at him. "Well. Do you believe me?"

He nodded, still panting.

"Don't worry. I saved Isabella. You don't have to try to rescue her."

He took a few deep breaths. "You—you saved *me*. Didn't you?"

I didn't want to brag, so I gave him a smile and shrugged.

He shook his head, more bewildered than he'd been when we added asiago to the menu. "Thank you."

"No need to thank me. Just promise you won't try to climb on any bridges?"

He put his hand on his heart. "Promise."

We gazed out at the river as Silas caught his breath. After a minute, he asked, "What are you going to do with..." He motioned to my purse.

The piece of crust was gone, melded back into the original calzone in my fridge, but Silas must not have realized that. Did he want it for himself after all? I searched his face for any hints of malice.

All I saw was his ridiculous grin as he said, "You can

help *so many people* with that thing."

Holy cow. Silas really was a saint.

And you know that voice inside your head? Not the one that tells you to eat the same slice of cheesecake two-and-a-half times, and not the one that tells you that you're an idiot for thinking you'd like having short hair. No, I mean the voice that tells you to do good things.

I heard it, clear as day: *That calzone's at least two servings.*

I had wanted to share my secret with someone, right? Silas knew it now. And the soft, curious look in his eyes...

I cleared my throat. "You really think I should help people?"

"Well, it's your calzone." His forehead crinkled. "I guess you can do what you want with it." He didn't say it, but he'd think less of me if I kept using it only to goof off. And he'd probably be right to judge me.

But could I, Kate Malone, really do something good? Where would I even start?

I bet Silas had some ideas.

"Well..." I paused for effect. "Figuring out who to rescue and how to change the past sounds complicated. I'd probably need someone to help me. And I hear you write apps? Maybe you could make one so we could keep track of things?"

His face lit up brighter than the flames of a pizza oven. My brain started playing the Mammoth Moolah mix of "Don't Stop Believin'," as if to tell me that things would work out.

With some luck, maybe Silas and I really could make the world a better place.

But I don't really need luck, do I? I have a time-traveling calzone.

Biography

Julie Bihn is an Arizona native who writes heartfelt, emotional, occasionally silly speculative fiction featuring friendship and love. When she first typed #TimeTravelAuthors, it spawned a community and changed her Twitter timeline for the better. Julie is the author of the novel *Titanic Voyage*. A theme park employee finds he can travel back to the *Titanic*, where he falls in love with, and tries to save, a heroine who perished in the sinking.

VISIT JULIE AT:
  https://juliebihn.com/

THE FUTURE,

and beyond

BLUE SKIES

NATHANIEL SWIFT

THE WIND WHISTLED past Eddie's ears and raced across his goggles as he looked down. About two-and-a-half miles below, a rough patchwork of farms, fields, and baseball diamonds looked back at him. He imagined kids in the middle of a game, the pitcher pausing mid-delivery to look up and wonder just what the heck those old guys were doing up there.

"You're doing great, Eddie!" his instructor, whose name he couldn't remember, shouted over the roar of the wind and the plane's engine. She wasn't an old guy at all; none of the instructors were. "You can take your clip off if you're ready!"

He looked up. The carabiner at the end of his safety line was still clipped to the pole that ran along the ceiling of the small plane. One of his hands held tightly on the line; the other held onto the homemade charm necklace Annie had given him this morning for luck. It was full of pink and glitter, and Eddie had felt foolish wearing it earlier, but he was grateful for it now. He put it back in the pocket of his jumpsuit and zipped it safely away.

He tried to back up a few steps, forgetting for a moment that his instructor was attached to his back for the tandem jump. She took a step back with him, and then planted her feet. Eddie stepped forward again. He wasn't sure if he was ready, but he had promised Dave. They all had.

He looked at Dave and offered a nervous thumbs up. Dave grinned back, loving every second of this. He shouted something that no one could hear and clapped a couple of times. Eddie and the others clapped back. Dave unhooked his clip, gave a sloppy salute, and then he and his instructor disappeared through the open door.

Happy birthday, you lunatic.

The rest of them looked around at each other, four middle-aged men with thin hair and big bellies, trying to remember how they had ended up here.

It was Dave, of course. It was always Dave. Every five years, he gathered them all together, and every time it was an adventure. They had all expected the big Five-Oh to be something spectacular, but they didn't expect this. Eddie thought Dave was kidding when he first suggested it— Aren't we all a little too old to start skydiving? he had said with a laugh—but Dave didn't kid about adventures. And Eddie couldn't say no, even though Annie was almost ten now, and maybe he shouldn't be attending death-defying birthday parties anymore.

But he had signed up, waived his rights to sue anybody, and sat through a half hour of training. Apparently, that was all it took for some company's legal team to decide you're ready to jump out of an airplane.

Austin, always quick to follow Dave's lead wherever it went, jumped next. Mark said something quickly and quietly, probably a prayer; he and his instructor followed suit a few seconds later. Eddie looked at Geoff, who was usually the last to commit to the craziest of Dave's ideas. Geoff looked a little sick.

"Are you going to be okay?" Eddie shouted.

Geoff tried to smile and gave Eddie a weak thumbs up. "I'll be right behind you!"

Geoff's instructor nodded, and Eddie looked down through the open door. Human beings, friends of his, were falling through the air below them.

This is nuts.

Okay, let's do it.

A black and white goose flew by the plane, looking at the open door with curiosity. Eddie thought for a moment that it might just fly right in.

Eddie took his clip off the pole. He walked with his instructor, awkward contestants in a four-legged race, to the open door. He thought for a moment about grabbing onto something, anything, to stop this crazy thing from happening, but he felt the comforting weight of Annie's necklace in his pocket, and the feeling passed quickly.

They jumped.

The plane was suddenly gone; there was nothing but spinning clouds and the ground far, far below. Eddie could feel his instructor shift her body to slow the spin, and he tried to relax his body to help her.

The sky was everywhere and everything, and the world he had always taken for granted was so far away.

I'm not on it.

I'm looking at the whole damn world, and I'm not on it.

Eddie laughed. He wondered where Annie was down there, and if she was watching him.

His instructor was struggling to shout in his ear. Even

though she was only inches away, he could barely hear her over the roaring wind. He had learned the hand signals they used to communicate while diving, so there shouldn't be any need to shout. Something must be wrong.

"I can't...pain in my...my whole arm feels like...you need to release the..."

She coughed a couple of times, and her head dropped forward. Eddie couldn't turn around to see her, couldn't tell what had happened, but he knew she was dead.

Eddie's heart and mind were both racing.

What now?

He was strapped to a dead woman, free-falling through the sky, about fifteen thousand feet above the ground.

Allison. Her name was Allison.

They didn't cover this in the thirty minutes of training.

The first thing was to release the clips that held the two of them together. That must have been what she was trying to tell him. Then, he'd be able to use his own emergency parachute and let Allison fall to the ground. He started to unscrew the first clip.

"You don't want to do that," Allison said.

Eddie screamed.

"Sorry to startle you. I'm not Allison."

Eddie screamed again.

"Right. I'm Trevor-14, and I'm from the future. I won't say how far yet; I know it's a lot to process already. This whole thing is a mess."

Eddie stopped screaming. The wind was oddly calm. Below him, he noticed three parachutes opening, puffs of white against the greens and browns of the earth.

Three? Shouldn't there be four?

"Anyway, you don't want to do that. You don't have a—"

Trevor-14 stopped as something buzzed by Eddie's ear,

reminding him of the buzzing-noise at the top of the tree in those Winnie-the-Pooh stories Annie always made him read to her.

But, this wasn't bees or whatever it was at the top of that tree. This was a bullet, and after whizzing right by Eddie's ear, it planted itself into Allison's forehead, or Trevor-14's forehead, or whoever it was Eddie was still attached to. Blood gushed from a hole in the back of her head—*his head?* —and floated in midair, keeping pace with Eddie and Allison as they fell.

Eddie screamed again.

What the hell just happened?

Whatever happened, he was still falling, and he was still attached to a now twice-dead body.

He tried to ignore his screams, which seemed to belong to someone else, and opened the pair of clips that were supposed to keep him safe. Allison's body drifted away, but not before giving Eddie a much better view than he wanted of her disfigured face.

He unzipped the pocket that held his emergency parachute ripcord, and gave it a tug.

Nothing happened.

He gave it a much harder tug.

Still nothing.

Parachute.

That's what Trevor-whatever was about to say. You don't have a parachute.

The ground below, which had looked this whole time like it wasn't getting any closer, suddenly started rushing toward him. Eddie wasn't sure if he was still screaming or not. He was thinking of Annie, loving her desperately, hoping she wasn't watching anymore.

If I ever get the chance to do this again, I'm going to pass on the skydiving party, thanks very much, Dave.

Or, at least, remember to use Allison's parachute.

I'm sorry, Annie.

Goodbye.

Luckily for him, for everybody really, Eddie was gone before his body hit the ground.

———

THE WORLD WAS dark and cold, filled with a cacophony of unrecognizable sounds that echoed and over-lapped. An incessant high-pitched beeping sound, or maybe more like a chirping, cut through the chaos and hammered away at Eddie's ears.

I have ears?

So, this is it? This is what being dead is?

Eddie tried to open his eyes but couldn't; they were too tired, it seemed.

"Don't try to open your eyes. It's too soon," a voice said. "You know that. You're acting like it's your first rat hunt, Journey-72."

The voice was familiar, but also not. Eddie recognized the rhythm, even though the sound was different.

"Trevor?" Eddie whispered. Something heavy and metal clattered noisily on the floor.

There was a rustling sound, and the familiar voice was right next to Eddie. "Who are you?"

Eddie tried again to open his eyes, to see the source of the voice, but they still refused to comply.

"I-I'm Eddie."

The voice considered this for a long moment.

"Eddie?"

"Walters. Eddie Walters. Is this heaven? This can't be

heaven, can it?" He hadn't seen anything yet, but this didn't sound like heaven. It didn't really feel like the other place either.

Another long pause.

"What is 'heaven,' Eddie Walters?"

Eddie tried to sit up. His body stubbornly continued to do nothing.

"Where am I?"

"New Jersey."

Eddie laughed. "Not heaven, then."

A sharp pain shot through his left shoulder, and the world swam away.

WHEN EDDIE WOKE UP AGAIN, the world was quiet. No, not quite. He could still hear the awful chirping, but it was distant and muffled.

He told his eyes to open, and this time they followed orders. The ceiling, low and dirty, had a single dim light-bulb in a dusty cage. Spiderwebs, thick with unlucky flies, filled the corners of the small room.

He told his body to sit up. It followed orders too, except it didn't feel like his body. He raised a hand.

What the hell is happening?

The hand that Eddie was looking at was small and dark, with skinny fingers, broken nails, and rough calluses. A long, jagged scar ran from the base of its thumb through the wrist, trailing off halfway up the thin, hairless forearm.

This is not my hand.

He raised another hand, and that one wasn't his either. He looked down, hoping to see familiar legs but knowing better.

Eddie stood up. Whoever's body this was, he was in control of it now.

The room was tiny—only a couple of steps, and he'd run into a wall in any direction. One of those walls had a solid wood door, and Eddie knew it wouldn't open before he tried it. He pounded on the door, and immediately his hands ached.

He sat down against one of the walls and cried. He hadn't cried since Annie was a baby, but this body needed a good cry.

A few minutes later, he heard locks clicking and tumbling. He wiped his cheeks with the back of his hand —*whose hand?*—and tried to prepare himself for whatever might be on the other side of that door.

The doorknob turned, and the door swung into the room, revealing a dark hallway and a small group of kids. A boy who looked about Annie's age, dressed like a soldier complete with a rifle slung across his back, seemed to be the leader. He was flanked by a pair of small soldiers on each side.

Their eyes all shared the haunted look of those that have seen too much suffering.

"How did you get here, Eddie Walters?" the boy asked in a familiar voice.

"You're Trevor?" Eddie asked in response.

"That is...partially correct. I am Trevor-14. We met in the Projection Room, and prior to that, in 2020 during a failed mission. But, you are not answering my question. How did you get here?"

"I don't have a clue," Eddie answered. "I don't know where 'here' is, or whose body I'm walking around in, or why kids are playing dress-up with uniforms and guns. What is going on here?"

One of the other kids, a girl with short, braided hair and a scar on her cheek, spoke before Trevor-14 could answer. "You don't know how you got here?"

"I died. At least, I thought I did. And then, I woke up."

The kids all looked at each other, clearly worried. Something was wrong.

Everything is wrong.

The kids huddled together, and Eddie could hear strange phrases rise out of their urgent whispers:

"Is that possible?"

"...only one-way..."

"Journey-72 must be caught in the current..."

"...someone else was there?"

"The Professor isn't going to be happy."

One of them, Eddie couldn't tell which, whispered very quietly for a long time, and then they all turned back to him.

"Come with us," Trevor-14 said crisply. The kids turned in unison to face the door, which had been open the whole time, and walked out of the room.

Eddie gave a sarcastic salute, unconsciously echoing Dave's farewell, and watched a stranger's hand snap to his forehead.

By the time he got to the door, the kids were already dozens of yards down the hallway, illuminated by dim lights running along the bottom of the walls. He caught up quickly, though; the legs he was running on felt young, strong, and full of energy.

As they walked, the kids ignored his questions: "Where are we going? Where are we? What do you mean we met in 2020? What year is it now? Who are you? Who am I?"

Eddie kept asking until they turned a corner and the view shut him up.

The room was enormous. Its low ceilings made it difficult to know just how enormous, but Eddie guessed it was the size of a football field at least. Lights ran along the floor, casting creepy shadows on the ceiling. Every five yards or so, there was a small hospital cot surrounded by machines and cables.

On every hospital bed, a small human body lay perfectly still, with their eyes closed and tubes connected to their body in all sorts of ways. Some of the tubes ran up to the ceiling. A few children walked among the bodies slowly, rifles bouncing on their hips, occasionally stopping to look closely at one of the machines.

Trevor-14 carefully scrutinized Eddie's face. "Now do you know where you are?"

Eddie closed his eyes. He shook his head.

I don't want to know.

"I told you," the girl said flatly. "Journey-72 is gone."

"She's not gone!" shouted a small boy, on the verge of tears. "We can get her back!"

Trevor-14 put a hand on the boy's shoulder, and the girl scowled at him. He smiled back at her and turned to Eddie. "This is the Projection Room. You've spent most of your life in this room—physically, at least. Except apparently, you haven't. Journey-72 has, but you're not her, despite the fact that you are inhabiting her body."

"What? I'm...what?"

"We're taking you to the Professor. She'll be able to explain it to you."

The kids suddenly turned and walked through the grid of bodies on beds, passing about a dozen bodies before making a hard right turn. Eddie kept up, too many questions in his head for him to ask any. As they walked, he noticed tags on the foot of each bed, each with a name and a number: Legend-22, Zaphod-42, Serenity-17, Constance-31...

More questions.

Finally, the room ended, and two of the kids slid a wide, heavy wooden door to the side, exposing a small room with a single desk and a very old woman sitting on a chair, hunched forward over the desk with her head resting on her arms. She was snoring a bit, and a little river of drool ran across the desk to bead up at the edge.

Eddie squeezed into the small room along with the kids, who closed the door behind him. They were all practically touching elbows as they circled the desk with the sleeping woman.

"Sit there," Trevor-14 said, gesturing to a chair on the other side of the desk. Eddie sat. Above him, a metal panel slid open, and a small machine descended straight down to land awkwardly on his head.

"What—"

"Don't speak. It might kill you."

What?

Thin cables grew from the sides of the machine and inserted themselves into Eddie's ears. They moved as if they were alive. His body stiffened, and a scream caught in his throat. His eyes closed, and he gratefully passed out.

Except, he didn't.

———

IN HIS MIND, Eddie was sitting along the third base line at Fenway Park, with the Green Monster towering over him, and the wind blowing out to right. The ballpark was empty, except for a young woman with thick horn-rimmed glasses and a Red Sox cap sitting a few seats away, cracking peanut shells and letting them fall to the concrete floor. The sunlight was bright, and the air smelled like freshly cut grass. Eddie looked at her blankly.

"This is your favorite place?" she asked, popping a few peanuts into her mouth. "What is it?"

Eddie nodded slowly and blinked several times, trying to make sense of anything. "It's Fenway," he said quietly, an aching loss in his voice. The woman shook her head and gestured for him to continue. "Fenway Park. It's where the Red Sox play baseball."

She shook her head again.

She doesn't know what baseball is?

He tried to explain. "It's where I spent time with my dad growing up. Now, I take my daughter there at least once each season. We've had a lot of good days here."

"People played games here?" She was looking out across the infield.

"Yeah. Some pretty amazing ones."

"Interesting." She looked for a long time, taking it all in, before she continued. "Do you know why you're here?"

"Not a clue. Do you? Please tell me you do."

"Not entirely. I do know some things that I need you to understand right away, but they're not going to be easy."

Eddie laughed. "That's good, because I don't understand anything. What year is it? Where are we? Let's start there. Oh, and your name would be great too. I'm Eddie, but I'm betting you already knew that."

The woman smiled, but her eyes stayed serious. "My name is simply the Professor. I haven't used any other name since I was a little girl, and that was a very, very long time ago. Today's date is November 19, 2142. We are currently sharing a current of consciousness, so the 'where' is complicated. Journey-72's body, and mine, are currently resting about a half mile underneath what you would remember as New Jersey. Does that answer your questions?"

Eddie looked around. "Is there beer here?"

The Professor shook her head.

"No, there's no beer? Or no, you don't know what beer is?"

The Professor didn't answer. "In July of 2050, an asteroid hit the Earth. We tried to knock it off course, and we did, but not enough to save the world. After it hit, survivors went underground, governments formed out of tech companies and aspiring autocrats, and they sent robots to the surface to rebuild so we could move back home someday."

"But you haven't."

"No. The robots got too smart, just like everybody said they would, and realized they could work faster if they forced people to work for them."

"So, in a hundred years, we're all slaves to robots?"

"Not all of us," the Professor said, conceding the larger point. "Some people escaped and went deeper, into secret tunnels and caverns. Some of us held out hope, in the face of everything."

Eddie could sense the Professor's growing confidence. "And now, you found a way to fight back?"

The Professor nodded. "In 2112, I had a breakthrough in my research on human consciousness. It would take years to fully explain, but essentially, I discovered currents of consciousness and figured out how to 'ride' them. Twenty years later, we learned how to jump to different points on the current."

"You're talking about time travel?"

She smiled. "Yes, although we don't call it that. Your physical body doesn't travel through time; your consciousness travels through the currents, allowing you to see a glimpse of a moment from a different time."

"That was more than a glimpse," Eddie interjected.

"That," the Professor said delicately, "was a disaster."

Eddie thought about Allison's heart attack, the bullet, the fall to the earth. He thought about Annie.

Yeah. Yeah, it was.

"What happened?" he asked.

"Sometimes things go wrong." The Professor crushed the handful of peanuts she was holding and let the crumbly bits of shell and nut drift to the ground. "Sending your consciousness across time can be unpredictable. This time, there was another actor involved in the situation—a circumstance we did not anticipate."

"Whoever shot Trevor wasn't supposed to be there."

She crushed the shells under her foot, taking her time before answering. "That is correct. You will be joining Trevor-14 and Meena-12 on a mission to repair the damage done by that actor."

Eddie shrugged.

Sure, why not?

"What's so important about Dave's birthday party?"

"You're not prepared for that answer yet."

Eddie could tell she was right. "What's with the numbers after everybody's names?"

She popped the last peanut in her mouth. "You're not prepared for that answer either."

She touched Eddie's forehead, and Fenway disappeared.

HE BLINKED, and he was back in the small room, surrounded by kid soldiers and the Professor's perpetually sleeping body. The cables slithered out of his ears, and the terrifying little machine whisked itself back up into the ceiling.

"Welcome back," Trevor-14 said. "Did the Professor answer all of your questions?"

Eddie laughed. "Not even close. But, I think you know that. What's next?"

Trevor-14 smiled, and Meena-12 stepped forward. "Follow me," she said, and quickly opened the door to the Projection Room. Eddie followed her and the other kids through the narrow path between the bodies, which Eddie now saw were each connected to the same kind of machine that had just defiled his head.

Meena-12 stopped next to a group of three empty beds.

"Hang on," said Eddie. "I don't want one of those things jabbing itself into my brain again."

Meena-12 looked at him without sympathy. "You grow accustomed to it in time," she said simply, and she lay down on one of the beds. "Please, lie down. This is the only way."

"The only way to what?" Eddie asked, but Meena-12 was already hooked up to a machine.

"The only way to save the world," Trevor-14 answered.

"Okay, then." Eddie lay down on a bed. "Hey, shouldn't we talk about the plan or something?"

But Trevor-14 was already gone, and Eddie's machine was rapidly descending.

EDDIE'S EYES OPENED. He was in his own body, but not in control; he tried lifting an arm with no success. He was sitting in an airplane hangar, along with Dave and the rest of the guys. A young man with a long bushy beard was reviewing safety instructions.

I remember this. Why am I here?

Mark caught Eddie's eyes and nodded knowingly, making Eddie feel even more confused.

The young man with the beard—*Vince? Victor?*—wrapped up his presentation. "It looks like we're blue skies this afternoon, which means perfect conditions for your first jump. If you stick around, you'll learn it means more than that. It's how we say hello, goodbye, and, most importantly, good luck. And now it's time to get ready, so...blue skies, everybody!"

"Blue skies!" Eddie shouted in response, along with his friends. They all stood up and traded high-fives and back slaps. The phrase rang a bell somewhere in the depths of his mind, but he couldn't quite place it. Eddie remembered all this, could feel himself doing it, but this time he was just along for the ride. Just an observer.

After the group broke up to put on suits and gear, Mark sat down next to Eddie, a little closer than Mark usually got.

"Eddie, I need to talk to you," Mark whispered.

"Sure, bud. What's up?" Eddie heard himself say.

"Here's the thing, Eddie. I'm not actually talking to you. I'm talking to an Eddie from the future who is in your consciousness right now, hearing what you hear. He's the Eddie I'm talking to."

Eddie understood now, even as he heard himself say, "What the hell are you talking about?"

Mark ignored the question. "Eddie, this is not Mark. This is Meena-12. You've figured that out by now. Mark will wake up when all this is over, and he won't even know what happened."

Eddie felt confusion and disbelief twist through his body.

"You can control this body's movements, but it will take effort. It's easier if someone is unconscious or dead, but you'll need to learn quickly. I need you to help Trevor-14 identify his shooter and stop the bullet from reaching its target. The original Eddie must survive this day. Can you do that?"

Eddie felt his head shake from side to side, but he knew that Meena-12 knew what he really meant.

Mark/Meena-12 clapped Eddie's shoulder and laughed. "Eddie, I'm kidding! I've been working on that one for weeks. You should see the look on your face. Come on, let's go."

Eddie laughed. That did sound like something Mark would do.

A little over an hour later, Dave gave a sloppy salute again and jumped out of the plane with his instructor again. Austin and his instructor followed a few seconds after.

Quietly, almost like a prayer, Meena-12 spoke in Mark's voice: "You'll only have a few seconds to find them. Good luck, Eddie."

Mark/Meena-12 jumped out of the plane, along with an instructor who had no idea he was jumping with a time traveler.

Eddie looked at Geoff. Geoff looked sick.

"Are you going to be okay?" Eddie shouted.

Geoff tried to smile and gave Eddie a weak thumbs-up. "I'll be right behind you!"

Eddie looked out the open door.

He jumped again.

Allison died again.

He tried to tell himself not to unscrew the clip again, but he was doing it anyway.

"You don't want to do that," Trevor-14 said.

Eddie heard himself scream.

"Sorry to startle you. I'm not Allison."

Eddie heard himself scream again.

"Right. I'm Trevor-14, and I'm from the future. Future Eddie knows this; you don't need to understand."

Eddie got his hands to stop unscrewing the clip. He tried to ask Trevor-14 about the plan, but he couldn't make himself talk. Three parachutes puffed open below them.

"Now, on the count of three, I need you to point your head down to the ground and tuck your arms and legs in. Can you do that?"

Eddie nodded.

"One...two..."

A buzzing sound approached quickly. Too quickly.

"Thr—"

The bullet found its target. Eddie's hands had returned to the job of unscrewing the clips, and Allison's body floated away.

Another bullet whizzed by, and then another. Eddie went into a dive again to make himself a harder target. He twisted his body to get a view of the shooter.

Geoff was diving down from above, a small handgun aimed at Eddie as he fell. His instructor was gone, and he was laughing.

"I don't even have to shoot you, Eddie!" he shouted. "I took out your parachute!"

Still laughing, Geoff pulled his own ripcord, and his canopy billowed out above him, pulling him up and out of Eddie's view.

The ground got closer.

Geoff?

Eddie blacked out before his body hit the ground again.

EDDIE OPENED HIS EYES. He looked down and saw himself, frantically unscrewing the clips that held him to the body that Eddie was now controlling. Allison's body. The Professor must have tried again.

"You don't want to do that," Eddie said.

The other Eddie screamed.

"Right, crap. I'm sorry. This is all pretty crazy. Dive with me."

Eddie dove, angling Allison's body toward the ground, and the other Eddie went along for the ride. A faint whizzing sound went by above them. Eddie flattened their bodies to slow their fall, and looked for Geoff. It felt good to be in control of a body again, even if it wasn't his.

He scanned all around. Nothing but blue skies, all day long.

Of course.

He had sung the classic song to Annie as a lullaby, always mixing up and making up the words. He hadn't thought about it in seven or eight years at least. Right now, he wanted nothing more than to sing it to her again.

Meanwhile, the other Eddie had succeeded in his attempts to unscrew the clips, and Eddie drifted away from his old body.

"No!" Eddie shouted. "You don't have a—"

Eddie chased the other Eddie all the way to the ground, hoping the Professor would be able to try again.

EDDIE'S EYES OPENED. He was in a different place; something must have gone wrong. His—*her?*—young legs were pumping furiously across a rocky desert, fueled by fear and desperation. Arms swung up into view, and he recognized them as Journey-72's arms. At least he assumed they were hers; they looked the same, except that the long scar on her right arm was missing. She turned her head back as she ran, and Eddie refused to believe what he saw.

Thankfully, she turned back to watch where she was running.

A sign for Exit 8 on the New Jersey turnpike was still standing amongst piles of rubble. The rocky landscape wasn't a desert. As he looked more closely, Eddie could see the hollowed-out remains of sleek cars and flattened buildings. The ground was the broken cement of a road that hadn't been used or repaired in decades. Brown grass grew through cracks in the pavement, spreading out to make the whole world look brown. Thick acrid smoke held any sunlight at bay; the sky was as brown as the earth.

She ran on, Eddie a captive passenger on a terrifying ride.

Behind them, a few dozen enormous metal things were catching up quickly. They were each at least eight feet tall, with sharp red claws at the ends of six arms, and they were fast. Rugged wheels, clearly designed to handle a post-apocalyptic wasteland, rolled over the destruction. They looked like they were built to destroy, and then adapted to kill.

Within seconds, the first robot had caught up, and swept her feet out from under her, knocking her to the ground. Eddie felt the pain of the landing, but also her resilience. She jumped back to her feet instantly, ready to take on a whole army of robots.

It reached for her head with one of its arms, and she

ducked under it and kicked the robot hard, right where one of the lowest arms connected with its body. The arm snapped off easily. Eddie could tell that she knew what she was doing.

But there were too many of them. She managed to duck and dodge and kick out three more arms before one of the claws pierced her right forearm, dragging itself through her skin and muscle all the way to her thumb. Eddie felt her skin ripping apart and screamed along with her.

Another arm reached for her head, and long cables like the ones in the Projection Room slithered out of the robot's claw and into her ears.

"Journey-13 has been terminated," Eddie heard an artificial voice say dully. "Prepare for reset procedure."

Journey-13? She won't escape until she gets all the way to Journey-72?

Eddie passed out.

EDDIE OPENS HIS EYES. There is a large silver thing in front of him, with a huge hole in its side. It's flying fast, but it's not moving its wings. Strange things with round heads crawl out of the hole in pairs and drop to the ground.

This is strange.

Eddie thinks about flying up to that hole and right into the silver thing. For some reason, he wants to stop the round-headed things from dropping, but he can't work out just why.

His mind wanders off to wonder where the rest of his flock is, and he flaps his wings, circling around the silver thing to head south.

EDDIE OPENED HIS EYES. He was Allison again, with 2020 Eddie unscrewing the clips again.

What was that?

"Don't do that!" Mark's voice shouted from nearby. "You need her parachute!" Mark/Meena-12 came close enough to grab onto 2020 Eddie's arm. "Also, that's not Allison."

"He's right," Eddie said. "I'm not. I'm—"

He was cut off by a buzzing sound. A hole suddenly appeared in Mark's throat. Blood floated all around them.

Meena-12 managed to say one thing before leaving Mark's dying body: "Save Eddie."

The other Eddie, 2020 Eddie, was still screaming. Eddie looked around for Geoff, but didn't see him anywhere.

"Hold on tight, old friend," he told 2020 Eddie, and pulled his ripcord. The white canopy burst out from the pack and slowed their fall. Eddie couldn't remember how to land safely, but Allison's body knew what to do. They hit the ground a little more roughly than it looks in the promotional video, but not too bad. The other Eddie wrestled himself out of the clips and turned to face Allison/Eddie.

"What the hell is—"

The buzzing again. The other Eddie fell to the ground, a red mess spreading through his hair.

Eddie looked up to see Geoff, still in the air, pointing a gun at him. Another buzzing sound, but Eddie didn't stick around to see if it hit him or not.

EDDIE OPENED HIS EYES, and even through the goggles, the wind was blinding. He was falling. By himself.

Then, it's too late. And I can't do anything in this body anyway.

He moved an arm to make sure, and he was surprised to see the arm move. His arm. It had been a while.

His relief was cut short, though—the ground was about to get closer very quickly, and he had no way to survive this fall.

On the baseball field below, a teenage girl on the pitcher's mound stopped mid-delivery, took off her faded Brewers hat, and pointed up at the sky. She held up two fingers and shouted at the other players and coaches. A few parents in the stands were already calling 9-1-1, reporting two people falling from the sky.

Eddie couldn't see or hear any of this, of course, so he was surprised when Allison's foot kicked his shoulder. He started to spin, and his foot collided with Allison's head. Her body turned, and without thinking about what he was doing, he grabbed her harness and pulled her ripcord.

A parachute sprang from her pack, jerking her body up as it caught the wind. Eddie almost lost his grip, but he held on tightly. He tried to grab her toggles so he could steer their descent, but he couldn't let go with either hand long enough to grab somewhere else.

A buzzing sound got close and then faded away.

Eddie wrapped his legs around Allison's body, and let go with both hands. They both started spinning, and another bullet whizzed by. He grabbed first one toggle and then the other, and pulled them out of their spin.

Geoff was falling a few dozen yards away, his parachute keeping pace with Allison's. His gun was fixed on Eddie despite the turbulence. Eddie suddenly had an idea.

This is a really bad idea.

Eddie let go of Allison's toggles, and straightened his body into a dive. The parachute holding up Allison's body drifted away. Geoff lowered the gun, surprised. He tried to evade the body hurtling towards him, but Eddie closed the gap too quickly.

Geoff went back to aiming the gun at the last moment, firing twice. A bullet ripped through Eddie's left arm, just below his shoulder, sending a burning pain up and down his arm. The other landed in Allison's leg, spraying blood across the sky.

Eddie crashed feet-first into Geoff's stomach, knocking the wind out of him and knocking the gun out of his hand. He was falling too far and too fast; he almost fell right past Geoff, but he managed to grab a handful of pants and crawl his way up Geoff's shocked body from there.

Geoff laughed. "You're crazy!"

Eddie laughed back. "It's been a crazy day."

Geoff squirmed and swung his arms, but he couldn't break Eddie's grip on the straps of his backpack.

"They're all crazy days," Geoff said. "Ever since the asteroid, everything is crazy. I used to project back into this time just to enjoy breathing the air."

"What happened to Geoff? Who are you?"

"He'll be fine. I'm not the bad guy here, Eddie."

"That doesn't make any sense."

Geoff, or whoever he was, looked down calmly. The ground was getting closer.

"I'll try to explain quickly. I'm Journey-72, and I think you and I got tangled up in the current somehow. The Professor found me and sent me to fix Trevor-14's mistake after the three of you went back."

"What mistake?"

"Saving your life."

Eddie looked at his old friend Geoff's face, looking for something familiar in his eyes and finding nothing.

Journey-72 continued. "Your daughter, Anne, will become the president of the United States in 2048. She will lead an effort, along with everyone else on the planet, to stop a massive asteroid from hitting us. She will fail, and the asteroid will destroy life as we know it."

Eddie had heard most of this from the Professor, but he was having a hard time with this new detail. "Annie?"

"Yes. The Professor has been sending us on missions for years, trying to establish a timeline where she does not fail. We have been making small changes in key moments, giving her the tools to succeed. The Professor thought that saving your life would help, but now we know that was a mistake."

"How is saving my life a mistake?"

"Your death was, of course, a tragedy for her to live through. She watched you fall after your instructor's heart attack, and it almost broke her. But she did live through it, and as she grew up it became part of her political identity. With her father by her side, Annie grows up to be healthy and happy, but she never becomes president."

"So, the asteroid gets us anyway."

"Actually, that leads to all sorts of problems before we get to 2050. That's why we had to reset today's events. Once we fix this, we can get back to work on giving Annie the tools she'll need while she's President."

The ground looked very close now.

"Does she miss me?" Eddie asked, as his tears were whisked away by the wind.

"Every day."

Eddie thought about Journey-13's desperate run, the brown skies, the red claws, and the things that slither in your ears. He thought about the twelve times she must have tried and failed before that run, and the fifty-nine times she must try again before she escapes. He decided.

He looked down, wondering where Annie was and hating what he was about to put her through. "And she's going to save the world?"

"I promise you, we will make sure she does."

I love you, Annie.

Eddie let go of Geoff's body and let gravity take hold. His body, the other Eddie's body really, spun and somersaulted as it fell.

Journey-72 watched Eddie all the way to the ground.

"Thank you," she said, but Eddie couldn't hear her.

———

SHADOWS WERE STARTING to stretch across the carefully mown grass as the Yankees took the field for the bottom of the sixth. It was a warm late summer afternoon, the kind announcers have been calling a "beautiful day for baseball" for two hundred and fifty years.

Trevor stood up to cheer on his Red Sox, to let them know he believed they could come back after the hated Yankees added two more to their lead in the top of the inning. They had just barely lost the 2141 World Series, after all, and he knew they could go all the way this year. Meena stood with him, and together they started a chant of "Let's Go Red Sox" that spread all over Fenway.

Journey took a sip of her beer and smiled at her brother, who grinned back at her and stood up to join Trevor's chant. She loved spending an afternoon at the ballpark.

An old woman with horn-rimmed glasses, a Red Sox

cap, and a bag of peanuts smiled at them from a few rows away and stood up to join in the chant.

The shortstop walked out from the dugout and crossed to the plate. She knocked a bit of dirt from her cleats and looked out at the pitcher. She took two pitches, both low and away, before jumping on the third, a fastball that floated up a bit as it came in.

The crack of the bat hitting the ball reverberated through the ballpark, and forty thousand pairs of eyes followed its trajectory up toward the afternoon sun.

Nothing but blue skies, from now on.

Biography

Nathaniel Swift (he/him) is a writer, artist, teacher, dad, and pet parent living in Chicago. He currently teaches elementary & middle school drama and writes as often as he can. Right now, he's working on a sci-fi series about a group of kids who move to Mars and save the universe, a time travel novel that explains how the Cubs won the 2016 World Series, along with a bit of haiku. Nat is also an award-winning actor and director, former Artistic Director of Eclipse Theatre Company, and has years of experience working with playwrights and ensembles to develop stories on stage.

VISIT HIM AT:

https://sites.google.com/view/writernatswift

MILADY

MARC HENNEMANN

PATTY CHIEN FELT a bump in the journey, like every-thing had switched off for a moment and then switched back on. "Damn," she thought. "I told Jessica not to base the machine in California with its unreliable electricity, but *no*! She had to have it in San Francisco. As long as I've been married to that girl, I'll never understand her devotion to that pla—" Another bump, harder this time. "Fuck! What the hell is going on? One more like that, and it'll throw the whole timeline out of place, and who knows where I'll wind up!"

A third one, so hard she brushed against the silver and iron bars. The energy contained in them crackled, knocking her to the floor of the time machine. As her consciousness ebbed, she thought she saw a woman's hands reaching for her.

"Mademoiselle Clarisse, *ça va?*"

"*Qu'est-il arrivé?*"

"*Je ne sais pas. Elle a du s'évanouir.*"

"French?" she thought. "Why are they speaking French? And why do I understand it? I don't speak French. And who is Clarisse? And why is she saying I passed out? It was the bump in the time machine. I must've brushed against the bars. Lucky I'm not dead. Maybe I'd better stay passed out until I figure out what's going on here."

"Suzette," said the mysterious woman whom Patty dared not open her eyes to see. "*Prends ses pieds et aide-moi a la remettre sur le lit, s'il te plait.*"

"*Bien sûr,* Kitty."

"So, your name is Kitty," thought Patty, still pretending to be unconscious. "And you're in charge, at least at the moment." As the two women moved her, Patty smiled inwardly, thinking "Yes, put me on my back. That's where I've done some of my best work."

She had to struggle a bit to keep the smile inward as she remembered how she had seduced Jessica when Jess accompanied her father on a wine-buying trip to China. Admittedly, it hadn't been a difficult seduction, Jessica being not only experienced but more than willing.

She decided that night that she would rather have Jessica and work as a contract assassin for the Central Intelligence Agency than do the same job for the Chinese Ministry of State Security and have to constantly guard her sexuality. She used Jessica and her father to contact the CIA station chief at the United States embassy in Beijing, and the Agency got her out.

"Where am I now?" Patty thought. "Some place that doesn't believe in washing, that's for sure. This bed cover smells like it hasn't been washed in weeks, and these two women smell like they haven't been washed in weeks either.

Even their French stinks. Hell, I can speak better French than that. Now that they've got me up on the bed, maybe I'd better come back to being conscious. Okay, brain. Switch over to French."

Patty groaned softly, and her eyes fluttered open. "Where am I?"

"Mademoiselle Clarisse, are you okay?"

"What happened to me?"

"You fainted, mademoiselle."

"I know I fainted, you stupid cunt," thought Patty, "but where and when the fuck am I?" But she said, "Where am I? I don't remember anything."

"You are at the home of your late father, in Paris. Phillipe Francois Faxicura."

"Phillipe Faxicura?" thought Patty. "Who the hell...? Oh, yeah, right. I read about him in China. That must be his French name. He was the first Japanese ambassador to Europe. His name was...um...Hasekura Tsunenaga, I think. Yeah, that's it, Hasekura. And do they think I'm his daughter? An ambassador's daughter is okay, I guess, but I hope Jessica and Don Jose are working to get me back home. This isn't where I want to stay for the rest of my life.

"DON JOSE, what happened? Where's Patty?" asked Jessica.

"To answer your questions in order, I'm not sure, and I don't know," replied Jose. "Something happened to the electricity. It cut out at least three times, and somehow, we lost Patty. I don't know where she is, and I don't know when she is either."

"Can you find her?"

"Jessica, I honestly don't know. I'll certainly do my best, but no promises."

"If only we had Miguel here."

"I'm not sure what he could do either. Look, let me work out the math, and maybe I can pin down where she is, and when she is, at least a little closer than we have now."

"Ok, but please find her, Jose, and bring her home."

"I'll do my best." And with that, Dr. Jose Sandoval went to work on his mathematical calculations. Thinking aloud, he said, "Well, what do we know? First, she was returning from Arthurian England, back at the end of the fifth century. She was investigating Morgan le Fay to see if she was indeed the modern-day Morgana Laffey. So, we can safely assume Patty is somewhere between the sixth century and the twenty-first. If we follow the Einstein-Hawking formulation, and presume this is a safe case to eliminate the middle, which the formulation itself says is almost always safe, then we should be able to locate her pretty accurately."

"Doesn't the time machine have a homing beacon?" asked Jessica.

"The homing beacon can only be used by someone at the same time as the machine. Patty could use it to find the machine, presuming it's at the same time she is. It doesn't help us any."

"What about the locator beacon?"

"We can use the locator beacon to locate the machine if it's in the same timeline we are. The answer to that depends on what the electrical fluctuation did to the computer's time guidance system. Let me run a security and function scan first to make sure the flux didn't cause any physical damage.

Once we've determined that, we'll see if we can link up with the homing beacon."

Five minutes later, after studying the numbers on the screen, Jose said, "Some of the readings are slightly deviated from the norm, but everything seems to be functional. The security scan shows no timeline breach, so the machine should be aligned with our timeline."

"When and where is it?" asked Jessica.

"The machine's coordinates are 48.86 north and 2.35 east."

"Where is that?"

"Hang on a minute while I look…it's in Paris."

"Paris? What is it doing in Paris!"

"I don't know yet," said Jose. "Let me find out when it is, and maybe that'll tell us. Ah, the machine is in 1627 AD."

"Is Patty there too?"

"Unless the electric flux was greater than it now seems, Patty is probably in 1627 Paris also."

"Wouldn't she be with the machine?"

"Jessica, we've never had this happen before. I just don't know all the answers yet. You'll just have to be patient."

"Patient my ass!" said Jessica, raising her voice. "Find her and bring her home!"

"And a cute ass it is, too," thought Jose. What he said, however, was "I will do both as soon as I can. Raising your voice at me won't make things go any faster."

"I'm sorry, Jose. I'm just anxious to get her home."

"I know you are, and so am I. And we will, I promise."

"Will her French be okay in 1627 Paris?"

"It should be. That's during the time when French became the official language of the French court as opposed to Latin and other languages. It would have been what's now called *Classical French*, but it's similar enough to modern French that Patty should be able to get along in the language."

"Okay, but what is she doing there?"

"WHAT AM I DOING HERE?" thought Patty. She had chased Kitty and Suzette, who were apparently household servants, out of the bedroom. Alone for the first time since she had "arrived" in Paris, she pulled up her long skirts, only to find she wore no underwear. "So," she thought, "apparently at least some of the more scandalous allegations of French women in the sixteenth or seventeenth century, or whenever the fuck I am, are true."

She smiled, and then steadied herself as she reached into her most intimate area and withdrew what appeared to be an ordinary tampon. Carefully opening one end of it, she pulled out what looked like a small pen. "Let's hope the damn locator beacon still works," she thought. "If not, I'm in a world of shit." Clicking one end of the device, she was relieved to see the small LED light up green. "Okay, you still work. Now tell me where the machine is." The locator beacon, however, was not to be hurried. First the digits 1*6*2*7 scrolled across the miniature screen, then nothing. "1627. Fucking wonderful. I already figured something like that. At least, now I know for sure. Now where's the machine?"

The green LED faded.

"No!" thought Patty. "Don't you dare fade out on me, you piece of shit." Just then, the LED came back on, only yellow this time. "Yellow! The damn machine's gone nontemporal. Pain in the ass! I hope Don Jose is getting this and he can re-temporize the machine. If not, I'm stuck here in sixteen twenty-fucking-seven forever!"

She got off the bed, walked to the window, and looked out between the drapes, but saw only fog and the rain she had heard pattering on the roof.

Interrupting her thoughts, there came a timid knock on the door.

"Now who the fuck is it?" thought Patty, quickly hiding the locater beacon in a convenient pocket. Her response, however, was merely "*Entrez.*"

It was Kitty. "Mademoiselle, there is a messenger from le Cardinal de Richelieu."

"Cardinal Richelieu?" thought Patty. "Just what have I gotten myself into?" Then, she answered, "Tell him that I shall be down in a moment and receive him in the parlor." As Kitty turned to go, Patty said, "Wait. Come down with me in case I faint again on the stair."

"And," she thought, "you can show me where the stairs and the parlor are."

Once set in the parlor, and after a furtive check of the locator—which showed nothing new—Patty received the envoy from Cardinal Richelieu. He turned out to be just a member of the Cardinal's Guard, wet from the rain and tracking mud on his boots. His ostrich plumed hat looked bedraggled as he bowed. "I bring messages from His Eminence, milady."

"Do you indeed? Well, give them to me."

The guard handed her an oilskin pouch, designed to keep out the rain. "His Eminence specifically directs that you read this one first."

"Then, I shall do as His Eminence directs," said Patty, untying the pouch and taking out the paper within. She read to herself:

3 décembre 1627

MILADY,

IT HAS COME to our attention that the Duke of Buckingham intends to reinforce and resupply the rebels at La
Rochelle by sea. This must be prevented at all costs. You
will accompany the Comte de Rochefort to Calais. Passage
to England awaits you there. You will prevent Buckingham
from dispatching his reinforcements. How you do so is your
affaire. Just ensure you are more successful than in the
matter of the diamond studs.

Richelieu

PATTY TOOK THE SECOND POUCH. Inside she
found:

3 décembre 1627

IT IS by my order and for the good of the state that the
bearer of this has done what has been done.

Richelieu

"OH, MY FUCKING GOD," Patty thought. "I'm in the middle of the *Three* fucking *Musketeers*!" Then she felt the locator vibrate.

"GOOD NEWS, JESSICA," said Jose. "The time machine has gone nontemporal."

"What does that mean?"

"It means that the machine has gone slightly out of phase with its current time. It's in 1627, but nobody can see it."

"Not even Patty?"

"Not even her."

"Then, how can she find it?"

"We'll have to re-temporalize it from this end," said Jose. "You see, the machine is normally nontemporal when it is traveling through time. That's why it seems to materialize out of nowhere when anyone returns from a time journey. Both the machine and whoever is in it are nontemporal while they are time traveling. The electric fluctuation must have temporalized Patty but not the machine. The problem with re-temporalizing it from this end is that it will temporalize at the same location where it last was temporal."

"English, Jose. English!"

"I'm sorry, Jess. What I said was that the machine was last temporal in Arthurian England, that is, the England of King Arthur's time. When the machine has to travel geographically as well as through time, it usually takes the most direct geographical route, so it should have come direct from Camelot to San Francisco."

"Then, why didn't it? How did it get to Paris?"

"The electronic flux must have knocked it offline,

allowing it to drift. There were three fluctuations. The first must have put it in 1627, the second one in Paris, and the third one must have temporalized Patty. It's a good thing it went the way it did. I would hate to consider Patty temporalizing over the Atlantic. Now, however, it should be nontemporalized somewhere near ancient Camelot," said Jose.

"But, no one knows where Camelot was."

"When Patty went on her exploratory trip, she located it near the current village of Whaddon, in Buckinghamshire."

"Is that where they filmed *Keeping Up Appearances*?" asked Jessica.

"No, that was filmed in Warwickshire, around Coventry."

"Well, it doesn't really matter. What can Patty do with it? I mean, if she's in Paris, and the time machine is in England..."

"If she still has the locator beacon, and it's still working, it should tell her what year she's in and her geographic coordinates. The best thing to do is temporalize the machine for a moment and then make it nontemporal again. If we do that, it will automatically send its location to the locator that Patty has. Then, all she has to do is get to it."

"Which may not be so easy."

"Patty is very resourceful. She should be able to get from Paris to Buckinghamshire, even in 1627."

"Oh, my God!"

"Jessica? What's wrong?"

"I think I figured it out."

"Figured out what?"

"Patty! Wait here. I'll be right back."

And, with that, Jessica turned and ran from the basement room where the time apparatus and supporting equipment were located. Jose could hear her footsteps as she ran up to the second floor. Moments later, he heard her running back down. She burst into the basement with a book in her hand.

"I know what's happening with Patty. It's *The Three Musketeers*! I was reading it last night."

"What do you mean 'It's *The Three Musketeers*'? That's fiction."

"I'm telling you, Jose. It's the only thing that makes sense."

"Jessica, how can it be *The Three Musketeers*? It's a story; it's not real."

"Look, Jose. I was reading it before I went to bed last night. Milady de Winter was sent from Paris by Cardinal Richelieu to kill the Duke of Buckingham in December of 1627. Patty is going to have to go from Paris to Buckinghamshire in 1627. Don't you see? It all fits together."

AFTER DISMISSING Cardinal Richelieu's messenger and reminding Kitty that too much curiosity killed the cat, Patty quickly returned to the bedroom. Taking the vibrating locator out of her pocket, she pressed a particular spot to stop the vibrations. "The LED is green again," she thought. "Jose must have re-temporalized it. About fucking time!" A series of numbers scrolled across the tiny screen. "This damn thing always hurts my eyes, but I need these numbers. It's the machine trying to tell me where it is." The numbers scrolled once again, and she looked around for something to write them down with. "Not even a fucking feather pen," she thought. "I'll just have to remember them. Not that hard. 52 north and 0.828 west. Now, where the fuck is that?"

She thought for a moment, and then it hit her. "Camelot! The machine went back to Camelot. And now, in 1627, that's where the Duke of Buckingham lives. *And* I'm being sent there by Cardinal Richelieu. I'll be able to get home! Even if I do have to travel to Calais with this Comte de Rochefort character. I hope he doesn't look like Christopher Lee."

Then the LED turned yellow.

AFTER HER TRAVEL TO CALAIS—DURING which she learned that the Comte de Rochefort really did look like Christopher Lee with an eye patch—she took a small boat to England, when she learned that it was *much* more comfortable to take the Chunnel. Of course, the Chunnel wouldn't exist for another four-hundred-plus years. She also found out that there was a very delicately balanced—and very sharp—throwing knife built into the bodice of her travel outfit. It would come in handy.

"YOUR GRACE, the Baroness Sheffield is here. She wishes an audience with you."

"Baroness Sheffield? Is that the name she is using now? Indeed, Felton, show her into the small salon and tell her I shall be down momentarily. And smile, Felton. She is beautiful, even though she is a deceitful liar, as treacherous as the Devil, and possibly a murderess in the bargain."

"Yes, Your Grace." Felton went back to the foyer, and

showed Patty into the small salon.

Patty took the only available chair and gave Felton the once-over. "A Puritan," she thought. "He looks just like the paintings. I wonder if...Nah, I'm not Faye Dunaway, and I'm really not interested. Besides, I need him to help me find the machine." Then, shaking her out of her reverie—

"His Grace, the Duke of Buckingham. Your Grace, The Baroness—"

"Yes, Shelton. Lady de Winter and I know each other well. You may go." Turning to Patty, the duke said, "Had I known you were coming, I would have had you turned back at Dover. You cost me ten thousand pounds when last we met. By rights I should have you tried and hanged for murder. Now, say what you came here to say and be gone."

"Ten thousand pounds?" laughed Patty. "Couldn't you get your lover King James to reimburse you?"

"At least I don't kill my lovers like you, Lady Black Widow. Now, what have you come to say?"

"His Eminence, the Cardinal Richelieu, has learned that you intend to send a naval expedition to relieve the Protestant rebels at La Rochelle. This will, of course, cause war with France, a war you should not fight, and cannot win."

"I shall do both," responded the duke. "Is that all you came to say?"

"It is not," said Patty, all the time thinking: Thank God I read that damn book. Six hundred and fifty pages of boredom. Now, what did Dumas write? Ah. "You might do well to reconsider, Your Grace."

"Why in the name of Heaven should I reconsider? King James is dead. You and your Cardinal have nothing on me."

"I refer not to your past love, but to your current one."

"I have no love but England."

"And the Queen of France, Your Grace. Do not forget the Queen of France. After all, was it not for her you spent those unreimbursed ten thousand pounds?"

"What has Queen Anne to do with the rebels at La Rochelle?"

"With the rebels, nothing, Your Grace. With you, everything. The Cardinal has vowed that he will destroy her reputation with both the King and the commoners. She will be paraded in disgrace, expelled from the Court, and perhaps even beheaded. Now, what say you, Your Grace?"

"Disgrace the King of France before all the crowns of Europe? Not even the mighty Cardinal Richelieu would dare. What say I to your Cardinal? Tell him that France may do her worst, England shall do her best, and we shall see which one prevails. Now be gone, ere I lock you in the Tower. Felton!"

"Your Grace?"

"Felton, you will take one of my carriages, a driver, and two mounted escorts, and you will conduct Lady de Winter to Dover, where there will be a ship waiting. Go as quickly as possible, purchase horses, food, whatever you need along the way. This woman is not to leave the coach for any reason except to attend to her bodily functions. If she escapes, you will not like the result. That I promise you. Now, take her and be gone!"

"Yes, Your Grace," said Felton.

The duke returned to his previous business, and Felton arranged for the carriage and escort while Patty waited in the small salon. Alone for the first time since she arrived in the vicinity of ancient Camelot, Patty very surreptitiously took the locator beacon out of her pocket and switched it over to homing function. She was instantly rewarded with a steady red LED. "Good," she thought. "That means I'm within a mile of the machine. The closer I get the faster the LED will blink."

Once in the carriage with Felton, with the driver perched on his seat and the two armed guards following behind, Patty very carefully transferred the locator beacon —still on "homing"—from her pocket into the muff in which she had both hands. She held it in such a way that she could see the reflection of the LED on her hand but Felton couldn't see it at all. It remained steady for about half a mile along the road to Dover, then began flashing at an ever-increasing rate.

"If you please, Master Felton," said Patty, "His Grace said I would be permitted to attend to my bodily functions, and I need to do so now. Could you please stop the coach?"

Felton signaled the driver to stop and had one of the guards take Patty behind a clump of trees a bit of a distance from the road. "Would you shame me, sir, by watching me?" said Patty.

"I have to make sure you don't escape. I'm not turning my back on you," responded the guard.

"Well then," said Patty with a teasing smile. "Perhaps there is something we could do together. I am originally from France, and you do know, don't you, that French-women wear no undergarments? Would you like me to show you?"

"You can show me anything you want, but I'm still not letting you go."

Patty coyly unbuttoned her long skirt at the waist and let it drop. The guard's eyes bulged when he saw that she was naked underneath. "There, you see? The stories are true," she said as she bent over to pick up the now discarded skirt. At the same time, she withdrew the throwing knife from her bodice and, quickly straightening, threw it underhanded so it buried itself in the guard's neck, cutting his carotid artery. "Take a good look," she said quietly. "You're never going to see a naked woman again." He was dead within fifteen seconds.

Patty collected her throwing knife, wiping it on the guard's jacket. She quickly stripped the guard of his boots and bloody jacket, which she discarded, and his pants and shirt, which she put on. As soon as she finished dressing, she ran away from the road and turned the locator beacon back to "locate."

JOSE GROANED and opened his eyes. What had awakened him? He had only put his head down for a moment...

"*¡Ay, Dios mío!*" he said to himself in the Spanish he used now with decreasing frequency, "the locator is actively homing. Patty must be near the machine!" He grabbed the direct line to Jessica's bedroom. It rang as soon as he picked it up. She answered on the second ring, sleep still in her voice.

"Yes, Jose?"

"Come down quickly. Patty has found the machine."

She didn't bother to answer, but he heard her feet flying down the stairs. "Is she here?"

"No, not yet. She seems to have located the machine, and I would think she'll be on her way back as soon as possible."

Jessica, ignoring the fact that she was only wearing a robe, grabbed Jose and hugged him, saying, "Thank you, thank you, thank you."

Jose, not minding in the least the fact that Jessica was wearing only a robe, disentangled the two of them. She was tempting, but he was sixty-two, and she was thirty and his boss. She paid him a huge amount of money, enabling him to live quite well, thank you, in one of the most expensive cities on earth, but there was nothing there, and he knew it. "Save it for Patty, Jess. I'm sure she'll be looking forward to getting back."

Jessica looked at him, still smiling. Then suddenly, she couldn't see him, and then, just as suddenly, as the generators kicked in, she could again.

"Son of a bitch!" swore Jose. "There goes the damned power again. Why in the hell can't PG&E keep the electricity on?"

"It's their stupid green energy," said Jessica.

"Well, I hope their green energy hasn't made us lose Patty again."

Jessica's face went pale, even in the emergency light. "Oh God, Jose. Check."

Performing the same calculations he had earlier, Jose quickly determined that Patty was in 1628, at a location of 50.48 north and 01.05 west. "She's in Portsmouth, England, in 1628," he said.

"It still fits," said Jessica.

"What does? That *Three Musketeers* stuff? Come on, Jess. That isn't real."

"Jose, I showed you yesterday. It does too fit. She went from Paris to Whaddon near ancient Camelot, but also where the Duke of Buckingham lived. Now she's in Portsmouth where the Duke was murdered in 1628. Don't you see? She's Milady de Winter!"

"Jessica, I've read *The Three Musketeers*, too. Milady de Winter didn't kill the Duke of Buckingham. John Felton did. In August of 1628. That much is real life. The rest of your conjecture is just that: conjecture."

"Oh, my God," exclaimed Jessica, as if she hadn't heard anything Jose said, "Jose, we've got to get her back home again, and really fast. After the Duke is murdered, she goes back to France and poisons d'Artagnan's girlfriend, Constance, and gets tried by the musketeers and sentenced to death, and then the headsman of Lille cuts off her head! We've got to get her back."

"Jessica, we'll get her back. I promise. All we have to do is temporalize the machine again just like we did last time. Then she can find it and get back here."

If PG&E can keep the electricity on for more than five minutes at a time, he thought.

AS SOON AS Patty found the machine, she quickly checked it for damage. Finding no obvious problems, she entered and set the controls to return to the twenty-first century. As she entered into the time continuum, she heard the cries of the other guard as he discovered his murdered companion. She laughed, thinking, "Too late, cocksuckers. I'm going home!" As soon as the thought formed in her mind, she felt another of the now-familiar bumps, much like the one that landed her in Paris. "Shit!" she thought. "Now fucking what?"

She opened her eyes, regaining consciousness. She couldn't see very much, only the wooden wall in front of her. "Horse shit?" she thought. "Why do I smell horse shit?" She sat up and looked around her, quickly discovering the answer. She was in a small horse stable. "Well, that explains the smell," she thought. "Now, where and when am I?" She carefully arose and looked out through a narrow space between the wallboards of the stable. "Well, judging from the way people here are dressed, I'm still in the seventeenth century. Summertime, I would guess from the green leaves on the tree across the street, and still England by the language."

Patty checked her immediate surroundings, too. No sign of the time machine, but she was still dressed as before and still had her weapons: the throwing knife and the knife she had taken from the dead guard.

She didn't have the locater! Oh, thank God—yes, she did. There it was, almost buried in the hay where she had lain. She turned it on, and it immediately scrolled the digits 1*6*2*8 and then 5*0.4*8*N*0*1.0*5*W.

"I'm getting really tired of this electric flux shit. Now, the damn machine has probably gone nontemporal, and I'll have to wait for Jose to temporalize it again. At least I know when I am and have some idea where." She carefully buried the locater under a pile of hay and horse manure in the far corner of the stable. "Now," she thought, "let's go and see exactly where we are."

She cautiously opened the stable door, and then went out into the street. There were groups of armed soldiers, mostly heading toward the waterfront. She couldn't exactly see the water, but she could see the forest of tall masts, which told her she must be in... "Portsmouth," she thought. "I'm in Portsmouth. In the summer of 1628. I wonder if this is the date of Buckingham's murder. If so, then Felton is somewhere close by, and he will recognize me. Maybe I'd better just wait in the barn until Jose re-temporalizes the time machine."

Before she could turn, however, she felt the sharp point of a sword in her back, and then another. "Turn very slowly and carefully, Milady de Winter. I'm sure His Grace, the Duke of Buckingham, will be delighted to see you again." It was the voice of Felton. "And he'll give me quite the reward as well."

Her first thought was to run, but she immediately dismissed it. They knew the city, and she didn't, and she needed to know exactly what she faced. She turned to face Felton and the guard from the carriage, both with drawn swords. Then, she felt another sword point in her back. "You needn't look over your shoulder, Milady. The sword you feel is wielded by the brother of the man you killed last winter. Ironic, isn't it, Lady de Winter, that the two brothers of the man you killed should now have you cornered? I know not how you fled the scene of your foul deed before the day of our Lord's birth, but you shall pay for your crime when I present you to His Grace, the Duke of Buckingham. Come, he holds court in yon public house."

Felton led the four of them back to the main street, up to the door of Ye Spotted Dogge Inne. Patty thought the doorway would be her first chance to escape, but there she was taken by the arms by two very large, very strong men and, with two swords now at her back, she was almost thrown into a chair, her two knives taken from her. "If what's coming is what I think is coming, I'll escape in the chaos," thought Patty.

Just at that moment, the Duke of Buckingham came out of the kitchen. "God's bones, but I tire of having to instruct the cooks in their jobs! And what have we here? Felton, have you finally brought me Lady de Winter? You managed to lose her easily enough during the winter, you bloody bobolyne! It only took you eight months, cumber-world that you are, to find her, and in Portsmouth, too. Had you thought to look here at the start of the new year, you might have kept your commission. Be, however, of good cheer, Felton. For you have brought me this day a prize I have long sought, and one that will hang in the public square ere the sun sets. There, or off the mainmast of my flagship. You were little more than a smell-feast, Milady de Winter, and now you have become a rakefire. Your fire will be put out with the setting sun, that I vow!"

While everyone else was watching Buckingham, Patty was watching Felton and thinking, "He thinks the duke will give him his commission back, but he won't. Oh, my God. He's picking up the knife I took from the guard! He's going to stab the duke with it! This is my chance to get away!"

Felton came towards the duke, holding the knife by his side. When he stood near Buckingham, Felton said, "Am I to understand, Your Grace, that you will not return me my commission, even though I have brought you that which you so desire?"

Buckingham gave Felton a withering look and said, "Return you your commission? I return you nothing, lubber-wort. Away, you scullion, you rampallian! I care no more for you than a fart." Then, he turned away, fixing his attention once more on Patty, who was still being held down in the chair.

He had barely taken one step towards her when Felton was upon him, grabbing him from behind, his arm around Buckingham's throat. "Scullion, am I?" Felton cried. "Rampallian? You'll refuse me my commission? I'll give you a fart, Your Grace, and this too!" And with that, Felton buried the knife up to its handle in Buckingham's side.

Felton dropped Buckingham to the floor and ran towards the kitchen, even as the dying duke cried out, "Villain! Assassin! You have made worms meat of me."

Momentarily forgetting about Patty, everyone else gave either chase or aid to Buckingham. Everyone, that is, except the brother of the dead guard, who stood between her and the street. Little did it do him, as she very quickly kicked him where it would do the most good and ran past him as he grabbed himself and fell moaning to the floor.

"Murder most foul!" cried Patty as she ran through the door. "His Grace, the Duke of Buckingham, is dead! In the tavern he lies, grievously wounded!" Having turned the attention of everyone in the street to Ye Spotted Dogge Inne and away from her, Patty ran to the stable, hoping to retrieve the locater and find the time machine.

When she got there, she could hear the horses all stamping and snorting inside. "What the hell?" she thought, as she unbarred the door from the outside. She had to jump aside as the horses all ran, panic-stricken, into the street.

As she cautiously peered around the door, she let out a bit of a yelp and ran inside. "The machine! Thank you," she offered silently to her ancestors. "Whichever one of you did this! Now, I can get out of this fucking place and go home!"

She quickly grabbed the locater from its hiding place beneath the manure, did a cursory check for damage, set the controls once again for 2022, and headed home.

JESSICA AND JOSE both sat in the basement and waited. "Jose," said Jessica, "has the AC gone off again? It's getting awfully warm down here."

Jose sat up as though he had been stung. "No!" he cried. "The machine is returning."

Jessica jumped up, and Jose warned her "Remember, stay away from the machine until the electric charge is drained out of it. That's what killed that poor woman from the CIA, right in this very room."

"I'll remember," said Jessica, as the heat quickly became almost unbearable. Then, with a clap of thunder, the machine arrived. Patty was home!

Once it was safe, Patty and Jessica rushed into each other's arms, Jessica smothering her wife with kisses. "Jessica shall thank thee, daughter, for us both," thought Jose, paraphrasing Shakespeare. When Jessica and Patty finally separated, he said, "Welcome back. That's not the outfit you left in."

Afterwards, as Patty downed an ice-cold bottle of Tsingtao, she filled Jose and Jessica in on what had happened. "Yes, you do smell a bit of horse shit," said Jose.

"Very funny, Jose," said Patty. "Just for that, Jessica and I are going upstairs to enjoy ourselves, and you can hold your own."

IN THE MORNING, Patty slipped quietly out of bed without awakening Jessica. She didn't shower because she didn't want to smell like soap where she was going. She dressed in clothes fit for fifteen-hundred years earlier, and went down to the basement. Jose was waiting for her.

"Remember," he said. "You're going to check out Morgan le Fey, to see if she is actually Morgana Laffey."

"I know my job, Jose. Let's get me out of here before Jess wakes up." Patty entered the machine, and Jose set the controls, twisting both into the continuum.

Just after Patty disappeared, Jessica came down. "So, Patty's on her way?" she asked. "Good. We need her information. God, Jose. I had such a weird dream last night. It was all about Patty, and she was stuck in seventeenth century France..." Then, she stopped abruptly and stared at the table where her copy of *The Three Musketeers* lay open.

"Oh my God, Jose. It was a dream...wasn't it?"

Biography

Marc Hennemann and his wife live in Nevada with their dog, Ozzie, and their Maine Coon cat, Sugar. The only time traveling he has ever done is from his birthday in 1950 until now. *Milady* is his first short story.

FREE WILL

GREGORY B. TAYLOR

—————

TIME TRAVEL WAS NOT ONLY possible, it had already occurred. Once she accepted that basic premise, everything else fell into place.

This was the truth that led to Marie staring at the six computer screens that afternoon, which displayed the results of her latest calculations. She leaned back in her chair, drawing some strands of her long, dark hair to her mouth to nibble on.

It was a bad habit, but it beat nibbling on her fingernails, which she had long ago decided was worse. Besides, it hardly mattered if this gave her split ends. It's not like anyone came out to visit her anymore.

"So, that's how it's going to be," Marie concluded. She pushed away from the desk in her basement, standing up and heading for the stairs.

She stopped partway. *He*, at least, deserved to know, before she left. Right?

She walked back, grasping the small grey cube next to

her central keyboard. Her personal electronic device. Her constant companion. Not constant since birth, but even then, the six-centimeter-long sides reminded her of the old Rubik's cube she had once played with as a child.

She activated the device, gave the command to follow, and then opened her palm. Her companion now hovered in the air next to her, like the drones of olden times.

Marie turned to stride across the room again, the cube keeping pace. "I'll be leaving shortly, Al," she stated.

"For how long?" the familiar not-quite-electronic voice asked. The sound was accompanied with pulses of a red inner light that more or less synched up with the words.

He sounded male, and was an artificial intelligence—AI —hence her cutesy name for him, 'Al.' As if short for 'Albert.' And while voice technology had advanced to the point where a companion device could sound perfectly human, she preferred to be reminded of the fact that Al was, indeed, artificial.

Did that make her a traditionalist? Was she simply stubborn? Did any of that even matter anymore?

"For forever," she answered, starting up the stairs.

Her companion reacted at first with silence. Seconds passed, at least for her. For Al, this had to be an incredible amount of time in electronic terms. Marie briefly wondered again to what extent such mannerisms had been preprogrammed in, and to what degree Al had simply adapted to her own expectations over the last thirty odd years.

Thirty years.

The thought made her stop in her tracks. She had received Al at fourteen, and he had been her only constant companion ever since. Now, even that was going to change. Was she ready for that?

"Have I displeased you?" Al questioned at last.

"Nope," Marie asserted. She resumed her walk up the stairs, banishing the thoughts from her head. After all, it was not like she had any choice in this. Not now.

"Are you gravely ill?"

"I hope not." She reached the main landing of her house and headed down the hall towards her bedroom.

"Are you getting married?"

Marie stumbled and nearly fell. The unexpected question, combined with the very thought of a permanent hook up with *anyone* these days, of either sex, made her laugh out loud.

She regarded her device, finding she needed to lean up against the wall outside her kitchen until her giggles had subsided. He waited patiently as she did so, rotating around on his axis while floating silently in the air.

"Why, Al. I never knew you had such a quirky sense of humour."

"Marriage is the next most likely reason for you to want to terminate our association," he countered. "Seeing as your new significant other would want you to spend your time with them, and not with me."

"Al, when was the last time I had a real date?"

"One year, two hundred, and thirty-two days ago."

Marie pursed her lips. Damn. Had it really been that long? Who had that even been? James? Sue? "I think that was a one-night stand."

"You called it a date."

"Yeah, well. I tend to use a lot of the wrong words when it involves other people," Marie grumbled. "Since people are such jerks."

"You say that a lot lately. I am starting to wonder if it is for my benefit so that you can sneak off and see people when I am inactive."

Marie eyed him. "Al, come on. You know I have no need for people. If they're not displeased about my sexuality, then they're attacking my ethnicity instead. Or, if it's not those, the issue is my personality. Hell, the only thing people don't attack me for these days are my scientific calculations. Because they know that's one argument they'd never win."

"I understand. Yet is that not what you would say to me if you were inclined to go out and see people on the sly when I am inactive?"

Marie slowly shook her head. "Al, I wish I could figure out when you're actually joking."

"Me too," Al agreed. "I am constantly refining my humour subroutines in order to amuse you."

"Keep working at that."

"It will be difficult to do once you are no longer around."

"Oh. Point," Marie granted. She pushed off the wall and resumed the trek to her bedroom. "Sorry."

Her device kept pace. "So, why are you leaving?"

"Because I have to travel back in time to convince myself that I can invent time travel. Which is, of course, a one-way trip."

"Your efforts have been successful then?"

"Yeah."

"Congratulations."

Marie looked over her shoulder. "One moment. Al, why was marriage a more likely scenario to you than me succeeding in my research?"

"Merely because I did not realize that you would leave immediately upon your success. Speaking of which, why is it you need to leave today?"

"Predestination paradox. Look it up."

Al went silent again. This time, he was probably connecting to the Cumulus Cloud or whatever they called the information branch of what used to be the World Wide Web these days. She hated that human beings had this need to constantly update the perfectly good names they had already decided on for technology. As if they were trying to escape the past. For all the good that ever did.

Marie reached her bedroom. She pulled the curtains closed, then kicked off her slip-on shoes.

She idly wondered why she had even bothered to cover the window. She had no neighbours, not this far out in the woods. Her latest food delivery had come two days ago. There was no reason for anyone to be out there.

What was she worried about, peeping squirrels? Seemed like the societal expectations regarding impropriety were inescapable, even now.

"This does not compute," Al concluded.

Marie began to undress, pulling down her jeans. "How do you figure?"

"I have found no reason you need to leave today."

She straightened to pull off her shirt, kicking her pants aside. "The hardware for the time machine is already in place, you know that. The problem was the equations. And I solved them today. I even double-checked, just to be sure."

"But, you did not expect to solve them today."

"I guess not. How is that relevant?"

"You are changing your clothes."

"No duh, Al. What of it?" Marie threw her shirt overtop the little device. The cube's hover position descended by about a half metre. It had to be another attempt at a joke; the extra weight was not sufficient to affect Al's hover capabilities that much.

"A predestination paradox, or causal loop, is a form of

paradox that occurs because there is no apparent source for an item or concept," Al clarified. He was trying to make his voice sound muffled.

Marie rolled her eyes. "Stop clowning around. Also, I already knew that. Obviously." She headed for the closet, deciding not to bother swapping out her underclothes.

"For instance," Al said, more clearly, "you are given a ball today, and at some future point, you travel back in time to give yourself the ball. The item hence has no origin."

"Al, you don't have to explain it back to me," Marie said. "It's what I used to complete the equations. Once I realized that I was the one who spoke to me back when I was twelve, everything else fell into place."

She pulled out her red dress. Not an item of clothing she would normally choose to wear. It's not that the skirt portion was too short, or that the neckline was too low—in such cases, she never would have bought it in the first place—she had simply never found dresses to be comfortable.

She looked to her jeans on the floor, then back to the dress. Between it and the conversation with Al, this was becoming more real.

Al spoke again. "You claim to recall a sharing of information with yourself rather than a concrete object. But whether the paradox is information or an object, you seem to have missed out on the fact that you retain certain aspects of free will."

Marie fingered her dress. "Except I don't," she asserted. "It's funny. My family has always told me to give up this research, right? Telling me that I was wasting my life. That I should find a nice full-time job, become more social, and basically turn my mental capabilities and quirky nature towards something of actual material worth. Which is the same messaging I then got from colleagues and prospective dates as time went on."

She half smiled, pulling the dress against her body.

"Except for that one time, when I was twelve. The only time in my whole life that anyone, adult or otherwise, *ever* believed I had this in me." Her smile vanished. "So of course, it turns out that, by listening to the older lady in the red dress and by believing in her words that day, I sealed my own destiny. And in all my life, the only person who ever had faith in me...was future me. A closed loop." She swallowed. "People are such jerks."

"This still does not compute."

Marie shook her head to clear it. "You're not making sense," she objected. She began pulling her dress on, over her head. "I fixate on this random woman's faith in me. I eventually solve the equations. I travel back in time to tell myself to never give up on time travel. Loop closes, end of story. So, what's your beef?"

"There is no reason you need to leave today."

"I just *told* you—"

"There is no reason you need to leave *today*," Al insisted.

Marie finished pulling her arms through and adjusted the shoulder straps of her dress as it fell into place. A dress she had only bought because it had reminded her of that woman who had spoken to her, in her youth.

She then eyed her shirt, still hovering at waist level, before walking over and snatching the article of clothing off her personal device. Al rose higher into the air again.

"Wait. You're saying that, when I got dressed this morning, because I didn't choose to wear the clothes I'd be wearing to time travel, that means I don't need to time travel?"

"Correct. Not today."

"What the hell is the point in waiting?"

The red light inside her device flashed silently a few times without vocalization. Was he trying to find the right words? "What the hell is the point in not waiting?" Al finally asked.

Marie found she could only stare.

"Besides, the human memory is fallible," Al added. "Perhaps that dress is not, in fact, accessorized the same way as it was when you saw it over thirty years ago. Perhaps your hair is not yet the correct length. Perhaps you need to take more time to think things through. There is no reason you need to leave today."

"Y-You can't be saying you'll *miss* me," Marie protested, dumbstruck. "I'll deactivate you. You won't know! Besides, I'm always either grousing and complaining at you, or whining and moaning about how lonely I am and how much I need to stop reading those god-awful romance books in my free time. You should be glad to be rid of me."

Al rotated in the air. "I am not emotionally impacted by your departure one way or the other. I am merely saying that there is no logical reason for you to leave today."

"I can't figure out why you're saying that."

"Nor can I," Al admitted.

Marie realized she was chewing on her hair again, and she made herself stop by forcing her arms to her sides. She went to grab the tool that would allow her to zip up her own dress at the back. Seriously, the sum total of all human knowledge was now accessible via a simple verbal interface, yet there were still no pretty dresses that could self-zip.

"Look, I can't take you with me," Marie sighed. "All electronics get fried. I figured that out years ago. It's a fundamental aspect of the time journey, and the reason why it's one way only. Not even a microchip can come along. Five more days of study, heck, five more years, it won't change that."

"I understand."

"I mean, shielding, maybe," Marie yielded. "You're not that big. But, that's not my area of expertise, which means not only having to *talk* to people again, but also years, *decades* more work. And it wasn't some grey-haired grand-mother talking to my twelve-year-old self. I know that much."

"I am not saying you have to take me with you."

"Then, what *are* you saying?" Marie demanded, now fully zipped. She flung the wire tool towards her bed without even looking, aware that she had become irra-tionally angry.

Again, a pause, then, "I am saying that there is no reason you need to leave today."

"Oh, for goodness—give me something to *work* with here, Al! Do you want a better send off? Should I give you to some nice young girl out there who will appreciate you more than I ever did? Though, it would more likely need to be some thirty-something, because you're not exactly state-of-the-art anymore, even with your upgrades."

"I am fine with being deactivated."

"So, why are you being so damn *argumentative* about this?" She brushed down her dress and placed her palms on her hips, glaring back at Al.

Her personal device now rotated around its axis several times, a sign that Al was struggling to find a human way of parsing a particular concept. At last, the red light pulsed. "You are special," he concluded.

Marie was sure she had misheard. "I am *what*?"

"You are special. If you leave today, no one will know this. Except for me, and I will have been deactivated."

"Oh, I'm special all right. As in special needs."

"That is not what I meant. Perhaps I did not find the correct word."

Marie pinched the bridge of her nose. "Is that what this is about? You think I should be rubbing this discovery in the noses of everyone who told me my research was pointless? That I should stick around to publish a paper? Because I can tell you exactly how *that* will go."

She sat on the edge of her bed.

"My relatives will smile at me, but have no idea what I'm even talking about, like normal. My colleagues will pat me on the back, then rush to apply my methods while hoping they won't ever have to speak to me again, like normal. My detractors will immediately discredit me, pointlessly attacking my sexuality and ethnicity instead of my work, like normal. I won't even score a relationship out of it, because most of the world's population will believe I'm unattainable, while the rest will—like normal—think I'm some hopeless undateable geek!"

Her fingernails dug into her palms.

"Though, apparently, it's been 597 days since my last major night out, so I guess romance should matter less to me these days, huh? God, why do I still read those books?" Marie shuddered. "I don't need a lot of new stress in my life, Al. I don't." She then began to chew furiously on her hair.

"I know. I did not mean to distress you."

"I know you didn't." Marie bit down more gently, before gradually pulling her hair out from between her pursed lips. She stared at the floor. "I know. I'm sorry. Look, I can't stay here. I can't. Now that I know, it has to be today. I need to get out of this life that I created for myself."

Al did not say anything. Marie wondered if it was another extended pause for her benefit, or whether he, in fact, had nothing to add. "I understand now," Al said at last.

"Good."

"But, I do wish others could have seen you as I see you."

Marie curled down towards her knees, pressing her palms to her face. "Yeah, well, surprise. We don't always get what we want in life."

"Indeed. People are such jerks."

She went from being on the verge of tears to laughing out loud, and looked back up at her personal device. "Al, have I ever told you that you're wonderful?"

"Not since our second year of association, when you were fifteen."

"Oh." She realized she felt rather bad about that. "I'm sorry again."

"Do not distress. You have used what I would consider to be synonyms."

"Have I? Well, you're wonderful too. And I should have said that more often."

"You are also wonderful. Perhaps that is the word I was searching for?"

"Perhaps." Marie looked up at him. "Thanks for being here for me all this time. Really. I appreciate it. Even if you didn't have much of a choice about it."

"You are welcome. In fact, I do not think I would have chosen otherwise, had I been given the option." Her personal device floated a bit closer. "May I ask one last thing?"

She nodded and gestured at him to continue.

"What will you do with yourself after you fulfill your predestination paradox?"

It was a good question. "Dunno," Marie admitted. "But

it doesn't matter. Whatever I do, it's already happened, yeah? It's not like I can change the past. Everything's predestined." She stood, drawing in a long breath. "In fact, I'd rather not think about it. Just...I'll be deactivating you now. Okay? And as I said, there's a good chance this farewell is forever."

"All right. Goodbye, Marie Melendiez. It has truly been a pleasure."

"Yeah." She plucked him out of the air, running a finger along one of his edges. "Yeah, it has been for me too. Goodbye, Al. Thank you."

His light pulsed once more, with no accompanying voice. Marie's grip tightened slightly. She unset the follow command, and once it seemed like he would not say anything else, deactivated him.

She then stood there for at least a minute, looking down at the inanimate cube in her hands, before giving it a little hug. Another silly societal expectation, perhaps? But to not acknowledge all their time together in this way, that would have felt wrong.

She carefully placed Al down onto her bed.

"I guess, through it all, you had faith in me as well," she murmured. "And that's not something I ever programmed in. So, I don't know why I never acknowledged it."

She looked over at her desk. Should she leave a note? No, anyone who knew her would deduce what had happened. And anyone who did not know her would not care.

She looked at her closet. Were there any nonelectronic things she should try to bring along with her? Again no, there really was no point. Was there?

She slipped her shoes back on, tapping her toes on the

ground. Should she have a snack? No, no. The longer she waited, the more anxious she might become.

"This isn't a big deal. It's all predestined," she reminded herself aloud.

Once she walked out of the bedroom, she never looked back.

With the hardware already in place, it only took a few hours to configure the system, based on what she had now discovered. Namely, a way to target a point in space-time. Without that target, she might have finished her time trip on the wrong side of the sun, seeing as everything moving through time also moved through space as well.

Now? She simply had to aim for her twelve-year-old self. Which she could do, as they both had the same genetics. Which was why she was the only one who could even make this trip.

In retrospect, Marie wondered how could she have missed this piece for so long.

The only hitch was that she could not target the exact time her younger self had been in the park that day. There would be a margin of error of several minutes or more. Not helping was the additional human concepts, like daylight savings time. Seriously, whoever had invented that one needed a slap upside the head.

Still, Marie was not too concerned as she stepped up on the platform. She had not even run a test trip, as she knew this would work. It had no choice *but* to work. Right? Predestination. Her trip was fated to work. It had to be so.

The timer hit zero before she could reach for her hair.

Marie saw, more than felt, the bizarre sensation of the world accelerating out from underneath her, even as she stood perfectly still. She quickly closed her eyes, surprised to have not lost consciousness.

The next thing she knew, she was falling. She landed on the earth, somewhere outside, in a bush.

"Ow," she mumbled. She slowly picked herself up, brushed herself off, and looked around. Yes. Yes, this was the park she remembered. She had done it.

And yet, there was another surprise. Not the landing itself, as she had been aiming high. Targeting the ground would have been as difficult a task as targeting an exact minute.

No, the surprise was that the sun was lower in the sky than she had anticipated.

How could the margin of error have dropped her off so late? Should it not have been early instead, to give her time to get into position? Was it possible to have misremembered aspects of this pivotal event in her life?

The initial surprise, however, was nothing compared to the reaction she had upon catching up with her younger self.

Because there she was, young Marie, sitting on the park bench. Talking to a woman in a red dress. A woman that was definitely someone else. A woman who was a bit taller than Marie remembered, with hair that was a bit too short, plus the dress was a different shade of red, and what the hell did this mean?

Wait, *had* someone else truly believed in her back then?

Marie's eyes watered as, all at once, she realized something. How every individual's own perception of the world could become full of distortions.

Which left her here. The equations had worked, and yet she had retained free will.

This changed everything.

Biography

Gregory B. Taylor is a serial writer and high school mathematics teacher living in Ottawa, Canada. His interest in time travel comes from growing up with *Back to the Future, Bill & Ted* and *Quantum Leap*. He has contributed numerous articles to the Time Travel Nexus (TTN) online, and was once a top finalist for Ink & Insights—Apprentice submissions.

He has been personifying mathematics equations (math-tans) since 2011, and maintains a website with regular updates for serial fiction at: https://mathtans. wordpress.com/

UNLICENSED CHILD

SUSAN HANCOCK

DOMUM-ORBIS in the Auriga Constellation

Liv

When your mother was a convicted spy, and your father was just some poor, unsuspecting man she'd tricked into having sex with her—hypnotised him 'til he thought she was his wife—you could be forgiven for growing up with a jaded view of life and your place in it. Oh, and did I mention they were both executed—at different times—in the no-where, no-when rift in the tower the elite-women use as a training facility? The rift held at bay with a force field; the one rift that can never be closed.

My other mother, my mother's life-partner Isabel, did her best. She loved me, like she loved my birthmother, but I was an unlicensed child. An abomination who had not been granted permission to exist, according to the ruling military.

She tried to hide me in the basement tunnels of the Elite-Women's Facility (the legendary EWF), but we were betrayed. Not all the women on short-term training contracts were loyal to her. When I was six years old, soldiers supporting the Central Committee dragged me off to one of the compulsory worker-training academies that consented to teach unlicensed children. I wasn't permitted to see her after that.

At the academy, we were a rough lot, a mixed-gender bag of random anomalies, slung together to prevent us from contaminating those with pure bloodlines and fixed, graded abilities to contribute to the workforce. When they'd taken me away, Isabel had whispered to me to hide my inherited empathic abilities. If they thought I might understand too much about those in authority, hypnotise men as my birth-mother had, the Central Committee would have had me hauled up in front of judges; those who could be guaranteed to find an easy excuse for why this child and that shouldn't live to perpetuate their parents' so-called crimes.

At the academy, I found I wasn't alone in hiding my birth gifts: Vess was the unlicensed daughter of a rift-opener. Her father was a nobody, and her mother wanted nothing to do with any unlicensed offspring who might mess up her ambitions for a future, which included an advantageous ultra-elite match. She'd paid bribes to keep it quiet, sending Vess to a baby farm for low-grade workers. Like me, Vess had been warned to keep her mouth shut and hide her potential talent. Two misfits with secrets, thrown together in a harsh system that despised us all. Friendship was inevitable.

Beyond our initial bonding, it was soon clear that friendship was key to survival in the harsh institution in which we were trapped. Gradually, we two became four, became six, as others I'd initially dismissed as boring and ordinary proved trustworthy and essential to the wellbeing of our group. My reading of emotions came in handy when checking out those who joined us. We gelled well together, keeping ourselves as separate as possible from anyone we feared might tell tales to the authorities about our inborn abilities.

Our other bond was that we were all equally determined to escape before the end of our tenth and final year of schooling. After that milestone, any of us could be terminated or sent to the deadlier work camps, those with lower than six-month survival rates, or worse, worker-breeding programs. Escape would be difficult, but it was feasible. Vess and I had the combined mind-skills to make it happen. Quinn, Tibor, and Gus had muscle if it was needed. Aelia was sneaky and clever. We could do it. If we could only get to the EWF tower, Isabel would help us. Assuming she remembered me. She loved me, she would definitely remember...

***

GROUNDS of the academy for unlicensed children, Domum-Orbis central landmass: present-day for Liv, aged fifteen years

***

Liv

Tibor found us a new meeting place. There was work going on in the basement boiler-rooms, where we usually met, so they were ruled out. Honestly? I couldn't help but be relieved, since I'd hypnotised the technician there too many times already. He thought I fancied him—entirely my fault—making him overfond of taking little liberties when no-one was around. But gloss over that—I didn't want the others to know my interference with his mind had potentially unpleasant consequences for me. Quinn would definitely have objected to me taking the risk again if he knew. So close to the end now. This night was to be our last meeting before "Escape Day", as we'd prematurely named it. We would all be turning sixteen over the next few weeks, so it was now or never.

It was only going to be a planning meeting, so we had nothing with us. Not that we owned much, but we had augmented our meagre possessions with pilfered items: survival rations, clothing, and six official ID blanks, stolen from one of the many boxes stored in the basement. They were ready to create actual ID cards for leaving students, and I thought we could probably forge something for ourselves. But none of these useful items were with us as we crouched behind the maintenance man's equipment store—the place Tibor had suggested.

The store was in a hidden corner of the grounds, next to the security fences of the inner perimeter, and seemed as good as any. But—no excuses—we were overconfident, careless, and hadn't reckoned on the possibility of there being an extra patrol. Thank goodness for Aelia's sharp hearing and whispered warning. Today was going to have to be "Escape Day." Ready or not.

"Do it, Vess. They're bound to spot us. If we don't get away now, they'll make sure we're locked in the cell block until we're transferred." Tibor spoke for us all.

Vess was shaking, but she stood, closed her eyes and reached her arms out, releasing the power-entity living inside her to tear open a rift. I'd seen it done before, in the

EWF tower, but I was the only one who had. More importantly, this was the first time for Vess's inborn power to manifest itself, a do or die moment for her. We stood in a protective ring around her, but standing made us visible against the skyline. Could've done without such bright twin-moons on this of all nights.

Of course, the approaching guards saw us and broke into a run, shouting as they pounded across the hard-packed earth, weapons drawn. The other four continued to shield Vess as she struggled to pierce time and hold the rift open. I stood apart and focused on the minds of the guards. To give Vess time, I had to soothe the level of aggression—make the guards feel as if we might legitimately be there, doing something totally innocuous. My vision flashed and blurred with the effort as I forced my mind to grapple with theirs. Far too many of them for me to be wholly successful, but I could sense a definite response: at least now they were hesitating and ready to ask questions, rather than firing to kill, as they'd intended when they initially spied us.

It bought Vess sufficient time to open a way through, but lurking in the back of my head, even as I released the guards' minds so I could follow, was the horrible realisation that I hadn't had time to implant the tower coordinates in her mind. It had been on the agenda for our meeting. Where else could she take us? Vess, literally, had no "where" to go to. Her only option was a "when" on this exact spot, a some-when which could be guaranteed to pre-date these existing buildings. The snag? Travelling into the past on Domum-Orbis was illegal and supposedly incredibly dangerous. The illegal didn't matter so much—escaping from the academy was illegal enough to potentially cost us our lives anyway—but what if the rift opened into no-when, a time before this world existed? Like the one in the tower.

Liv, hurry, I can't hold this much longer; the others are through. Vess's voice seemed like a strange echoey sound inside my head. I felt hands yanking me bodily into the grey, shimmering oval of the doorway. Quinn. Violent pain shot through my leg, then darkness.

DOMUM-ORBIS CENTRAL LANDMASS: a time long before the academy for unlicensed children existed

---

Quinn

It was horrible. First thinking the soldiers would catch her, then hearing the shot and her scream, now seeing Liv lying unconscious on the grass with blood flowing from a wound in her leg. Judging by the wild surrounds—I'd never seen the like before—there wasn't going to be any help for her here. Wherever "here" was. Somehow, Vess had got us away, and she was collapsed on the ground too, exhausted by her incredible feat.

Goodness only knew how far back we were in the past of our planet. Not what any of us would have chosen. It was simply what we had to deal with, and Liv's life might be the forfeit if we couldn't find some way of helping her. It looked as if the hole in her leg had been ripped open by some kind of projectile. The sort of old technology the military was reportedly trying to re-develop, because elite-women could now interfere with the mind-operated weapons they'd been using.

Stripping my tunic off, I made a thick pad of it to staunch the bleeding. While I held Liv in my arms, Aelia tied the pad in place with strips torn from the tunic Tibor had also contributed.

Before we were done, Vess had recovered and was anxiously hovering over us. "How bad is she? If she recovers consciousness, she'll be able to transfer the EWF tower image and coordinates into my mind, like we originally planned. If I can transport her there, I know her mother will help."

"Are you sure you'll be able? What if we've changed something by travelling so far back? It's supposed to be dangerous." Gus sounded gloomy. "What if we're stuck here with no food, shelter, or water? Liv'll die first, and then the rest of us."

Tibor gave an angry snort. "That's cheerful. I'll scout around, see what's here."

Before he could leave, Liv moaned and shifted in my arms, opening her eyes. Vess leaned forward to grab her attention.

"Liv...we need to get you to the tower. Let me into your mind, and I'll know where to open the rift to."

Liv made a weak sound, blinked, and looked straight at Vess. The intensity of Vess's gaze made me hope the transfer had taken place. That, and my crossed fingers.

"If you open the rift, I'll carry her through. We'll have to take a chance. The soldiers may already be there looking for us." No way was anyone else taking her. Fortunately, no one objected.

Tibor lifted Liv, and I stood up so that he could transfer her back into my arms. Vess was already in her trance, arms outstretched and total concentration on her face as the power pulsed through her. It took so long...I didn't dare imagine how far back in time we were. Then, a room shimmered into misty view beyond the doorway in front of us.

"It's the tower," Liv whispered.

I launched us through the rift. Vess was struggling with the effort again, and I felt it close behind us. I hoped, for the sake of the others, that someone in the tower could breach the distance back to them.

EWF TOWER, Domum-Orbis: later on, "Escape Day"

Liv

Ten-years-away faded into nothing in my mind as Quinn laid me down on the familiar couch in the dream-creation laboratory. The outer door burst open, and Isabel was there, together with another woman I didn't recognise.

"Liv! You're hurt. You know they're already here looking for you?" My other mother rushed towards me, while her companion stood back, with the door partly open, presumably checking the corridor outside.

"How long do we have?" Quinn spoke before I could. "There may be something lodged in her leg, something the soldiers fired. And we've ended up so far in the past there's no help available. It's a wilderness—crammed with tangled bushes and massive trees. Nothing like the indoor trees the ultra-rich families buy as ornaments."

"Flavia, get me an emergency medical kit from the infirmary, please. I'm going to move us back a week. Follow the trace through when you've collected everything necessary." That was Isabel. My mamma. Always ready for anything.

"It was quiet here last week. No dream-creation contracts—the Central Committee has put a temporary ban on our work in creating habitats. They want to revive old, manual building techniques, cutting us out. My last intake of students completed their training and moved out a couple of weeks ago, so we should be undisturbed. I can work out the times when I wasn't in here." She opened a rift in her easy, lazy style, and ordered Quinn to carry me through.

And then I was on the same couch, but a week earlier. I didn't feel any different or better. No miraculous undoing of the injury, but that wasn't how rifts worked on living individuals. If it had been, we'd have died long before reaching the past my friends were currently waiting in. It was an effort to control my breathing as the pain pulsed sharply. Isabel stroked my hair.

"Flavia will give you something to make you sleep, and she'll deal with your injury. I'll take your friend back to next week and return him to the others in your group with supplies to help you survive."

"How did you know there were more of us...?" I wondered aloud, in a weak voice that didn't seem my own.

"The soldiers came here almost as soon as you escaped. They were looking for three females and three males. But I've been on edge all year, waiting. I knew you'd find some way to avoid the final-year transfer to the camps." Her "efficient" voice softened down to a whisper. "I've missed you so much, you and Blanche. I'm sorry Liv. I could do nothing to save either of you."

"Not your fault." I answered gruffly, the salt of tears in my mouth.

Quinn cleared his throat. "Will you be alright if I go back before you can?" He looked reluctant to leave me.

I waved him away with a pathetic gesture. "I'm fine. Help the others. Isabel will send me back as soon as I'm fit."

I'd not registered, but Flavia had already returned. Done with talking, I took a flask of the drug she held out to me and drained it.

Next I knew, I was tucked up on the bed-shelf in Isabel's room, presumably still safely ensconced in the week before my escape. While my leg was sore and bandaged, and my head still felt fuzzy, I was a lot better than I'd been when I arrived. Hopefully, I would be well enough to return to the others before the week Isabel had carved out for me was up and the soldiers would...had?...come searching. I went back to sleep again.

DOMUM-ORBIS: several thousand years before present day, 1,065 days since "Escape Day"

Liv

I leant back against the bark of one of the more solid tree trunks circling the wet and muddy clearing which housed our camp, preferring to observe the argument raging. Tibor was loud and annoying, as usual, winding Vess up, trying to have the rift-opener in his pocket. Or perhaps his bed. Tibor definitely fancied her. I once suspected Quinn might have felt that way about me. I wouldn't have objected. But Quinn hid his mind, and I didn't force him to open up, as I could have done. Problem was, I had once picked up a stray thought of his concerning my particular skills. A thought which suggested that although he wasn't averse to me, he would never dare take a relationship further because, in the words in his thoughts, *Empath-hypnotists are fucking lethal.*

Wincing at the hurtful memory, I focused back on Tibor and Vess, who were still squabbling. See, that proved the point: I *could* have manipulated their minds, but I would never do that to any of them. *So there, Quinn. Don't judge.* I mentally flipped the finger at him.

"C'mon Vess. Gotta give it a shot."

Tibor was trying his best and getting nowhere. Stupid oaf wasn't going to get his way by bullying. *Shut up Tibor.* Since the debacle of our arrival, Vess was timidity personified, justifiably, even if she did secretly admire Tibor. That was something she'd told me in secret. *She* never suspected me of reading her. I just wished Quinn had given me a similar trust...Like I cared...

Anyway, if he got his head straight, Tibor would be in with a chance of life bonding with Vess. He only had to learn when to shut up. Back in our own time, he'd never have been licensed to bond or breed with anyone. Flamered hair and blue eyes that actually matched the blue upper-body markings we all had? No chance. Those in power aimed to stamp out any deviations from the standardised dark hair and brown eyes—like mine and Vess's, Gus and Aelia's. Rumour had it that blond hair was the latest slated for breeding out, so Quinn would have been unlucky too. Red had been outlawed long since. Tibor and Quinn were both lucky to have ended up in the academy rather than sentenced to the termination rift as unfortunate aberrations. *If* any part of being at the academy could ever be considered lucky.

Thoughts of changing our luck, though, was the very reason I wasn't supporting Vess—love her as I did—and didn't disagree with Tibor. We needed to be somewhere else, somewhere offering more than this half-life. Here, nearly three years on, we were existing, make that *barely* existing, living hand-to-mouth in a permanent scrubby, shitty campsite, part of a wild landscape we'd none of us experienced before. Not our fault, coming from a future where animals and plants had either been killed off or banished from all inhabited areas of land. When we'd first arrived, it had been so strange to see feral trees, bushes, and animals. Now everything was simply judged as potential food and shelter. Without it, we wouldn't have survived.

The argument continued without me...

Vess glared up at Tibor. "You do it then. You give it a shot, as you call it. I'd like to see you opening a rift to some other time and place in the universe, with no charts or mental images to guide you."

"You fucking well know I can't." Tibor scowled at her. "You're the only one. Just saying...If you don't want to make Liv take endless, risky trips to beg for essentials, then you need to come up with a better plan. That stuff Liv brought back last time is almost gone." As if to prove a point, he jabbed a finger through a ragged hole in his tunic.

Quinn was silent, faking neutral, which had to do with words I'd whispered to him earlier. Yes, we badly needed provisions, but Vess did her best. She was scared shitless at the prospect of launching herself over greater distances into the unknown. Essential if we were to flee off-planet. And who wouldn't be afraid? It was bad enough watching her steel herself to open a doorway into the tower for supplies; we were so far back in time. And the risks of me being caught were staggeringly high, since she could never be sure the tower was secure. It was sheer luck we'd not run into soldiers when she first opened the way after my injury. Isabel always covered for me and gave us plenty, but she couldn't guarantee my safety, and we hadn't wanted to take advantage. Only six trips to scavenge provisions in all the time we'd been hiding in the past.

I'd had enough of the quarrel. This was the moment to air my plan, the one I'd shared with Quinn in a quiet moment. He was expecting it and moved forward when I winked. I crossed fingers and spoke as calmly and quietly as I could.

"How about we ask Isabel to lend us one of the EWF rift-openers? She may even come herself. If you send me to the tower, I could bring her back with me. You can talk to her, Vess, try to find a destination she can help us travel to. They still have star charts in the dream-creation room. When my leg was healing during that stolen week, I heard mention that they'd rescued some of the otherworld-history books and other gear when the university was destroyed."

I felt the emotional support of Quinn silently applauding my words, waiting to see who'd be in and who'd need persuading.

"How can we be sure anywhere's safe for us? It's too much of a risk for all six of us to suddenly appear together in some strange place. Suppose we run into Aurigan soldiers visiting that same planet and time on one of their searches for work-camp slaves? You told us your father was once kidnapped from another world." Gus sounded dubious, with the worried frown that was always on his face carving even deeper lines than usual.

"I'm with Liv." Tibor made his views felt forcefully. "We have to take the risk. We can't go on like this. There aren't enough of us to create a viable colony. We can't go back and live in our own time either. We're fucked unless we can get off-planet."

"The longer we're settled here, the greater the chance of

us doing something that messes with the timeline of our planet. Better to get away and leave the past in the past." At last, Quinn joined in, using the argument I'd already put to him.

"There's no one and nothing here to mess *with*. And at least we'll still be alive." That was Aelia, and she was clearly against.

"No, we won't be alive," Tibor said angrily. No prizes for guessing that Aelia and Gus were getting on his nerves. "We'll get sick from the poor diet, or we'll catch some disease and die. We risk our lives every day, just by being here."

He was right. So far, simply to survive, we had to spend all the daylight hours hunting, fishing, foraging for just about anything to supplement the dried field rations which Isabel scavenged for us from the EWF allocation. Even with her help, there was scarcely enough to eat. Right from the beginning, we'd have been sunk without everything she provided: survival camping bubbles to live in, clothing, water purification tablets, crates of vacuum-packed food-supplements, otherworld hunting equipment. Tibor might not be the most tactful one of us, but he was the most realistic, and wasn't afraid to speak his mind.

Vess gave Tibor one of those looks, sighed, and capitulated. "Fine....We'll send Liv to the tower and see what she can negotiate for us." She gave me a sidelong glance. "So long as nothing happens to me, we can always come back if we end up somewhere worse than this." No smile for me, definitely angry I hadn't confided in her. She was getting more and more prickly as our stay here stretched out, knowing she was the only one who could change things. Perhaps I was prickly too, knowing I couldn't.

Time enough to mollify her later. Now that Vess agreed in principle, the argument was surely won.

"I know Isabel will do everything she can," I tried to reassure everyone. "She's offered before. It's only that Vess wasn't ready to make such a huge leap."

Fuck. I didn't mean to criticise, but I could see that was how Vess was taking it, so I hurried on. "I don't blame you, Vess. It would have been madness for us to go unprepared. We'll completely depend on you to get us back if it all goes wrong. It's a lot of pressure. Goodness knows, we're grateful to you for saving us when we first escaped, and I'm totally in debt to you for saving my life when you got me to the tower after I was shot." Hopefully, that would do it, and Vess would take the olive branch. This was one of those times when it would have been useful to have put aside my scruples and used my skills to bring Vess fully on board. But I wasn't going there. That was an ethical line I wasn't prepared to cross.

"Votes for asking the tower to help us travel to another time and place." Quinn was fed up with the arguing and took the initiative. "I vote yes." Gradually every member of the group raised a hand. We were going to try.

It was the only option that made any sense.

THE EWF TOWER: present-day, 1,065 days since "Escape Day"

Liv

Quinn and I entered the rift quickly. I hadn't wanted

him there, but he'd insisted. Trying to dissuade him was more trouble than it was worth. I turned to look back through the haze swirling in to fill the space behind me. We'd have been lost without Vess, however scared she was. At least she could close the rift for now. Isabel would open the return one when we were ready.

The tower was deserted, but I was certain some kind of alarm activated when an incoming rift opened. Each time we'd arrived, Isabel had joined us almost immediately. It was safest not to go looking for her in case of soldiers. I could probably handle them myself, but Quinn would be a problem, since I was always best working alone. And I didn't want Quinn to see what I might need to do if challenged. Hypnotic seduction was the most common trick an empath-hypnotist had available—an intrusive interference with another's mind, body, and emotions. Not pleasant to see, or do, but strictly necessary to keep loved-ones safe from the ever-suspicious soldiers who supported the regime running this god-forsaken world. It was annoying and humiliating the way people admired everything a rift-opener could do, while my birthmother's legendary ability to distract the guards while the work-camp rescues were in progress—that was regarded with distaste and sneers. My father's wife was the hero of the day, my mother was apparently a slut, and it was her skills which I'd inherited. I was proud of them. So, don't ask me why I didn't want Quinn to see them in operation.

As predicted, no sooner did I think of Isabel than the door opened, and she walked in with an old friend. Seeing their smiles, we moved out from the shadowy corner we'd retreated to when the footsteps neared. Quinn's arm had wound around my waist in our brief alarm, but I detached myself from him and ran to hug her and her companion. I remembered Mathias from my childhood, and there he was —scarcely looking his fifty-plus years. Isabel's shadow-protector.

She eyed me anxiously. "You're looking thin and tired. It's been a long time since you last came for supplies. How are you finding your camp? Is it too rough?"

"That's why we're here today. We're in a state, come to beg you to get us away somewhere else and destroy the trace of our destination. I know you have all the star charts here."

"There's always Earth," she said thoughtfully. "I don't know where Kat and your father sent the contingent from there, but Matt..." She hesitated and turned to him. "You must have images stored from that time and place in your head. Perhaps move the dates a little further forward in the lives of friends who chose to settle away from the complex Kat constructed."

Mathias smiled at me and nodded. "Reckon between us, we could work something out... not risking the exact location, but getting somewhere safe that's near and lines up my bodily age now with what it would be if we were following my timeline on Earth."

"Vess is nervous. Could we travel from the past, where we are now, and borrow one of your people to actually open the rift? I know...before...when they...when my father and his wife had to do what they did... you were worried about the soldiers making you give up their coordinates."

"We were all under siege then. Nowadays, the soldiers assigned to the facility have grown bored, and those in charge are too short staffed to keep such a close eye on us. No one knows you were even here, so no one will come asking if you leave. Add the fact, you're travelling from deep in the past, and I can't imagine how it could attract any attention. You'll still be on their 'wanted' lists, but the initial hunt has long since died down. Tell your friend she won't have to open the rift. Someone here can do that for you. But remember, if you run into problems once you're there, she'll be your only hope of returning. If you're heading for seventeenth-century Earth, it's a massive leap in time and space. Your half-sibling, Liss, and her mother, were exceptionally talented. Not every untrained rift-opener would be capable of doing what they did."

"Well, I'll try not to frighten Vess with the thought of all that responsibility." I gave a wry grin. "She's flaky enough about us doing the deed, without more worrying thoughts to hold her back." I felt the warmth of Quinn's arm return around my waist again.

Isabel nodded, and Mathias spoke reassuringly, "Don't worry. Let me chat with her. I'm sure I can help a lot with destination images and contacts for you to make when you get there. If you like, I'll travel with you. I make a good protection detail—not too old to fight if need be. There are ruffians on Earth, same as everywhere. Your Vess knows the coordinates, so she can send me back as soon as I've introduced you to everyone and got you settled."

The flaw in that would be if Vess couldn't hack the return. I knew I should say, *"No, we'll be fine,"* but the thought of him being with us was too comforting. Quinn didn't seem to find it comforting, though. He was holding me even closer, and I had the feeling he was not comfortable with either Mathias or Isabel. Possibly because they were a part of my life from before I even knew he existed? There were emotions I could have processed near the surface of his mind, but I kept well away from them. No one else questioned his silence or the way he held tight to me.

It was ages since I'd seen Mathias. I wasn't going to pretend not to be happy at the thought of him coming with us. He'd given up the freedoms of Earth, when he could have escaped, to assist with rescuing others who fell foul of our military rulers. Ethical reasons. But he definitely craved the adventure too. He knew the warren of illicit basement tunnels here like the back of his hand and was always prepared to engage in skirmishes with the soldiers to get those in danger to the hidden underground entrances to the facility and away, later, to safe dwellings. He'd made Isabel's life's mission a hell of a lot more secure and better than it would otherwise have been. And now he was willing to help us to escape.

"Your camp in the past?" he asked unexpectedly. "You've had no problems with travelling there and back to it? Tell me more about what it's like?" I wondered why he was so interested.

"Spartan's the best word. Lake instead of showers, primitive toilet facilities. You would not want to fill in the used holes in the ground when it's your turn, believe me. Unlike the dried and vac-packed stuff from here, food has legs or fins or wings...and moves. We've given it our best, but there are too few of us, or too many, depending on your point of view. We're still reliant on the survival bubbles Isabel gave us for shelter! With the supplies from here, it's manageable. Without, it's not."

Isabel looked disappointed. "I've seen pictures from other planets showing vegetation and animals. Surely it must be beautiful?"

I screwed my nose up. "Beautiful at first sight, maybe, but we're too permanently exhausted to appreciate it. And the dangers are real too. Not all the creatures are friendly— plenty of teeth and claws."

Isabel shut up quickly, looking at Mathias, but not before the germ of an idea had been planted in me. If we were to escape from so far back in the past, our camp might be a viable interim way of hiding those hunted by the authorities—ultimately getting them safely off-planet without leaving a telltale trace. If all the illicit star charts and otherworld-history books were hidden in the past too...? Neither Isabel nor Mathias would ever pressurise us into helping. There were people here capable of dream-creating habitats. But I could help. If we only dared risk the timeline issue and created only a small alteration to the past? And there was no overlap, no chance of being in the same place more than once.

The idea tapped into feelings of guilt. I was doing nothing to aid hunted misfits like me, and everything to find a way for my own privately selected group to leave our problems behind us. If Isabel hadn't been my other mother, we wouldn't be alive. Others deserved life too.

Yet there was the horrible unsatisfactoriness of what we had now. My stomach cramped with anxiety. I was so tired. What if Earth didn't work out for us? I already knew we'd have to disguise the blue markings on our upper bodies, like all Aurigans had to do in more primitive places. If it wasn't viable, we might end up having to return to our camp to find some other way to make it work.

Isabel had decided. "I'll send Flavia with you. You've already met, and I trust her completely. She came with the intake a couple of years back and stayed to help. Kat once chided me for allowing evil to happen. Never again after her...their...sacrifice, and Flavia agrees with me, always at my side."

Isabel stopped and looked at me. An unusual hesitation. She was always such a positive person. Then I felt her emotion and understood: my birthmother had been replaced. I tried a smile to help her go on.

Encouraged, she spoke, almost shyly, "Perhaps you might give us both your blessing. Your mother will always be my first love, but Flavia loves me and makes me happy."

I hid the emotion, but it was a bombshell. It shouldn't matter all this time since her death, but it felt like another reason to be gone from here. Perhaps Isabel wanted to be rid of me and the unwelcome memories I must awaken in her.

She wasn't an empath, but she must have sensed my thoughts. Next thing, she had me in a hug and opened her mind to me, allowing me to see the love for me and for my birthmother, love which had never gone away. I was comforted, perhaps even more guilty at the thought of leaving her behind.

DOMUM-ORBIS: several thousand years before present day, 1,066 days since "Escape Day"

Quinn

Before we returned, Isabel gave us access to a secret stash of clothing from our proposed destination. Presumably a legacy of those who'd come and gone from its shores in the past. Before our war, Earth had evidently been a favourite short-stay visit for anthropologists in the otherworld-history department. Afterwards, most of the University was ransacked and destroyed, but not before Isabel's followers had stolen away everything relating to useful time periods and places. All really helpful to us now.

Flavia was the rift-opener who returned with us. Liv's special friend, Mathias, came too. He made me feel uncomfortable, like he was Liv's dad and I was some boy found wanting. Probably my imagination, but Liv worshipped him as if he was this legendary figure. I wondered if she'd look at me like that if I volunteered to stay behind and fight. Neither of our visitors looked very impressed with the encampment. Let *them* try to do it any better.

How he managed it I don't know, but in a very short time, Mathias ironed away all Vess's doubts, and Tibor, watching Mathias, *finally* got the message that Vess did better if she wasn't being pressured. His turnaround to being ultra-supportive was nothing short of miraculous. It helped that Flavia was taking Vess through all the training she would have received at the EWF if she'd gone there as a licensed elite-woman.

While I never knew what I'd done to make Liv so wary of me, I was working on changing her mind. I cared about her too much to give up. Looking at Tibor and Vess's new relationship was encouraging. If the others paired up, it could do no harm to my chances.

Time was speeding past, and the two from the tower kept us better supplied with food and clothing. Even so, there was still nothing here to recommend staying on.

1,095 days. I was counting. And then it was time.

Flavia opened the rift. I could appreciate it more since this wasn't Vess riddled with nerves; for once, we weren't being rushed. The air crackled with the heat of an almost invisible flow of flame from Flavia's fingertips, as the power-entity inside her swelled and ruptured the atoms of the air, bursting through, ripping a hole in the substance of space-time. It was awe-inspiring, watching her hold the nothing-ness between the stars at bay as the power tunnelled outwards to its destination. And then, it was done, and she was holding a precarious balance.

"Go through now." We sensed Flavia's effort, running forward to obey. No orderly queue, but a mad dash to be some-where and some-when else entirely. Hopefully, a new and better stage in our lives.

ILFRAYCOMBE, England, Earth: seventeenth century in the Earth timeline

---

Quinn

I was stunned into silence. A sea, a ferocious sea, smelling of salt and seaweed and something indefinable, was crashing, hissing, and sucking on the narrow rim of sand, as we stood in the entrance to the cave through which we'd arrived.

Mathias wouldn't let us get our breath back. "Minor miscalculation. The tide's coming in fast. We need to get up from the shore before our access to the cliff path is cut off. Come on, beyond the rocks there. Hurry!" He pointed, and we set off at a jog. Fortunately, we were used to running. Living in the wild had hardened our bodies from the scrawny kids we'd been when the rift first dumped us there.

I looked for Liv to hold her hand, and my heart practically stopped beating. I knew in an instant that she'd made a choice, and I wasn't it. She wasn't there. Not that I couldn't understand how she felt. I felt guilty about leaving, too. But for her to plan and do it without talking to me. Didn't we always talk things through?

Mathias propelled me forward. "Help me with the

others. We can talk when everyone's safe." I hated him. I'd have bet money Liv had talked to *him*.

Aelia was shortest, so Mathias, bringing up the rear, swooped her into his arms since, with each wave, the water surged further and further up our legs. Gus ran with him, and Tibor was almost dragging Vess, who would otherwise have been slower in her water-soaked hampering skirts. I rushed forward, helping him. It was so much easier in the breeches of the day; the skirts the women had to wear were a life-threatening challenge in these circumstances.

Once we were safely onto the cliff path, with the waves lashing at our heels, I turned to Mathias. "Did you know she wasn't coming?" My words sounded belligerent to my own ears. But he seemed to take them in good part.

"I didn't know for sure, but I'm sorry. I did suspect the idea had taken root in her heart."

"When you go back...you *are* intending to go back, aren't you? When you go back, I'm going with you."

"She won't want you to put yourself in permanent danger just because she feels she owes a personal debt to Isabel. You don't have obligations of the kind she feels she does."

"She made a choice for me without asking. She had no right to do that. I love her. If I go back with you, she can tell me to my face if she doesn't want me."

Mathias looked as if he understood. "When everyone is settled, and Vess tries to send me back, I'll warn you. If you still want to come with me, then you'll have the opportunity. But you may change your mind in the meantime." Softening his words, he squeezed my shoulder. "If it helps, I think she should have told you, but I think she did it this way so that you wouldn't feel obligated to stay if you didn't want to. If I know Liv at all, she would have wanted you to be happy. Plus, I suspect she's always feared you don't wholly like her, because of her mind-skills. A lot of people fear and despise empath-hypnotists. Her birthmother suffered constantly from the censure of people who didn't understand her brand of courage. Liv won't want you to return if you can't see beyond what she *has* to do to keep those around her safe."

He couldn't understand that this promised refuge meant nothing to me without her. Sure, humans were compatible with Aurigans, and we could read their minds, giving early warning of suspicion. So what? I wasn't looking for a human female. I wanted Liv, only Liv. I wanted to be with her in a forever life bond. The blue of my markings pulsed and ached for her. What was the point of escaping without the woman...I...I loved? None.

DOMUM-ORBIS: several thousand years before present day, 1,137 days since "Escape Day" (42 days since Quinn left)

Liv

The weeks since my friends left had been busy, but I still missed them. That ache in my chest when I thought of them. But I wasn't being completely honest. Yes, I cared about the others, especially Vess, but what I was really thinking was that each of the forty-two days since Quinn had left felt unutterably lonely. He'd got under my skin stealthily. I was used to talking to him, laughing with him, discussing my plans. I might not have totally trusted him, given that once-expressed opinion on my kind, but it didn't change the threat of tears whenever I thought of him—out there beyond the stars, living in a time and place I would probably never visit. Sometimes my heart felt as if it was trying to stretch out wings and fly into the distance. Hoping to feel his heart beat against mine one more time. I had to hide my shameful sniffles from Flavia and from Isabel when she visited.

But at least I no longer felt guilty. I told myself this endlessly when regrets about my decision prevented me from sleeping, and all I wanted was to persuade Flavia to open that rift again to let me join him. But I couldn't do it. We'd already accomplished so much, she and I working here. And I would be useful back in the facility too...much, much more was needed...would always be needed.

Flavia, with my help, had dream-created a small, viable habitat beneath the ground in our soon-to-be haven in the past. Once the rock-burrowing grubs had done their work, she lay in a drug-induced trance in the remote tower, operating the machines which spewed out the shell of an underground environment in which people could comfortably stay before being helped along our proposed escape route. No one would be there long. This could never be an established community. Too much risk. If the ills of Domum-Orbis were to be addressed, it had to be in its present, our present. Isabel had persuaded me that there could be no safe way of interfering with the past. Too many lives potentially lost or unlived. We could not play God.

So, in my usual melancholy state, I was making a list of necessary equipment, seated on a fallen tree in the camp I once lived in with Quinn and Vess and—

"Look out, incoming rift." I heard Flavia call out from the entrance to our fledgling complex. Presumably,

Mathias had returned. I didn't really want to see him. He was part of the reason I was here and Quinn was somewhere across the universe. Mathias's bravery had inspired me, but he never had to give up a potential relationship like mine and Quinn's. Or, at least, I didn't think he had. That part of Mathias was a private space in which no one trespassed.

A shadow fell over the page I was reading. A familiar shadow? I looked up and saw clenched fists. My heart pounded.

"How could you leave me alone without telling me what you were going to do and why?"

Surely Quinn hadn't travelled all that way back to be angry with me? He was glaring as he thrust a hand through his wild mop of hair, jerkily, making it ten times worse. But his eyes were red-rimmed.

I stood. "How could I pressurise you into staying? You'd be in so much more danger than me. I can always hide in the tower. The soldiers can never tell us women, one from the other. How could I ask you to risk your life?"

"Crap. Didn't I have the right to decide for myself?"

"But would it have been your true decision? Or would you have felt too guilty to go if I'd asked you to stay?"

"Still my choice."

"Yet, you think I'm dangerous. I heard your mind once. I promise it was accidental."

"So that's the grudge you've borne against me all this time?" He sounded horrified. "Yes, I think you're fucking lethal, amazingly, fucking dangerous. It's one of the things I don't know whether to admire in you or feel jealous of. Doesn't mean I think you're dangerous to *me*!"

For once, I allowed myself to experience his emotions— he was so uncertain of my feelings for him, yet still cared about me. And he *had* come all this way back to complain about my decision.

Something halfway between a snort and a sob found its way from my chest.

It was the catalyst.

I was in Quinn's arms.

"I love you," he said shakily. "You aren't going to get rid of me. Meet the newest member of the Domum-Orbis resistance movement. Assign me my task for the day."

"Love you too, Quinn." I laughed and play-punched him. "Your only duty today is to let me make it up to you for not talking it over before I chose not to go to Earth."

"Don't ever do that again. You'll never know what it felt like, that moment when I knew I was somewhere across the universe and you were back here alone. Worst hurt in my entire life."

I felt his pain, but said no more. Talking was overrated, and the blue of our markings was pulsing to the beat of our hearts.

Biography

Susan Hancock, PhD, is a former University Lecturer who has written and published academic non-fiction over several years. She gave up teaching in order to concentrate on her battle with a cancer, which is now fortunately dormant. Fingers crossed. In a totally surprising move, she became obsessed with the idea of writing an adult novel and ended up writing five (so far), the Anstey's Kingdom sequence. She has discovered that characters are hard taskmasters, determined their stories should be told. It isn't uncommon to find her in tears at the laptop when something dreadful happens to one or other of them. But they and she understand some things can't be changed.

To follow the author why not visit her website: https://susanjenniferhancock.com/ or check out her author page: https://www.amazon.com/Susan-Hancock/e/ Bo8BTRVPN1

A NOTE FROM THE COLLECTIVE

Dear reader,

We hope you enjoyed *The Accidental Time Travelers Collective, Volume One*. These stories have lived inside our heads for a long time, and we're thrilled to share them with the world.

If you have time, we would love it if you posted an online review. It doesn't have to be long—a sentence or two will do! Reviews help books get noticed, and that means we'll be able to bring you more time travel stories in the future.

Or the past. We do both.

Thanks again for reading!

Signed,

The Accidental Time Travelers Collective

ALSO BY THE COLLECTIVE

Individual members of the Accidental Time Travelers Collective have published other books you might enjoy. Here's a sampling!